The Force of Fate

By Paul Bryers

In a Pig's Ear
The Prayer of the Bone
The Vatican Candidate: A Harper & Blake Mystery

Written as Seth Hunter and available from McBooks Press

The Nathan Peake Series
The Time of Terror
The Tide of War
The Price of Glory
The Winds of Folly
The Flag of Freedom
The Spoils of Conquest
The Sea of Silence
Trafalgar: The Fog of War

The Force of Fate

Seth Hunter

Essex, Connecticut

An imprint of The Globe Pequot Publishing Group, Inc.
64 South Main Street
Essex, CT 06426
www.globepequot.com

Distributed by NATIONAL BOOK NETWORK

British Library Cataloguing in Publication Information available

Library of Congress Cataloging-in-Publication Data
Names: Hunter, Seth, author.
Title: The force of fate / Seth Hunter.
Description: Essex, Connecticut : McBooks, 2024. | Series: The Nathan Peake series ; 9
Identifiers: LCCN 2024006526 (print) | LCCN 2024006527 (ebook) |
ISBN 9781493077847 (trade paperback) | ISBN 9781493077854 (ebook)
Subjects: LCSH: Great Britain. Royal Navy—Officers—Fiction. | Great Britain—History, Naval—18th century—Fiction. | LCGFT: Historical fiction. | Sea fiction. | Novels.
Classification: LCC PR6052.R94 F67 2024 (print) | LCC PR6052.R94 (ebook) |
DDC 823/.914—dc23/eng/20240403
LC record available at https://lccn.loc.gov/2024006526
LC ebook record available at https://lccn.loc.gov/2024006527

Contents

PROLOGUE

Mr Merry and Mr Burr

MR ANTHONY MERRY WAS NOT A HAPPY MAN.

Merry by name, merry by nature was the ironic crack among his colleagues in the British foreign office, usually following the receipt of one of his gloomy dispatches from the front, or from whichever unfortunate nation bore the burden of being his current host.

Monsieur Toujours Gai, Napoleon had named him with imperial irony during his brief tenure in Paris.

By the time of his appointment as the representative of His Britannic Majesty in Washington, Merry's reputation of being something of a diplomatic Jonah was firmly established. In every country that he had served as Britain's envoy—Spain, Denmark, and, finally, France—his period of office had ended with a declaration of war. Against Britain.

But it was not thought that he could do much harm in Washington.

'Nor does it much matter if he does,' his critics agreed complacently. 'The Americans having about as much clout from a military point of view as a slap with a wet kipper.'

This was a bit rich coming from the diplomats of a country that had suffered the ignominy of defeat in the American War of Independence, but at the time of Merry's appointment, the federal army had been reduced to two regiments of infantry and one of artillery—a total of just over three thousand men—and the navy comprised just six frigates and not a single ship of the line.

The federal capital itself was at that time very much a work in progress. Upon their arrival in the summer of 1803, Merry and his wife were confronted with a vast building site, a shambles of half-completed houses swathed in scaffolding rising up out of a morass of unpaved roads, mud, and stagnant pools, though to the jaundiced eye of the new arrivals, they appeared to be sinking into them.

The couple did their best to keep up appearances, however. They rented the biggest house they could find, acquired a four-horse carriage and a number of Negro slaves, and prepared to put on a show for the natives.

When the new envoy presented his credentials to Mr James Madison, the current secretary of state, he was dressed in full dress uniform with a surfeit of sashes and gold braid, a cocked hat with an ostrich plume, and a gilded sword that had been presented to him by the king himself. Doubtless overwhelmed by this display, Mr Madison delivered him to the presidential house for a formal presentation to its present incumbent, Mr Thomas Jefferson.

But Mr Jefferson did not greet Mr Merry in the manner to which he felt entitled as the representative of the first nation in Europe, whatever the pretensions of the Corsican bandit currently ruling France. There was no brass band, no military guard of honour, no flags or bunting. In fact, there was no president.

After inquiring among the staff, Mr Madison embarked on a lengthy search of the uncompleted building, taking the increasingly indignant Mr Merry in tow. After tripping in and out of several empty rooms, and others that were clearly used for storing building materials, they eventually found him in a small study reading a book. But it was what he was wearing that most offended the British minister, for as he later complained, far from being what one might expect of a head of state scheduled to meet an important foreign diplomat, it was more the kind of thing one might pass on to the under-gardener after discovering that the moths had been at it. Moreover, upon their entrance, their host heaved a weary sigh and marked his page carefully with a bookmark before rising to greet them. His subsequent manner was polite but distant. All of which the representative of King George considered to be a deliberate insult.

In fact, King George was very likely at the root of the problem. As governor of Virginia and a founding member of the Congress, Mr Jefferson had played a leading role in the rebellion against the king's rule, narrowly escaping capture and very likely a hanging when the king's troops burned down the state capital of Richmond. He had gone on to write the Constitution that replaced the royal authority with a republic, and had vigorously opposed all attempts by King George and his armies and navies to re-impose that authority, or to bully the new nation into subservience after it had achieved its independence. He was particularly incensed by the widespread practice indulged in by the king's navy of stopping American ships on the high seas and searching them for deserters or contraband, taking away many of their best seamen on the spurious grounds that they remained His Majesty's subjects.

Mr Merry was of course perfectly aware of Mr Jefferson's hostility towards the British monarchy and of his admiration for the ideals of the French Revolution. But he was particularly sensitive to what he considered to be a snub. Unlike most of his colleagues in the British foreign office, who tended to be of noble birth—or at least something approaching it—Mr Merry was the son of a London wine merchant, and although he might have succeeded in ingratiating himself with the right amount of grovelling, accompanied by the occasional gift of a crate of champagne, it did not help that he was something of a snob himself, and his wife, even more so.

A few days after this inauspicious beginning, however, the Merrys were invited to dinner at the White House. Mr Merry naturally assumed that this was the president's way of making amends, and that he was to be guest of honour. But this was not the case. Indeed, not only was it apparent that he was to be treated no differently from the other guests, he was horrified to discover that one of them was the representative of the emperor Napoleon. This, at a time when England and France were at war. At the very least it constituted a gross breach of diplomatic etiquette, if not a gratuitous insult. But this was only the start of the evening. Things were to get very much worse.

When it was time to go in to dinner, the president, who was a widower, gave his arm to Mrs Madison and not Mrs Merry, as her husband had been led to expect. Instead, it was the secretary of state who led her to the table, leaving the seething British envoy to follow on with the rest of the herd. To make matters worse, it was a *round* table, with no established hierarchy in the seating arrangements and not even any labels to indicate where the guests were to sit. The president explained with a smile that this was the new fashion of pell-mell. Sit wherever you like.

Mr Merry did not like it at all. After standing around for a while at something of a loss, he eventually stumped around the table in his finery, looking for a place where he might sit. He took the last empty chair.

The following day, Mr Merry was moved to make a formal complaint to Mr Madison, who only increased the offence in Merry's eyes by describing it as 'a matter of very little moment.' He then discovered that the president had referred to his wife as 'a virago,' which though in the original Latin meant a female warrior, was far more likely on the president's lips to have the secondary meaning ascribed to it in Dr Johnson's dictionary—namely, a word commonly used for an impudent, turbulent woman.

From that moment on, Mr Merry regarded President Jefferson as his mortal enemy and sought every opportunity to be avenged upon him.

It was not that easy, however, for his superiors in London were somewhat preoccupied with European affairs and were not inclined to take the president's slights, real or imagined, any more seriously than the secretary of state. Napoleon had assembled a vast army on the French side of the English Channel, and Britain was in mortal fear of invasion. But Mr Merry was storing up ammunition for the future, and Fate threw an unexpected weapon into his hands.

His wife, it appeared, had formed a friendship with a gentleman by the name of Aaron Burr.

Mr Burr had stood as a candidate in the last presidential election when he had been narrowly defeated by the present incumbent. Under the terms of the constitution then in force, he had been appointed vice president but had found this far from satisfactory. Indeed, he continued to maintain that the vote had been a fraud and that Jefferson had cheated him of the presidency. He concluded that this fraud had been achieved with the assistance of the leader of the opposition party, Mr Alexander Hamilton—partly to spite him, and partly because Hamilton feared Burr's rivalry much more than that of Jefferson. Such was the antipathy between these two men that Burr had eventually challenged Hamilton to a duel—and shot him dead.

Although in the hurly-burly world of American politics duelling was then considered an entirely reasonable way of settling a quarrel, or even a mild difference of opinion, it emerged that while Hamilton had deliberately fired high and wide, his opponent, after spending several days in serious practice, had shot to kill. As a result, he had been charged with several major crimes, including murder, and promptly fled to South Carolina, where he judged the officers of the law would be reluctant to follow him.

Although the charges against him were eventually dropped, Burr was unceremoniously dumped from his party's ticket in the next presidential election and found himself in the political wilderness. In high dudgeon he took himself off to the real wilderness, embarking on a well-publicised tour of the western frontier.

But now he was back, and he wanted to meet with Mr Merry.

'He has a proposal he would like to discuss with you,' his wife revealed. 'Something that might turn out to be very much to our advantage.'

Mr Merry was not overly enthused. Mr Burr was clearly a dangerous man. He was also a notorious womaniser—Mr Jefferson had referred to him as a 'voluptuary'—and Mr Merry was not at all sure about the nature of his relations with Mrs Merry. But he had heard that Burr shared his deep dislike of the president, who, in his view, had destroyed his political career.

He agreed to the meeting.

Mr Burr came quickly to the point. His tour had taken him into the territories acquired from the French and collectively known as the Louisiana Purchase—a vast tract of land extending northward from New Orleans to the Canada border and westward from the Missouri to the Rockies. Few people in the East knew much about it, other than that it contained a multitude of forests, mountains, and swamps, an unknown number of aborigines, and a few thousand French and Spanish adventurers, trappers, and out-and-out scoundrels on the run from the law, but it was believed to have a vast potential for settlement, and New Orleans was already a major entrepôt for trade.

'What would be the reaction of Great Britain should these territories declare their independence from the United States?' Mr Burr desired to know.

Mr Merry kept his expression carefully neutral, but his mind was considerably exercised.

'Is that a possibility?' he enquired.

'I believe it is,' Burr replied. 'Indeed, I can reveal to you in the strictest confidence that I have been approached by a number of people in these territories who wish to know if I would be willing to seek international support for such a venture.'

'People of substance?' enquired Mr Merry cautiously.

'I regret that I am not at liberty to name names,' replied Mr Burr, 'but they include some of the most respected citizens of New Orleans and the governors of some of the most important garrison towns and trading posts along the Mississippi.'

Mr Merry's knowledge of New Orleans and the garrison towns of the Mississippi was not extensive, but his interest had been considerably piqued.

'And what would be required in the way of support?' he asked.

'Initially, money,' declared Mr Burr.

Mr Merry was not, as we know, inclined to levity, but he may have permitted himself a secret smile at this point, for he suspected that Mr Burr was in need of money himself, and that this entire proposal was nothing more than an audacious attempt to acquire some. This did not end his interest, however. At the very least, it raised the possibility of being revenged upon Mr Jefferson for the slights that had been heaped upon him since his arrival in Washington.

But there were more strategic considerations. Divide and rule had long been the defining creed of his political masters in London. It had worked in Asia and in Europe, and there was no reason why it should not work in North America. Indeed, an attempt had been made to divide the northern and southern colonies during the Independence War, and it had enjoyed some success—until the unfortunate incident in Yorktown when an entire British army had been obliged to surrender to the insurgents and their French allies.

That evening he composed a carefully worded dispatch to London in which he outlined his new intelligence and the opportunities it presented for exploiting the divisions between His Majesty's former subjects, thus exploding the myth of a United States, preventing its further expansion to the West, and settling Mr Thomas Jefferson's hash once and for all.

[illegible] equipped Mr. Murray admirably [illegible]

[illegible] the most respected [illegible]

[illegible] and the presence of some of the most important [illegible]

[illegible] towns and trading posts along the [illegible].

Mr. Murray's knowledge of [illegible], and [illegible] was extensive [illegible]

[illegible]

Chapter 1

The Captain and the Ape

Gibraltar, November 1805

Meanwhile . . .

Four thousand miles across the Atlantic, two old friends sat on top of a rock watching the world go by. One wore the uniform of a post captain in His Britannic Majesty's navy; the other wore nothing, for he was an ape.

'Well, they are taking him back to England,' said the captain. 'Pickled in a cask of brandy. On doctor's orders, apparently, to preserve the corpse from corruption so that the public may gaze upon it one last time before it is laid to rest.'

The ape bared his teeth and delivered a series of whoops which could be interpreted as derisory.

'My sentiments exactly,' said the captain. 'However, he apparently expressed a wish not to be buried at sea. "Do not let them throw me into the sea, Hardy," he is reputed to have said when he lay dying in the *Victory*, though I did not hear him, and I was as close to him as I am to you now.'

He considered for a moment, then added, in the interests of truth: 'Well, not quite as close, perhaps, and there were a lot of others there. However, I must say I am surprised, for the sea was his natural element. On land he was hopeless, to be frank—in love, in business, even in battle. The land was where he lost his arm and the sight of his eye, not to speak of what happened in Naples.'

They both shook their heads over what had happened in Naples.

'There are rumours that the cask has been broached,' the captain continued, 'and that the people have been drinking it from a straw. Sucking the monkey, it is called. I mean no disrespect. I do not know why a monkey comes into it, but that is the expression. If 'tis true, I fear he will arrive in England in no fit state to be seen by anyone.'

They sat in silence for a moment, reflecting on the ironies of fate, the hapless quest for glory, and the inevitable ending of life's journey.

The captain was somewhat given to introspection. His name was Peake. Nathaniel Peake. He was thirty-six years old, dark-haired and -complexioned, and, despite the impression he may have given to the contrary, of sound mind. He knew it was unlikely that the ape had even the faintest idea of what he was talking about, but like many English gentlemen of his kind, he had been talking to his dogs and horses from an early age and felt more relaxed in their company than with many of his own species. An ape was in his view an acceptable substitute. Besides, it was all he had.

The creature had not disclosed its name, and may not have had one, but the captain addressed it occasionally as Jarvey, the London slang for a coachman and the nickname of Admiral Sir John Jervis, to whom it bore a striking resemblance—at least in Peake's view, who had at times fallen foul of the admiral's notorious bad temper. Its ancestors had lived on the rock since the time of the Moors and had survived the Spanish and then the British occupations. Although the British called them apes, they were in fact macaques, rightly classified as monkeys, which is what the Spanish called them. As they could never agree on anything, this was of little consequence. Certainly, it was doubtful the apes gave it a thought. Even if they were monkeys.

The rock was called Gibraltar, and though it was very nearly on the southernmost tip of Europe, it had long been at the crossroads of world history. A thousand feet below them they could observe the town and harbour of the same name, and across a narrow strait, Africa. The sun was rising where it usually rose, in the east, suffusing the sea with a golden glow.

'I should be going back to England myself,' said the captain after a lengthy silence. 'My fiancée is with child, and I am quite worried about her. I say fiancée, for I have written with a proposal of marriage, but I have not yet received a reply. Do you have children?'

The ape, whose mind had wandered, waved a languid hand in the direction of a troop of his associates who were disporting themselves, at a respectful distance, on some neighbouring rocks. They mostly appeared, to the captain's untrained eye, to be mothers with young children.

'What—all of them?'

The ape gave what might have been an indifferent shrug, or an indication of his lack of information on the subject.

'Well, it is a wise child that knows its own father,' Nathan reflected gloomily.

They lapsed into another silence.

'I expect I shall have to find a home in England for them to live,' Nathan resumed at length. 'I cannot send them to Sussex. Not with the situation my father is in. My mother would have them in Soho, but it would not be the thing at all. I sometimes think they have much in common. And the two of them together . . . ' He gave a theatrical shudder. 'I suppose you have the same sort of problems with your lot,' he ventured, but his companion, knowing nothing of Soho or Sussex or the more delicate matters to which his companion had referred, refrained from comment. He had, in any case, become distracted by a yellow bug with two distinctive black spots which was climbing laboriously up the rock towards them.

Nathan, for his part, had observed several figures, about the same size as the bug at this distance, moving along the mole that formed the southern boundary of the harbour.

'That will be my coxswain and his crew with the mail,' he confided, 'so I suppose I must be on my way.'

He slid down from the rock and dusted the seat of his breeches.

'Hopefully we will meet again before they decide what is to be done with me. In the meantime, I will bid you good day.' He touched the corner of his hat. 'Pray convey my respects to your wives and children, whoever the father is.'

He made his way down the steep slope towards the harbour, bounding stiff-legged when he felt himself to be unobserved, walking with quiet dignity at other times, and removing his hat to greet the occasional passer-by taking the early morning air on the lower slopes of the Rock.

The smell of coffee and fresh-baked bread assailed him as he walked through the narrow streets of the town, and he was tempted to stop at one of the several pavement cafés that were opening up for the day, but he did not care to keep his boat crew waiting without their breakfast down on the quayside.

He need not have worried, however, for having picked up the mail, they had made their own arrangements for breakfast, as boat crews invariably did, and were stuffing themselves with pastries they had purchased with the money he had given his coxswain, Mr Banjo, for their expenses.

'All well?' he enquired with subtle irony as he stepped aboard. 'I do not suppose you have saved me one of them.'

Mr Banjo silently handed him a bag which on inspection he found to contain a sticky kind of tart known as a *calentita*, a local delicacy.

'Back to the barky?' asked the coxswain.

'Back to the barky,' said Nathan, settling himself in the stern and breaking off a portion of tart, which was stickier than he preferred and best taken with coffee or some other beverage, but he was too hungry to wait.

'The barky' was in fact a thirty-six-gun frigate of the *Perseverance* class called the *Panther*, which had been under his command since the previous summer. Launched in 1783, she was obsolete in military terms—she had been superseded by the new *Leda* and *Lively* class frigates in the British navy—and on paper, at least, she was no match for the faster and more heavily armed frigates in the French or American navies. However, she had distinguished herself in a number of single-ship combats, most recently when she had taken the *Perle*, a forty-gun French frigate, off Vigo. However, Nathan did not expect to be with her much longer, for his had been but a temporary appointment, and he was aware that so far as the distant authorities at the Admiralty were concerned, it had not gone entirely to their satisfaction.

He was greeted as he came aboard by the first lieutenant, Mr Simpson, whose self-regard, in the captain's view, was combined with a contempt, even vindictiveness, towards lesser forms of life that had been in no way diminished by the loss of his left arm in their recent engagement with the *Perle*. The empty sleeve was pinned neatly to the front of his jacket like a battle honour, which it was, but the captain could not help but take it as an admonition for his own mistakes during the early stages of the encounter. They had lost fifteen men dead and twenty-five wounded, and though no-one else was complaining—except, possibly, them—the captain bore a heavy burden of responsibility.

'Shall I have the mail distributed immediately, sir?' the lieutenant enquired, in a tone that indicated such a decision would confirm him in his opinion of the captain's indulgence in such matters. What else the lieutenant would have done with it was beyond the captain's comprehension. Probably kept it until the end of the day to increase the virtues of delayed gratification.

'Oh, I think so, Mr Simpson, don't you? And if there is anything for me, perhaps you would be good enough to have it sent down to my cabin.'

It had taken considerable self-control for him to resist the temptation to rummage through the small stack during the short journey from the harbour, but he now had to curb his impatience for a few more minutes until his steward appeared with the single letter bearing his name. He did not recognise the handwriting and opened it at once, even before his servant had left the cabin. It was, as he had hoped, from Louise de Kirouac, the young woman he had described to his friend the ape as his fiancée, though this was, in fact, something of an exaggeration.

Mon chéri, it began promisingly.

But sadly, this was as good as it got.

She understood that his mother had sent him news of her recent arrival in London and of her present condition. She hoped this had not been too much of a shock for him. She was in excellent health and good spirits. Her position in France had become untenable for a number of reasons, which she could not commit to paper, but she wished him to know that she neither needed nor expected anything from him. She was perfectly capable of looking after herself and had the resources to do so. It was with some reluctance that she had communicated with his mother, lest it gave the wrong impression, but she had felt that it was the right thing to do.

Nathan took some time to think about this but was unable to come to any helpful conclusion. He read on.

She had found a house in Soho—in Meard Street—not far from where his mother lived. The name was amusing—*n'est-ce pas*—given her current circumstances.

This necessitated another pause, for he did not at first understand what was so amusing, but of course—she meant Meard in the sense of *merde*, which was French for shit, hence 'I am living in Shit Street.'

Ho ho.

In fact, he did not consider it at all amusing, for though the tenor was flippant, it was clearly a reference to her 'current circumstances.' When his mother had written to him, she had conveyed the information that Louise was living in the vicinity of the king's palace in Saint James's Park, which was one of the most affluent districts of London. She had clearly moved since then, and while Soho was perfectly respectable as a neighbourhood, it was not Saint James's Park.

The area abounds with French exiles like myself, and I feel as at home here as if I were in Paris.

He assumed this, too, was meant ironically. By her own account Louise had been the illegitimate daughter of a notorious playwright and pamphleteer called Olympe de Gouges who had been dispatched by the guillotine when Louise was barely fourteen years old, and she herself had been confined in the Carmes prison until the fall of Robespierre.

Your mother has been most kind and supportive, but I am quite able to look after myself and in no need of financial assistance, having access to funds lodged in a London bank. Please be assured that I very much value her friendship, however, just as I remain your adoring

Louise.

Adoring was hopeful, he supposed, though it might just be a neat way of signing off. She had to write something, and she possibly considered that it had to be rather more intimate than 'affectionate,' given the way they had disported themselves during their most recent encounter.

There was no mention of his proposal, but then he had only sent it a few days ago. It was probably still making its way across the Bay of Biscay in the Falmouth packet. Even so, he considered that she might have been more forthcoming about her future intentions. Also, the reason she had decided to come to England. Why had her position in France become untenable, and why could she not have committed it to writing? Did she think her letters were being opened by agents of the British government, and, if so, what reason had she given them to explain their interest?

Unfortunately, he knew of several reasons. Until recently she had been employed as sculptor to Empress Josephine at her home in Malmaison, just outside the French capital. The two women had formed a close friendship when they had met in prison at the time of the Terror. They were like sisters, he had been told, though Josephine was probably twice Louise's age. Had there been a falling-out between them, or had something worse happened?

In the not-so-distant past, Louise had been a member of a band of royalist insurgents in Brittany known as the Chouans, from their alleged practice of hooting like an owl as a signal to each other before an attack. Louise had ridiculed this as a myth. She nevertheless could hoot like an owl. She had demonstrated this accomplishment on several occasions, and he had found it impressive. Even more recently, she had been a secret agent of the British government. Or more specifically, of Sir Sidney Smith, who ran what was almost a private intelligence service on behalf of the Admiralty. Quite possibly she still was. He had called her his assassin—his *beautiful* assassin—and though he might not have been serious—he could have meant an assassin of the heart—it was open to question. There were always questions where Sir Sidney Smith was concerned. Louise, too, sadly. He knew it was best not to probe too deeply into any of her affairs, but it did not stop him torturing himself with suspicion.

He scanned the letter again in search of clues.

This reference to having access to funds in a London bank, for instance. Where had such funds come from? So far as he was aware, her father's estate had been confiscated by the revolutionary government. Perhaps he had managed to move his money to London before he died, but it did not seem likely, and certainly Louise had not mentioned this to him during their short but passionate acquaintance. It was possible, he supposed, that she had sold one of her sculptures. Empress Josephine—it was strange to think of her by that name; he had known her in Paris as Rose Beauharnais, a notorious femme fatale whose lovers included the president of the national convention and the vagabond Corsican artillery officer known by Rose's friends as Captain Cannon, who was now the master of Europe.

Rose—a much more appropriate name, in Nathan's view—had commissioned Louise to sculpt a statue of herself attired as a gardener, or a lady of leisure doing a bit of gardening, as most gardeners would have described it, to stand among the flowerbeds at Malmaison, but Rose probably had more debts than the Prince of Wales, and even if she had given Louise an advance, how could she have transferred it into a London bank at a time of war? He supposed there were ways and means, but apart from this, the only other source of income available to her was her intelligence work for Captain Smith. Or whatever else he was paying her for.

It seemed to Nathan that the whole gist of the letter was to avoid giving him the slightest sense of responsibility for the condition in which she found herself, or suggesting that there was any level of commitment between them.

Which, of course, made him wonder if the child was, in fact, his.

He stored the letter in the one lockable drawer of his bureau, stowing the key on its long chain in the inner pocket of his waistcoat.

But it would not stop him thinking about it. Or her. Every hour of the day and night, if his past experience was anything to go by.

He was temporarily diverted, however, by the entrance of a young midshipman bringing a signal from the admiral to attend upon him. At his earliest convenience, which of course meant immediately.

The captain, who was not a natural optimist, took this as ominous.

Chapter 2

The Tar from the Tyne

'Well, well, Captain Nathaniel Peake. As I live and breathe. Or is it his shade?'

The admiral regarded Nathan warily as he entered the great cabin of the frigate *Euryalus* and stood respectfully before him.

'Speak thou. How say you? If thou canst nod, speak too!'

Nathan had a vague idea that this was a quote, but its origin confounded him as much as the reason for it. He frowned a little but uttered a civil greeting. He could not decide if the admiral was in a jovial mood, or if this was the precursor of a rebuke. He was said to be somewhat unpredictable.

Vice Admiral Cuthbert Collingwood had been Nelson's second in command at Trafalgar, and his flagship, the *Royal Sovereign*, had been the first in action, but she was so battered about he had been obliged to shift his flag to the frigate *Euryalus* at the height of the battle. Either she suited his simple tastes or he had found nowhere else that would have him, for he was still here. He sat at the head of the captain's table, which occupied what space was not taken up by a pair of thirty-two-pounder carronades and a few bits of furniture. The pale November sunlight came streaming in through the stern windows behind him and motes of reflected water danced on the deckhead above while two bespectacled clerks made inroads on the immense amount of paperwork that covered most of the table, dipping and scratching with their quills like a pair of waders pecking for molluscs in the shallows of an estuary.

It was the first time Nathan had met the admiral in person, and he was somewhat taken aback by the tone of his greeting, which might be said to combine an element of wonder with sardonic censure, much as an entomologist might regard a rare specimen whose existence had been rumoured but was not definitely known to exist, and which he strongly suspected of being a fake. Had he been the confident, devil-may-care individual to which he aspired—somewhat in the mould of Sir Sidney Smith, perhaps—he might have replied: 'Well, well, Admiral Collingwood,' in the same sardonic tone, but still having some regard for his naval career, he did not.

Collingwood was something of an oddity for a naval officer. He did not drink, smoke, or gamble, and he did not appear to care much for food either. He was opposed to hanging and flogging; he was even against impressment, which, given how much weight the Admiralty attached to it—they had always claimed the navy could not be crewed without it, and they were probably right, for who else would be mad enough to go to sea—it was a wonder he had achieved the rank of lieutenant, never mind admiral. It was widely said of him that he would have made a good bishop.

For all his fabled piety, however, Collingwood had the reputation of being a puritanical old tyrant, though more so with his officers than the men, to whom he was something of a father figure. He was probably in his late fifties, but he looked ten years older and was said to suffer badly from rheumatics. Old Cuddy was the name by which he was familiarly known throughout the fleet, but some of his officers had been known to refer to him as Old Salt, Junk, and Sixpence, for he was supposedly quite poor due to his wife's 'excesses,' whatever they were, and his dinners were miserable affairs, with old meat and cheap wine, and a lengthy sermon if you were especially unlucky. He was a Northumberland man, born and bred on the banks of the Tyne, and although he had attended a grammar school and had been at sea since he was twelve years old, he still spoke the local dialect when he was so minded, though he usually reserved it for banter with his servants and the men of the lower deck, who were largely recruited from the same region and known throughout the fleet as the tars from the Tyne.

'Well, they be proper raged at you back in London,' he said now, 'and are after me sending you home in chains to be hanged, drawn, and quartered, or whatever else they have in mind for 'ee that is within the bounds of the law.'

'I am sorry to hear that, sir,' Nathan replied with an air of baffled interest. 'Is there a specific complaint?'

'Specific?' The admiral goggled. 'Specific, says he.'

He looked to share his astonishment with the two clerks, but they remained engrossed in their paperwork, or at least made a good impression of it, and he was obliged to return his scandalised gaze to the captain.

'Aye, you could say that, you cheeky bugger. They want to know what you were doing fighting for the French at Trafalgar—which I have to admit seems a reasonable enquiry in the circumstances.'

This finally penetrated the clerks' carapace of indifference, for they both looked up in surprise before bowing their heads over their books again, lest the admiral turn his wrath upon them.

'So, sit you down, sir,' he invited Nathan with an appearance of gentility that was paper thin at best, 'and take all the time in the world, for I am as keen to know as they are.'

'With respect, I was not fighting *for* them, sir,' Nathan replied, taking one of the two chairs available to him and suppressing a weary sigh, for it was not the first time this suggestion had been made, and he was disposed to resent it. 'I spent the best part of the battle hiding under a fire engine, and then—'

'You did *what*? A *what*?'

The two clerks bobbed up from the swamp to exchange arched brows, and one of them made a noise very like a snigger, upon which the admiral glared down the table so fiercely they ducked their heads once more, dipping and scratching as if their lives depended upon it.

Nathan did not at all blame them; Collingwood was famous for his bollockings. He'd once cut the pigtails off all his midshipmen with his own penknife, one after t'other, young and not so young, for not making the correct observations at the noon reading.

'A fire engine, sir,' Nathan replied with an air of polite condescension, for, despite the warnings he had received, an unfortunate spirit of rebellion, doubtless inherited from his American mother, led him astray on occasion. 'An adaptation of the normal bilge pump fitted with canvas hoses. Perhaps you are not familiar with it, sir. It is a Dutch invention.'

'I know what a fire engine is, sir. By thunder! Another remark like that, you dog, and I'll have you disrated for impudence and insubordination before I send you home in a cage.'

Nathan did not doubt it. He was sailing pretty close to the wind, and he knew it. There was no sign of the famous penknife, but there was a bottle of ink within reach, and he would not put it past the admiral to hurl it at his head.

'I beg your pardon, sir. But the fact is that, though they did not expect me to fight for them, they did insist on me helping to work the fire engine.'

'Did they indeed. Insist, did they? Well, if that is not fighting for them, I do not know what else it is. Our job, sir, as commissioned officers of His Britannic Majesty's navy, is to destroy the enemy, not put out fires for them. I am half in mind to hang you myself, let alone send you back to let their lordships have the pleasure.'

'Forgive me, sir, but I was obliged to keep up the deception of . . . of being an American.' He took the plunge into these deep waters. 'However, I took the first opportunity that occurred to hide under the device as soon as we were engaged in combat, and I remained there until I was dragged out by the boatswain and compelled to help pile up the bodies in the middle of the deck.'

The admiral had been staring at him as though mesmerised by a very clever charlatan, or a lunatic, but he finally recovered.

'What in God's name are you blathering about, man?'

'That is what they do, sir, so that they may give them a dignified burial at some later stage, whereas we, as you know, pitch them in the sea at once, which in my view is by far the better option, for seeing them all bloodied and knocked about and piled up like so much offal in the middle of the deck has a shocking bad effect on morale, and—'

'Damn your eyes, sir! More of this and I'll not answer for the consequence. Are your wits addled or what, for I swear by all the saints, mine are. I ask a simple question and I get a load of drivel that would not be out of place in Bedlam. Let me be clear, sir—let me be *specific*. What I and their lordships desire to know is what the fuck you were doing on a French ship of the line in the first place.'

'I beg your pardon, sir. I thought you knew that already.'

This seemed to deprive Collingwood entirely of the power of speech, but after regarding him in wonder for a moment, he shook his head as if to clear his brain and managed to get out a solitary word.

'What?'

'Only that I put it in my report, sir.'

'Your report?'

'Yes, sir. Which I wrote at the request of Captain Hardy, so that he might send it to you.'

The admiral swept an arm at the immense amount of paperwork that occupied the long table.

'Yes, well, as you see, sir, I have had rather a lot in the way of reports lately, besides having a great many other matters to deal with, so it may have escaped my attention. Perhaps you would oblige me with a brief summary.'

'Of course, sir.' Nathan scratched his head. 'Where to begin? Well, I assume you are acquainted with the action off Cape Finisterre at the end of August?'

The admiral stared at him in silence, but there was a light in his eye that put Nathan in mind of the spark in a short fuse just before it reaches the powder keg. He pressed on before the explosion.

'Well, after Admiral Villeneuve had broken off the engagement, he took refuge in the port of Ferrol. Our own fleet under Admiral Calder had been scattered by a storm, and we were concerned that they might come out before we had sufficient strength to—'

'We?'

'Myself and Captain Griffith, sir—that is, the Honourable Edward Colpoys Griffith, of the *Dragon*, which were then the only ships of the British squadron on station.'

'Were they indeed?' The admiral's voice was thoughtful, and the spark had gone from his eye. 'Go on.'

'We were concerned that they might continue with their journey northward to Brest. Which, as you probably know, was Napoleon's plan.'

A long, considering stare but no comment.

'That is to say, to combine the Mediterranean and Atlantic fleets so as to overwhelm our naval defences and proceed with his invasion of England,' continued Nathan helpfully. Still, no reaction. He pressed on.

'Well, in hopes of gaining some time for our forces to gather, I volunteered to venture into Ferrol aboard the brig *Grampus* of Philadelphia, which we had taken prize, my intention being to pose as the ship's master and provide false information to the effect that a large British fleet was assembled immediately north of Ferrol under the command of Admiral Lord Nelson.'

'Howay, man.'

This was at least something, though its meaning was unclear. In any case, Nathan had an attentive audience. Even the clerks had stopped dipping and scratching and were staring at him like two wax dummies, quills poised at the ready.

'My intention was to sail straight back out again and resume my command, but unfortunately I was taken prisoner, which is how I came to be aboard the *Redoutable* during the battle off Cape Trafalgar,' he concluded with a rueful smile.

A long pause, even longer than the ones that had preceded it.

Nathan let the smile fade and put his hand to his chin, rubbing at it reflectively.

'I see,' said the admiral at length. 'Well, I say "I see," but I am damned if I know what to make of it, Peake. I am not saying that I doubt you, for I do not at all, but—well, you see the difficulty.'

'Sir?'

'Well—the *Redoutable*, man.' As if this said it all. 'The very ship that was engaged with the *Victory* for the best part of the battle. And from which our dear admiral, God rest his soul, well, as you know . . . received his fatal wound.'

Nathan nodded gravely.

'I do not suppose you have a notion of how that came to be, so to speak?' the admiral enquired, almost diffidently. 'I mean, of who fired the fatal shot.'

'I am afraid not, sir.'

This was untrue. He did in fact have quite a strong notion. In his mind's eye, he saw the Neapolitan marksman they called *Lo Spettro* climbing the ratlines of the mizzenmast with his musket slung about his shoulder and a determined look on his face, but as he had no solid evidence and the killer was almost certainly dead, he was reluctant to share the image, or for that matter, the reasoning behind it.

'I did not know the admiral was wounded until I came aboard the *Victory*,' he revealed, 'and joined the mourners in the cockpit.'

'You were there when he died?'

'I was, sir.'

'He was my very dear friend, you know.'

'I know, sir.'

In fact, he knew no such thing. Although the two men had known each other for almost thirty years—they had served as lieutenants in the same frigate during the American War—it was said that there had long been tensions between them. They were certainly very different in character and temperament, and even more so in their approach to command. Collingwood was the senior in age by about ten years, but he had always been one step behind in terms of promotion, and there was a feeling among their fellow officers that he had always been in Nelson's shadow. But now he had succeeded him as commander of the Mediterranean fleet and Nelson was on his way back to England in a barrel of brandy. Or rum—there was some dispute on the subject.

It was significant, Nathan thought, that the very first thing he had done as commander in chief was to countermand Nelson's order—his last order, in fact—which had been to anchor the fleet and ride out the coming storm. Collingwood had decided to make for Gibraltar immediately, and as a result, they had lost all but four of their prizes to the sea.

'Did you ever meet him yourself?' the admiral asked now. 'Apart from when he was dying, I mean.'

'Once or twice,' said Nathan. 'When I served under him off Genoa, back in the nineties, and again after his victory at the Nile.'

This, too, was misleading, if not downright duplicitous, for he had served him in several other locations, though in circumstances and a capacity he did not wish to advertise to all and sundry. He had been with him on the *Captain* at the Battle of Cape Saint Vincent and the *Vanguard* at the mouth of the Nile, and it was Nelson who had sent him to India to warn the British authorities there that Bonaparte was heading their way. He had been a guest at his house in Merton during the short-lived peace, and he had even helped him choose the lining for his coffin. He would never have said they were friends, that would have been immodest of him, but he had known him as well as he knew any admiral, even his own father, and he grieved his loss as much as any man alive.

'We will miss him,' said the admiral. 'England will miss him.'

Then, after a decent pause, he added, 'However, to the present. The fact is, Peake, I am going to have to send you back to England to answer these . . . I will not call them charges, but there are some serious questions regarding your conduct, and I think you must respond to them directly.'

'By all means, sir.' Nathan hesitated a moment, but if he did not ask it now, it would prey on him all the way home. 'Am I to face a court-martial, then?'

'No, not at all, Peake. No, it is just an inquiry.' But any reassurance Nathan might have derived from this was entirely dispelled by his adding, after a small pause: 'At this stage.'

Nathan managed a bleak smile. 'Not a hanging, then.'

'No, sir. I am sorry, I spoke out of turn. But the fact is . . .' His eyes strayed once more to the clerks, and whatever he'd meant to say, he thought better of it. 'The best I can do for you is let you take the *Panther*. At least 'twill not look as if you are being sent home in disgrace, for it seems to me you acted with the best of intentions. However . . .' He shook his head, as if it was all beyond him.

'Thank you, sir, I appreciate that,' said Nathan, 'but I can quite easily go back on the Falmouth packet and save you the loss of a frigate.'

'No, no—you take your own ship, lad. And if it looks like they are going to keep you hanging about'—he winced at the unfortunate choice of word—'you can send her back to me under your first lieutenant and re-join us when you, when all this is cleared up.'

'Thank you, sir,' Nathan said again, meaning it. He stood up to take his leave. 'With your permission . . .'

But the admiral too was rising to his feet. 'I will take a turn on deck with you, sir. I could do with a bit of fresh air.'

It was clear that he had more than fresh air in mind, however, for he led Nathan to the weather side of the quarterdeck where they had a measure of privacy.

'I just wanted to say to you, Peake, in confidence, that there may be more to this inquiry than the matter of you being on *Redoutable* during the recent battle.'

'Sir?' Nathan went for baffled innocence again. It had served him well enough in the past, though there had been notable exceptions.

'I do not know the best way of putting this to you, but I have heard that you are acquainted with Bonaparte . . . and . . . and certain members of the family. His sister, for instance. The youngest.'

That would be Pauline, of course. How the hell had he found that out? And if Collingwood knew of it, how many others did?

'There were certain . . . activities . . . I undertook, from time to time,' Nathan floundered, 'at the request—the order—of my superiors. As to their nature . . .'

Collingwood raised both hands as if he were pushing him away.

'Not another word, sir. Far be it from me to . . . You know your own business.'

This was by no means true, not even near true, but Nathan did not contradict him.

'All I will say is that certain people in positions of . . . of influence have clearly misunderstood—or, I should say, they have not clearly understood—the circumstances. So, yes, you may have some explaining to do.'

'I have nothing to hide, sir.'

This, again, was far from true, but he had been ducking and diving for many years. He knew the art of evasion as well as any man in the service—bar one, perhaps.

'And there are those who would speak up for me, if it becomes necessary,' he added.

'Good, good, I am glad to hear it.' But the admiral clearly had something else on his mind. 'Would one of them be Captain Sir Sidney Smith, by any chance?'

He saw Nathan's expression and did that pushing-away gesture again with his hand.

'Keep your counsel, man, keep your counsel, for these are deep waters. I expect you know that Captain Smith has his . . . *detractors* in the service, in politics, even in—in higher places. There was that business with the Princess of Brunswick, for instance . . . '

He glanced at Nathan hopefully. It was another strange thing about Collingwood that for all his godliness and his moralising, he dearly loved a scandal, and Captain Smith's affair with the wife of the Prince of Wales was a very juicy scandal indeed for those with any interest in the subject.

But Nathan kept his mouth shut. He had served under Smith at the beginning of the present war, and though he did not particularly like the man, or trust him, he did not care to denigrate him. Not in present company, at least.

'Well, we all have our little weaknesses,' the admiral submitted awkwardly. 'And the Swedish Knight has . . . well, he is a man of many parts, as they say.'

Nathan maintained his discretion, but the admiral's use of the term 'the Swedish Knight' revealed his own prejudice, for it was a label pinned on Smith by his detractors. He had been knighted by the King of Sweden for services rendered during that nation's war with Russia back in the eighties, and though King George had recognised the title, out of respect for his Swedish cousin, few others did, certainly not in the service. Several British naval officers had died fighting for Russia in that war, and the part Smith had played in that would not be quickly forgotten, or forgiven.

'I would not wish you to be the—what is it, not scapegoat, but something very like it . . . ' The admiral frowned over the elusive word. 'Well, whatever it is, I mean the target for those who should properly be gunning for Smith.'

'I understand you perfectly, sir,' replied Nathan, 'and I will heed your advice, but, as we both know, a certain amount of subterfuge is necessary in war, and—well, sir, Captain Smith is a master of the art. People may not like it, but it is not all "Go straight at 'em," as Lord Nelson would have put it.'

The admiral stiffened. This could have been taken as a criticism, though it was not so intended. However, there had been a time when Nelson and Smith had competed for the role of national hero, and their rivalry had divided the service. Nelson had won that particular contest at Trafalgar, but now he was dead, and Smith, very much alive.

'Be that as it may,' the admiral concluded, 'I wish you safe passage back to England. And the best of luck to you when you get there.'

He did not add 'Because you are damn well going to need it,' but the thought lingered in the air.

Chapter 3

The Voyage Home

The start of the first dog watch, and the last drop of light bleeding from a dirty sky. The *Panther* was leaning into a heavy sea as close to the northeast wind as it would allow. Murky, squally weather, and a stinging slap of spindrift and salt spray in the face at every clash of wave and bow.

Nathan's mood was morose. Any chance of combat or of taking a prize had been dashed by the foul weather that had dogged them since leaving Gibraltar, though it did not stop him clinging to the diminishing hope. Anything to relieve the tedium of the journey home and take his mind off what awaited him at the end of it.

He was not thinking so much of Louise, though perhaps he should have been, but of 'the buggers at Admiralty,' as Collingwood might have put it, for though he was fairly confident that he could answer for his conduct before, during, and after Trafalgar, he could not answer for the prejudice of his inquisitors, or the level of antipathy they might feel towards him and his associates in the dark arts of espionage. And he was inclined to think that Collingwood had been right when he had hinted that this was the real reason for his recall.

He would not be the first to be judged on the company he kept, and no matter how reluctant he had been to serve under the command of the Swedish Knight, he had endured that dubious distinction for two years or more—since just before the start of the present war, in fact, and in a capacity that could cause him serious embarrassment, or worse, if its scope and implications were ever revealed to his accusers.

Of course, this all depended on who these individuals were, and how many state secrets they were prepared to unearth with their probing. But the very fact that they had been allowed to summon him home to answer their charges—for charges they were, no matter how they might choose to phrase it—was disturbing enough in itself. He was surprised that Lord Barham, or even someone senior to him in the Whitehall hierarchy, had not scotched such an inquiry as soon as it raised its head, for fear of what it might reveal. He was sure that William Pitt, for instance, would not wish the king to know what had been ventured in his name—and he certainly would not wish Parliament to know.

Nathan did not normally concern himself with the world of politics, but the closer they came to England, the more it pressed upon him. In the past, whenever it had threatened his equanimity—or his freedom, or his life—he had been able to divert himself with more pleasurable pursuits. The study of the cosmos, the prospect of a prize, the love of a good woman, and more frequently, the enjoyment of a good meal. He was a man of simple tastes and easy solace—in his own opinion, if not of those who knew him better—and the prospect of a decent table could cheer him up no end. But he had just eaten, and it had singularly failed to lift his spirits, and unless he succumbed to the temptation of toasted cheese and a glass of port for his supper, he would not be eating again until breakfast.

The other consolation he could usually count upon was friendship. In the company of friends, he could laugh at his misfortunes, or at least crack a grim smile, but in his present circumstances he felt very much alone.

This was not remarkable in the captain of a ship of war; it came with the job, so to speak. But he found his fellow officers on the *Panther* particularly difficult to get on with. Unusually, the three commissioned officers, and even the lieutenant of marines, were the sons of viscounts or barons and thus permitted to prefix their names with the title 'the Honourable,' at least in writing. This contributed to an inflated sense of their own importance, which was combined with a perceptible antagonism towards those who had attained high rank without this distinction, as if it were an affront to the natural order of things. Their conceit had conveyed itself to the midshipmen and warrant officers who aped the manners and arrogance of their superiors, and at times it seemed to Nathan that they all went about their duties as if a bad smell had afflicted them, and it probably emanated from the crew. His own more relaxed approach had led to some considerable tension between them, and he knew that they felt he was trying to ingratiate himself with those of inferior rank.

Nor did it help that he had been appointed as a temporary measure whilst their captain was on sick leave, and that for half the time he had been officially in command he had left the ship in the care of the first lieutenant. There were very good reasons for this, at least in Nathan's opinion, but his officers would probably classify them under the heading 'Consorting with the Enemy.'

Much the same as their lordships of the Admiralty.

The sound of the ship's bell recalled him to his current situation and the end of the first dog watch. It was also the signal for a change of personnel, and Mr Collins took over as officer of the watch. After a stiff exchange of courtesies, Nathan resumed his stance on the weather side of the quarterdeck, but it was now impossible to see beyond the light cast by the stern lantern, and all that showed were the sheets of rain and the occasional glimpse of an Atlantic roller as it made its relentless progress towards the coast of Brittany. They were probably some thirty leagues to the south-west of Ushant, he reckoned from his last observations, in one of the most dangerous seas in the world, made even more perilous in time of war by the proximity of the great French naval base at Brest.

Even so, he had no intention of staying on deck much longer. His port and his toasted cheese awaited him, or soon would—and he was about to announce his retirement for the night when out of the darkness and the rain to windward, a ship appeared.

'Appeared' as in apparition, for she was very like a phantom, and no sooner seen than upon them. A brief glimpse of a predatory beak and a billowing expanse of sail, emerging from the darkness on their starboard quarter. He heard himself shout 'Port your helm!' in an instinctive reflex, much as one might raise an arm against a blow, swiftly followed by an obscenity that was likely to be his last word on Earth. Then they were heeling hard over as the frigate took the wind on her beam, the helmsman wrestling with the wheel and a second hand leaping forward to add his weight to the struggle.

The phantom vanished into the darkness whence she came, leaving only the memory of her passing, the brief but striking image of a bearded warrior with a plumed helmet, a shield, and a short sword poised in the act of burying itself into the heart of an enemy—and the agitated voices Nathan had heard on the wind.

'Hands to the braces!' His own voice now, for Mr Collins stood frozen at the con, and they were canted over quite alarmingly with the wind on their beam and the weight of those great Atlantic rollers bearing down on them, threatening to roll her with them all the way to Brittany.

With painful slowness the bows came round once more to the wind, and Nathan ran stiff-legged down the slope of the deck, clutching at the larboard mizzen shrouds to halt his descent and peering out into the night, for he had the impression that the apparition had been on a course that would take her out into the Atlantic. He could see nothing, not even her stern lights. She was long gone, lost in the rain and the dark, as if she had never been—but it was firmly fixed in his mind that the words he had heard were French.

So, outside the realms of fantasy, she was most likely a cruise raider that had slipped out of Brest, evading the British blockade. Not impossible—others had done it—but where was she headed? Ireland, the Americas, the whaling grounds of the South Atlantic? Useless to speculate, for there was nothing he could do about it. It was highly unlikely that he would find her again in this bog of a night, even if he made the effort. And if he did, that brief glimpse had assured him that she was a two-decker, and she would have three times his weight of broadside. The sensible course would be to press on towards Ushant, where he might find one of the British squadrons engaged in blockading Brest, and he could report the encounter.

He was about to state this intention to Collins when there was a flash of light in the darkness to westward and the boom of a gun—a little muted by the weather, and most likely a signal gun. Probably from their late associate, but if so, to whom were they signalling? It could be the *Panther* herself, he supposed, but then there was another flash and report from the darkness to the north. So, he had his answer. There was another ship out there.

Then all hell broke loose. Flashes, bangs, signal lamps, flares . . . fireworks bursting in the night sky . . . Not quite a battle, more a celebration. Enough to tell him there was a whole fleet out there, or at least a squadron. Eight, nine ships perhaps, strung out across a mile or so of ocean.

A presence at his shoulder. The first lieutenant, Mr Simpson, doubtless roused by all the hoohah, fully dressed, too, in as much as Nathan could tell by the light of the stern lantern. Nathan apprised him of the situation, and he could tell from the way the officer peered out into the darkness and then at his captain that he had his doubts. A lone cruiser perhaps, but not a fleet.

'Beat to quarters,' Nathan instructed him, 'and clear the decks for action. But as quiet as we can. No need to bring attention to ourselves.'

For the next few minutes or so they ran blindly on, and the crew went to their action stations in the dark and with a great deal less fuss than usual. Whatever he might think of his officers in terms of their manner, there was no faulting their organisation, and the crew of the *Panther* were as well trained as any under his command. There was a fair bit of noise when they rolled out the guns, but otherwise they might have been padding around in dancing pumps. Possibly they were.

But still he could see no sign of the enemy. If enemy they were.

He looked out to windward again, wiping the water from his eyes. He might have been seeing things. Hearing them, too. How sure was he that the voices he had heard, or thought he had heard, had been French?

Sure enough, he thought. He was not going to retreat in the face of the first lieutenant's scepticism. They had almost been run down by a French ship of war, and there were a number of other ships out there. If they were French and they were signalling each other, it would be to pass on the news that there was a stranger in their midst. Most likely British.

He looked to his own lights. The big stern lantern, the two smaller lights at the top of the mainmast, and the dim glow of binnacle and belfry. It was probably best to douse them, he thought, at least at masthead and stern, and take the risk of a collision over the greater risk of making the frigate a target. He was about to give the order when there was a shout from one of the lookouts in the mizzentop, and he caught the word 'Astern!'

He turned on his heel to see another apparition bearing down on them, this time to larboard. It might have been the same one, circled back on them. The same impression of a warlike prow and a great mass of sail, just a little paler than the night. Then a great belch of flame as she fired on them.

He had no idea of where the shot went. High and wide, he hoped. There was no obvious sign of injury. He was tempted to fall off the wind and cut across her bow, for it was a perfect opportunity for a raking shot, but she was too close—she would smash right into them, and they would come off far worse from the encounter, for even the little he could see of her in the darkness indicated that she was a ship of the line. But what else was he to do? He could not go running on into the night, letting her knock bits off him, not least because he was likely to be one of the first bits.

Then he thought of the carronades in the quarter galleries.

He had caused them to be mounted shortly before their fight with the *Perle* because he had detected a blind spot in the *Panther*'s defences. The quarter gallery was where the captain had his own private seat of ease—two of them, in fact, one on each side for the convenience of his dinner guests—but Nathan had installed a thirty-two-pound carronade there with a range of fire that covered most eventualities. He had to squeeze past to relieve himself, but it was a small price to pay for the cover they provided.

He called out to one of the midshipmen and sent him below with instructions for the crew of the larboard carronade to fire at will. It must have been loaded and ready, for he had barely to wait more than a few seconds after the midshipman's hurried departure before there was a flash and a roar from the desired location. At this range they could hardly have missed, but there was no sign that they had done any damage, and he could see from the white crest of foam at her bow that their opponent was gaining on them. If she drew level they would feel the weight of her broadside—in fact, she had only to fall off the wind a little and they would be feeling it already, but perhaps her captain was afraid of losing them in the dark.

This reminded him of his long-delayed order to extinguish the stern light, but before he could issue it, the French fired again and did it for him. Nathan felt a sharp stab of pain in his left shoulder, and when he put his hand to it, he felt a shard of hot glass sticking out of his oilcloth. Another inch and it would have gone through his neck. He pulled it out without thinking and released a gush of warm blood.

He told one of the midshipmen to fetch him a wad from one of the quarterdeck guns and pressed it onto the wound. He seemed to be the only casualty, besides the lantern itself.

He could still see nothing in the sea ahead. Either their lights were veiled by rain or there was nothing there. But then something very like a starburst exploded in the sky and in its glow he saw them—at least seven or eight ships to the north, and half as many to the south, spread out across maybe a mile or so of ocean. He could see his own ship, too, the entire length of her, from the bowsprit to where he was standing, and if he could, so could they. What in God's name, or more likely the Devil's, were they using as a light? But then it was gone, and they were in darkness again, all the deeper for the brightness that had preceded it.

And in darkness they stayed. There was no further attempt to fire upon them, nor any sign of their pursuer, or any other ship. At the end of the watch, he had the guns secured and the men stood down. And they continued northward through the night.

Nathan stayed on deck until the end of the first watch and then went below to rouse the doctor, or one of the loblolly men, to have his wound properly dressed. Then he went to bed. He never did get his port and toasted cheese.

Chapter 4
Christmas

An empty sea it remained, even at break of day. A grim, grey day much the same as the last, with low scudding clouds, the same chill wind from the northeast, and frequent rain squalls. They had held their course throughout the night and by Nathan's reckoning were almost due west of the great naval base at Brest. But there was no sign of the French fleet—or indeed, of the British fleet that was meant to be blockading them there.

He summoned Simpson to his cabin and instructed his steward to bring them a fresh pot of coffee. It failed to strike a note of informality, much less companionship, but then there was nothing in their previous relations that had encouraged him to expect either.

'There is nothing for it but to make for Falmouth and send word to the Admiralty by land,' he proposed. 'It will be a great deal faster than beating up the Channel in the present conditions.'

Simpson nodded thoughtfully but said nothing.

'I cannot avoid my meeting in London,' Nathan told him. He had said nothing to his officers about the nature of this meeting, though it was possible they knew from other sources. 'So, the most sensible course is for me to carry the news myself, while you take the ship back to Gibraltar.'

There was no indication from Simpson's expression that he agreed with his conclusion or not, or what his own personal preferences might be. He might have been looking forward to Christmas in London with his family, perhaps. Nathan did not even know if he had family. Perhaps he should ask; perhaps he should have asked long ago. But now was probably not the time, not when he had already made up his mind that Simpson was taking the ship back to Gibraltar.

'If you encounter any ships of the blockading fleet, pass the news on to them, but otherwise, press on to Gibraltar to let Collingwood know.'

'You are assuming, sir, that the ships were French?'

Finally, a reaction, if not one that Nathan might have wished for.

'You think they were not?' he said.

'I do not think we can say for certain. Sir.'

'You think it was the British blockade?'

'There is surely that possibility.'

'Except for the French voices—and the signals.'

Simpson said nothing.

'Have you ever seen British ships signalling like that?'

'No—but . . .'

Nathan paused to let him finish, but that was it.

'If they were French, they will be well out into the Atlantic now, heading towards the Americas,' Nathan went on. 'I think that possibility must be acknowledged. So, I am going to take poste from Falmouth, and you are going to take the ship back to Gibraltar with my report.'

'Certainly, sir.'

Simpson tipped the remains of his coffee down his throat and reached for his hat.

And Nathan sent word for Mr Banjo.

The name was derived not from the musical instrument, as most of his shipmates assumed, but from a shortening of his family name of Adebanjo, whose meaning, as he had informed Nathan upon enquiry, was 'he who fits the crown.' He was in fact the eldest son of a Yoruba chieftain in the region of the Niger who had been sold into slavery after a palace coup by one of his brothers. When he and Nathan first met, he had been among the entourage of the Spanish governor of Louisiana. Nathan had purchased his freedom, and that of a number of his fellows, when he found himself in need of a crew.

Since then, they had shared a number of adventures on land and sea, and Nathan considered him a friend, in as much as the exigencies of the service would allow. Apart from his current role as coxswain, Banjo had served as bodyguard, spy, gunner's mate, and armourer, having an affinity for all forms of ordnance, the more complex the better. He enjoyed the rank of a warrant officer, but Nathan addressed him as George in private and tended to avoid giving him direct orders, rather framing them in the nature of a request, which he normally considered favourably, though not always.

He suspected this interview would be rather more difficult than the one with the first lieutenant, and he was right.

'Why is that?' demanded George, when Nathan informed him that on this occasion he would be travelling alone.

'You know why is that,' he replied tartly.

During the last war, when they were serving in the Ionian Sea, George had been accused of striking an officer—a hanging offence if it was proven. Witnesses said that there had been an altercation, and in walking off George had caught the officer with his shoulder and sent him spinning to the deck, but he would still hang for it if it came to a court-martial, and Nathan had been obliged to have him placed in irons. But later, in the heat of battle, he had freed him and arranged his escape. The navy never forgot a charge as heinous as striking an officer, however. Years later, on his return to England, George had been arrested by a notorious thief-taker by the name of Mellors, and Nathan had been put to the trouble of arranging a second escape.

He pointed out now that he did not want to take the risk of it happening again.

'We have risked it before,' George demurred, 'when we came back from France.'

'We had no choice,' said Nathan. 'This is different.'

'I could use a different name.'

Nathan shook his head. 'Apart from the danger to yourself, it would be a considerable embarrassment to me if you were discovered,' he said.

George did not know of the trouble Nathan was in—if he had, there would have been no dissuading him—but this last exchange took the wind out of his sails, and he reluctantly agreed to stay with the ship.

They reached Falmouth early in the forenoon watch, and Nathan secured a post chaise to carry him on to London. This took a few hours longer than he expected, the roads being especially bad at this time of the year. There was even a fall of snow that held them up for the best part of a day in Devon, which meant that they would be arriving in the capital late on the twenty-fifth. Nathan had not overlooked the advent of Christmas, but the festivities had not played a great part in his life for some years. Last Christmas he had been in the Temple prison in Paris.

He wondered what Louise would be doing by way of celebration. If anything. She might be an atheist, for all he knew. A republican and an atheist. Strangely, this was one of the many personal details they had not yet discussed.

The closer they got to London the more nervous he felt, not from fear of the inquiry he was to face, but with the anticipation of seeing her again. It was six months since the last time. Then, he had felt as close to her as anyone he had ever met. Now, he was almost afraid to meet her. He would know by the look in her eyes, he thought, whether she still loved him, and whether the child she was carrying was really his.

It was raining when they reached London, the streets unusually deserted. It was three in the afternoon and what little light there had been all day was fast leeching from the winter sky.

He instructed the coachman to take him directly to Whitehall, and to wait.

Admiralty House appeared to be as empty as the streets of London. He could see no light in the windows. He had to knock several times before the door was opened. An elderly man in some kind of naval uniform, possibly from a different era—Queen Anne's navy, perhaps. He carried a horn lantern and looked much put out by the disturbance.

'What is all this,' he complained. 'Knock, knock, knock.'

The porters at Admiralty House were notoriously disrespectful of the naval officers who so often came a'begging at their door, most of them being in hopes of a ship or a promotion. Nathan apologised for the intrusion, keeping his sarcasm muted, and asked if the first lord was in residence. Lord Barham, he knew, often slept here. But not on Christmas Day, apparently. He was at his home in the country, the porter replied, with his nearest and dearest, as every Christian soul should be.

'Is anyone in authority here?' Nathan enquired, his tone becoming increasingly sardonic. 'Only I have come a long way, and I have urgent news of the French fleet.'

This, possibly combined with the gold lace on his hat, did at least stop the man from closing the door in his face. He invited Nathan to step across the threshold whilst he enquired of 'Them Upstairs.'

It took a while, but eventually he returned with the news that the 'duty officer' would attend to him.

The duty officer turned out to be a young lieutenant by the name of Parker who occupied a room on the first floor. It was sparsely furnished but blessed with a small coal fire which was presently the only source of illumination. On the table before him there was a bottle and two glasses, half full, but whoever had been keeping him company had obviously made themselves scarce. Nathan doubted if it was the porter.

In a few words he reported his encounter with the French squadron off Brest.

'My goodness,' said the lieutenant, 'are you sure?'

'Perfectly sure,' replied Nathan coolly. 'At least eight ships of the line, possibly more.'

'Well, well,' said the lieutenant, scratching his head.

There was a short silence.

'I was surprised not to encounter a single ship of our blockade,' Nathan ventured. 'Else I would have reported it to them.'

'Ah. That is because they are not there,' said Parker, attempting a feeble smile.

'Why, is the war ended?' Nathan enquired.

'No, no. Ha ha. Or if it is, no-one has told me about it.'

He saw that this drollery was greeted with no appreciable change of expression.

'No, his lordship thought it so unlikely that the French would venture out, what with Trafalgar and the winter, you know, that it would be safe to withdraw the fleet to home waters.'

'I see,' said Nathan. This was very unlike Barham, but there might be other considerations he knew nothing about.

'Yes, well, but you say they are out,' the lieutenant pressed him.

'Well, a good few of them, at least.'

'I see. Well, I suppose I should send to inform him.'

'It would be as well,' agreed Nathan.

'Even though it is Christmas Day.'

'This is true.'

'Can I offer you a drink?' Parker gazed rather miserably at the bottle and the two half-filled glasses. Nathan wondered who his companion had been and where he was now. Or she.

'Not for the moment, thank you. Perhaps you would like me to write a report.'

The lieutenant brightened a little. 'Yes. Yes. That is an excellent idea. A written report.'

'You have a messenger available.'

'I do. I do. Well, I did do, not so long ago.' He looked about him as if he might have mislaid him somewhere in the room.

'And transport?'

'Yes, yes, I believe there is a coach—somewhere.'

Barham House was somewhere in Kent, Nathan recalled, possibly near Maidstone. A good forty miles or so.

'What about the first secretary, Mr Marsden?' he suggested.

Marsden was a Dubliner, but Nathan had an idea he had a house in London.

'Oh, good lord, yes. Mr Marsden. He lives in Kensal Green.'

'Considerably closer, in fact.'

'Yes, yes. It is.'

'Then might I suggest—'

'Of course, of course. I suppose—I mean—would you like pen and ink.'

'That would be helpful. Paper, too, if you have any.'

It took a few minutes to arrive, and a few minutes longer for Nathan to complete his dispatch. He accepted a glass of wine while he was engaged.

'I will send it at once,' declared the lieutenant. 'Is there anything else, while you are here?'

'No,' said Nathan. 'I will wait for Mr Marsden to contact me if he requires further information.'

He gave the lieutenant his mother's address and returned to the coach with the rather unsatisfactory feeling that he might have done more.

'Soho Square,' he instructed the driver.

The roads being clear, they were there within a few minutes.

Unlike the Admiralty, the house was brightly lit from top to bottom, and there was the sound of music from within.

His mother's footman, Vincent, answered the door. He was properly astonished, but then his pleasant young face spread in a delighted grin.

'Happy Christmas,' said Nathan.

'Well, it is now, sir,' said Vincent. This was so precisely the right answer that Nathan could have embraced him, but the poor fellow might have been embarrassed.

'Is my mother home?' he asked, stepping through the door.

This was not as absurd a question as it might have been in any other household, for his mother was often not at home, and Christmas would probably have increased her social obligations. As for the lights and music, it was perfectly possible that she had let the house out for the duration, or the servants were hosting their own celebrations.

But his mother was, apparently, at home, and entertaining guests.

Nathan did not know if he was up to guests. Not immediately, at least.

'Tell you what—I will warm myself in the kitchen and see if I can beg a drink and a bite to eat,' he said, 'while you let my mother know I am here.'

There was extra help in the kitchen and some faces that were strange to him, but enough people who knew him to have him settled comfortably by the fire while they fetched him something to eat and drink. He closed his eyes for a moment and might even have nodded off. Then he felt a hand on his shoulder.

He opened his eyes. It was not his mother.

'Are you real?' he said, for he might have been dreaming.

He touched her face to be sure, and she kissed him somewhat chastely on the forehead, but this would not do at all. He pulled her onto his lap and kissed her firmly on the mouth. There was rather more to her than he had expected, but he recalled that she was six months pregnant.

When she surfaced, she appeared slightly shocked. It was not, after all, something you were supposed to do in front of the servants, even with a Frenchwoman.

He had expected them to be shocked, too. What he did not expect was the applause.

Chapter 5

The House in Meard Street

'*Mon Dieu!* Will you stop pacing about like a large rat in a cage!'

'I am sorry. I do not mean to be so . . .'

Nathan would have preferred a different analogy, lion or tiger—even wolf would not have been anything like as offensive—but he flung himself down upon the nearest, indeed only, available armchair, shifting slightly to remove what turned out to be a chisel from beneath his left buttock. Lacking any other means of disposal, he placed it on the floor.

'It is a nautical habit, I fear, of which I am scarcely aware.'

'Well, please endeavour to wean yourself from it, at least when you are not at sea. You are even making the baby restless. It has been kicking the shit out of me since you got here.'

This conversation was conducted in French, the speaker's native tongue, which rendered the last sentence a little less vulgar than if it had been spoken in English, though this was unimaginable in any English lady of Nathan's acquaintance, but then, he had never heard them hoot like an owl either.

'Is it getting you down?' he enquired considerately.

'Is *what* getting me down?'

Her tone advised retreat; instead, he hazarded a cautious advance.

'Well . . .' He nodded in the direction of her abdomen.

Louise was, by her own account, some six months with child, but if it had not been apparent in her appearance, it was in her manner, which was unusually irascible. In the time he had known her, she had never been chary of expressing an opinion, even if it could be construed as critical, but he would never have described her as short-tempered or shrewish. Of late, however, she often appeared irritated by quite minor issues, and he attributed this to what he had described as her 'confinement.'

Louise no more liked being confined than he did—hence, the pacing—and she had probably spent more time in her rooms in Meard Street than any other place in her life, with the exception of the Carmes prison in Paris at the time of the Terror. He felt that she should get out more, and if she was reluctant to go out alone, or even with a servant, he was perfectly happy to give her the pleasure of his company. Whenever he had suggested this, however, she had appeared reluctant on the grounds that she did not want to be dragging her 'bump' around with her, as she indelicately put it.

He had his doubts about this, or at least about its being the only reason. Whilst his knowledge of the precise stages, symptoms, and effects of pregnancy was as informed as that of any naval officer, no more, no less, in her case they did not seem to him to be especially restrictive. In the first place, the 'bump' was not too difficult to disguise if she wore loose clothing, as now, and, more significantly, she did not appear to be the least embarrassed either by her condition or by the circumstance of being unmarried. It helped, of course, that she was French. When it came to ethical matters, there were fewer strictures on the French émigrés in London than there would have been on the native of the species. Besides, when she had first arrived in London, she had put it about that she was married to an English naval officer who was being held as a prisoner of war in France.

'And if people ask who *I* am . . . ?' Nathan had enquired when this subterfuge was revealed to him.

'Then I shall say you are his brother,' she had replied with smile.

It was as difficult to get a sensible reply out of Louise as it was to know if she was telling the truth, or guarding it with some elaborate fiction of her own invention—fibs, falsehoods, fairy tales . . . Nathan had several words for them, and they all seemed to begin with *f*.

He was sure, however, that her ambiguous status—and his—was the main reason she did not want him squiring her about the city, at least so far as social events were concerned, though she was amenable to the occasional walk or drive in Hyde Park, provided they did not stop to converse with anyone.

Which was easy enough at present, given Nathan's own social isolation.

'What is getting me down,' she said now, 'is the fact of your pacing about the room as if it is the quarterdeck of a frigate. Which is, I am sure, where you would much rather be.'

'That is not true,' insisted Nathan indignantly, though he would not have wished to be questioned on the matter by a skilled interrogator. He had not yet told Louise of his present predicament, and his fear that he might never get to pace the quarterdeck of a frigate—or any other ship of war, for that matter—ever again. He told himself that this was because he did not wish to burden her with his own problems when she had such a significant one of her own. Besides, he had heard nothing from the Admiralty since his return, which was almost two weeks since. Nothing about his report of the French fleet; nothing about the inquiry. He did not think they had forgotten him. The wheels of authority turned slowly, but they usually got there in the end.

Louise muttered some words in the Breton dialect which were mostly beyond Nathan's comprehension, but he caught their drift.

'Louise, I am happy wherever *you* are—you should know that by now.'

'Should I?' But she softened slightly. She smiled a quizzical smile. 'Even in Shit Street?'

He took this to be a comment on her condition rather than her address, and was disposed to resent it. He had repeated his proposal of marriage on several occasions since his return from Gibraltar, and her replies had been evasive.

She did not wish him to feel under any pressure, she had said. Or else, she did not care to marry someone who spent most of his life at sea. She said she did not wish to be 'a grass widow,' and 'to dwindle into a wife.' Both these phrases were said in English, and he was persuaded she had heard them from his mother, who had harboured her own resentments on that score when she was married to his father. There may have been other reasons she did not care to mention, however, and about which he could only speculate.

He permitted his gaze to roam about the room, this being less objectionable, he hoped, than if he paced about it. It was officially described as the withdrawing room, and was on the first floor overlooking the street, but as it faced north and Louise was, among other things, a talented sculptor, she had appropriated it as her studio; hence, the chisel and other tools that lay about the place, along with a great many lumps of clay and the bole of a tree which had appeared since his last visit, and whose origin he had not yet explored, other than enquiring as to how she had managed to get it up the stairs. ('I carried it,' she said, which he was not inclined to take seriously, as it looked as if it weighed as much as a twelve-pounder gun carriage. He could not help wondering, of course, who had found it for her.)

Propped against the walls at floor level were a number of sketches in charcoal, mostly of male and female body parts, and on a table were numerous pieces of rock, a mortar and pestle, a hammer, a mallet, and more chisels similar to the one he had sat upon. There was a smell that he vaguely identified as a mixture of turpentine, earth, and rotting wood, along with something else he could not put a name to—not what you might expect of a lady's drawing room, but not as unpleasant as the others.

Returning his attention to the tree—which was hard to ignore, as it occupied a large portion of the room—Nathan saw that it had acquired a breast, part of an arm, and the beginnings of a hip, but the rest remained in the state nature had intended, retaining most of its bark and even a quantity of ivy.

Although it was clearly in its early stages, it reminded him of their first encounter on the island of Jersey in the first months of her exile. It was not really an encounter, as he was fairly sure she had not been aware of his presence, being entirely engrossed in carving the statue of an angel in an old chapel. He had stood in the doorway, captivated not simply by the loveliness of her features, but by the rapt expression upon them—the total sense of absorption in her art.

The angel had, in fact, turned out disappointingly, in Nathan's view, largely on account of its features bearing a disturbing resemblance to those of his commanding officer, Sir Sidney Smith. He had not mentioned this to Louise, only that the face looked more demonic than one might expect of an angel, to which she had replied only that it was 'the Avenging Angel,' which did nothing to clarify the issue or resolve his suspicions. He imagined that it had remained behind on the island when she had abruptly departed for France. She may even have presented it to Smith as a parting gift.

'Did you ever finish the sculpture for Rose?' he enquired. 'That is, Empress Jose—'

'No, I did not.'

Clearly this was another subject to be avoided.

There were several areas of Louise's life that came into this category, not least the reason she had fled to England. The only time he had asked a direct question about it, she had said, possibly in a spirit of sarcasm, that she thought he might have been interested in knowing that she was carrying his child. He restrained himself from pointing out that there was no reason for her to believe that she would find him in London at the time. In fact, he had been at sea, as he usually was. It was true that she had made herself—and her condition—known to his mother, but as she did not expect him to marry her, and had refused to let him provide for her in any other way, he considered it reasonable to harbour doubts.

Wherever her money came from, she obviously had enough to pay the rent and to retain a pair of servants—a man and a woman, both Bretons, who attended to all of her domestic requirements—though Nathan detected a more complicated relationship than was usual between mistress and staff. Their names were Branoc and Bella—short for Belladyna—and they appeared to be in their late twenties. He did not know if these were their real names; they sounded too neat to him, too much of a pair. When he asked Louise how she knew them, she had said she had gotten them through an agency. Best not to ask anything about that either.

'I see you have started on a new project,' he ventured, this being a reasonably safe subject, though not without a number of pitfalls he might inadvertently blunder into, his knowledge of sculpture being limited.

'Yes.' They both looked at it, his expression bland, hers critical.

'What exactly . . . ?'

'A dryad.'

'Ah.'

'It is a character in Greek mythology,' she informed him after a moment. 'A spirit who lives in a tree and takes the form of a young woman.'

'Yes,' he said, 'I know what a dryad is.'

He wondered sometimes if Louise was coming too much under the influence of his mother, who seemed to think that because he had been at sea since he was thirteen years old, he was as ignorant of the classics as he was of any other form of learning besides the ability to tie knots and name many of the principal objects in the cosmos, accomplishments which she did not consider especially advantageous in London society.

He was still gazing at the object in the centre of the room. Although it looked as if Louise had only just started on it, it occurred to him now that she might mean to leave it much as it was, so that it appeared that the dryad was emerging from the tree, as if in the process of birth, or transformation. He was about to congratulate her on this concept, or if that was not her intention, to suggest it to her, when he thought better of it. There were times when Louise welcomed comments on her work, even ideas for improvement, but he sensed instinctively that this was not one of them.

'Would you not prefer to work in a studio?' he enquired.

'I am perfectly content where I am, thank you.'

Nathan sighed, shaking his head, and before he could think better of it, he said: 'Louise, I wish you would let me marry you.'

She observed him silently for a moment, and he tried to read what thoughts lay behind that thoughtful appraisal, but she was at least as practised in the art of subterfuge as he was.

'It is not that I do not wish to marry you,' she said.

'But . . .'

'As I told you . . .'

'Not while I am wedded to the sea.'

'I did not put it quite like that.'

'Perhaps not in so many words, but it was what you meant,' he persisted. 'Just as a nun is wedded to the Church. It is a false perception which I believe you share with my mother. In fact, the sea has come close to killing me on a number of occasions and will doubtless succeed one of these days, and I had as rather be wedded to it as to . . .' He sought a suitable example.

'An assassin?'

That was not the word he sought. The last time he had called her that, even in jest, she had been so little amused it had led to a furious row, and it was the last time he had seen her for a year.

'You would make a very poor assassin,' he said carefully, 'in your present condition.'

'Oh, I do not know. I think it might be much to my advantage in putting my victim off his guard, and I am as capable of wielding a dagger as I ever was, though I might choose the bludgeon over the blade. In fact, there are several objects within my reach at present that would serve as well as any.'

She gave him a wicked grin which after a moment he returned, though somewhat less wickedly. It was as difficult to remain cross with Louise as it was to know when she was being flippant or serious, telling him the truth, or beguiling him with one of her fictions.

She was probably not an assassin, he had concluded, but for at least half of her life she had inhabited a world in which violent death and deception was the normal expectation.

It had crossed his mind, of course, that the child she was carrying was not his. He had instantly dismissed this as unworthy of him—worse than that—but he could not stop it forcing its way out of that dark part of his mind where the demons dwelt. They had spent two weeks together at Malmaison after his escape from the Temple prison in Paris—an escape procured by her agency, and with the assistance of her friend, the empress. It was the last place the authorities would look for him, Louise had insisted when he had expressed his doubts on the subject. He had lived in seclusion in a cottage in the grounds where, despite the precarious nature of his situation, they had made love almost every day. As a means of preventing her present condition, she had used a sea sponge soaked in a mixture of vinegar and cedar oil, but he could not be sure that she had always worn it, and, in any case, he was no more assured of its reliability than any other form of contraception, though in his experience the French were usually rather better at it than most.

He saw that Louise was regarding him thoughtfully.

'What are you thinking about?' she said.

'You,' he said. 'And the cottage in Malmaison.'

He thought there was the hint of a blush.

'There is a bit more of me nowadays,' she said.

'But still as beautiful.'

'And what else?'

'What?'

'What else was on your mind? You were looking pensive.'

'Ah. Well, I was also vaguely wondering what we are having for dinner.'

This was a lie, but she frequently accused him of thinking too much of his stomach.

'A *terrine de faisan*, *soupe à l'oignon*, *bouillabaisse*, *cassoulet*, *crêpes aux amandes*, and a *tarte Tatin*,' she replied at once.

'Really?' He brightened.

'I have no idea. I just made it up.'

She dissolved into helpless laughter when she saw his face.

'I am sorry,' she said, eventually. 'I should not tease you, but it is irresistible at times. I confess I do not know what we are having, but it will be something nice.'

This was probably true. Whatever else Nathan might feel about the house in Meard Street, he could not fault the cuisine.

'A nice salad, perhaps,' she said.

She was under the impression that he hated salad. This was not true, though you could have too much of a good thing. But he did not rise to the bait. He considered he was fairly safe from salad in January.

'I do love you, you know,' she said.

'And I love you,' he said, as if he had countered a move in chess and awaited the next with interest.

She heaved herself up from her chair and crossed over to him and sat down on his lap.

He gave an exaggerated *Ouff!* (though she was, in fact, quite heavy).

'Are you going to spend the night here,' she said, 'or are you going back to Mama?'

She squirmed her bottom against him provocatively.

'Going back to Mama,' he said. He caught her wrist to stop her from slapping him.

'Because you do not care to sleep with a woman who is with child,' she said scathingly, 'even though the child is your own?'

'No. Of course not.'

This was true.

'Then why?'

'Because I am going to a funeral.'

She winced. She knew this. She also knew whose funeral it was. There was no-one in the country, outside of Bedlam, who did not.

'The funeral is not until the afternoon,' she said.

'I know,' he said. 'But we have to be at the cathedral first thing, because of the crowds.'

This was a lie.

Chapter 6

The Funeral

The real reason was to see Emma.

He had resolved that on the morning of the funeral he would pay his respects to the grieving widow—as she would doubtless consider herself, even if no-one else did. This meant a ten-mile coach ride to the house Nelson had purchased for them both at Merton, and where he had lived during the short-lived peace with France, initially with Emma and her husband, Sir William Hamilton, and then, after his timely death, with Emma and her daughter Horatia, who was widely believed to be his own. Nathan knew they had spent his last few weeks ashore here, before leaving for Trafalgar.

It was at least an hour's drive out of London, but despite what he had told Louise, he knew he would not have to take his seat at Saint Paul's before midday, and he figured that if he made an early start, he would have plenty of time to get there and back.

He rose before dawn, but the sky was a pale grey by the time he arrived, with streaks of pink and orange that suggested it was going to be a fine day.

A fine day for a funeral.

A servant showed him into the darkened drawing room where Emma sat alone in the bay window. She was swathed head to foot in black crepe, a dark veil covering the face that may not have literally launched a thousand ships, but had certainly turned Britain's greatest admiral into her devoted slave. The drapes were drawn and most of the light came from the fire, which threw monstrous shadows on the walls, not unlike the dancers in a Greek tragedy, or the Attitudes she used to perform for the entertainment of her guests in happier times.

As Nathan advanced into the room, he saw there was a bottle of what might have been medicine and a glass filled with a brownish liquid on the small table beside her. He also noticed a second figure, sitting in the far corner, but of so still and silent a presence it might have been the angel of death—though it was most likely her loyal companion, Mrs Cadogan, who had been with her in Naples and was thought to be her mother.

He made his bow to both ladies and murmured his condolences to Emma. She did not rise, but she lifted her veil to permit a chaste kiss upon the cheek.

Nathan was shocked by the change in her appearance. Red-rimmed eyes he had expected, but they looked to be set in clay, so grey and slack were her features. He had seen her play many a tragic heroine in the past, but for once he was persuaded that her heartache owed nothing to artifice. She looked at least a decade older than when he had last seen her, and he would not have recognised the beauty he had known in Naples at the height of her powers.

She gestured to the leather armchair opposite. It issued something between a belch and a sigh as he lowered his weight into it, and a lance of importunate sunlight penetrated the drapes to reveal the motes of dust circling mournfully in the stagnant air.

'Was you with him,' she said, 'at the end?'

'I was,' said he, though he wondered how much she knew of the circumstances, and whose version she had heard. How did she even know Nathan had been at the battle, never mind the deathbed, such as it was?

'And did he suffer much?' Her voice broke.

He had been shot through the collarbone, the bullet piercing his lung and shattering his spine, or so Nathan had been told later by Hardy. The particulars of the wound had not been made public, but one thing was for sure—the poor man had been in agony for several hours before he died.

'He had the comfort of knowing it was the greatest naval victory England has ever known,' Nathan murmured. Unwisely.

'Fuck his victory—fuck England and all it meant to him!' And here was the spitting tigress loosed, but her rage dissolved in broken-hearted sobs.

'His last words were of you,' he murmured lamely, and far too late.

In truth, whilst he had been present on the occasion, he had been too far back and the noise of battle too loud for him to hear much besides Nelson's injunctions to the doctor to rub his back or fan his face or give him water. It was only later that he had been told of his plea to Hardy to look after Emma. Reverend Scott had recorded his last words as 'God and my country,' but then he would; he was a chaplain of the Church of England.

'You are going to the funeral, I suppose,' said Emma, looking up, her voice more controlled but the anger still palpable.

'I am,' he said, bowing his head.

'You know I am not invited.'

'I did not,' he lied.

He was surprised to be included on the guest list himself, given his current disgrace, but perhaps Lord Barham had put in a word. Strictly speaking, having been with him at the Nile, he was one of the band of brothers, though as he had not been captain of one of the ships, his status was, as usual, ambiguous.

He met her eyes. 'I am so sorry, I—'

'Damned hypocrites,' she spat. 'And is it true they brought him back to England in a cask of brandy?'

It was what everyone wanted to know.

'It might have been rum,' he told her, in the interests of accuracy.

But she was wracked with sobs once more, and soon led away by her loyal attendant, leaving him to make his own way back to the carriage.

Damned hypocrites was right, he thought, as they took the road back to London, though in fairness it was probably the king who was the principal obstacle to inviting Emma to Saint Paul's. Whatever else you called him, he was probably not a hypocrite; he believed most of what he said, that was the trouble, and he had always been very strict on morals, even his own. Besides, it was always difficult to invite a man's mistress to his funeral when his wife was going to be there. It was probably written up in a book of etiquette somewhere.

His pity for Emma was combined with a degree of anger for the way she had been treated. Not just now, but for most of her life. She had been passed around from man to man since she was a young girl, when her face had made her fortune. But whether you were an heiress or a blacksmith's daughter, your fortune was always going to be in the hands and at the whim of the men you met along the way. She had probably been a lot luckier or cleverer than most women who relied upon their looks for advancement. Sir William Hamilton had been enough of a gentleman, or held her in sufficient esteem, to marry her, thus giving her the protection of his name, his position, and a title, whilst Nelson had loved her enough to leave his wife, offend his sovereign and his peers, and find himself shunned by what passed for civilised society.

Until he was dead, of course, when they all wanted to claim his acquaintance.

But not hers.

Nathan recalled when he had first met her in Naples, back in '97 when everyone wanted to know her. She had been at the height of her powers, wife of the British envoy and friend and counsellor to Queen Maria Carolina, sister of Marie Antoinette and consort to the king of the Two Sicilies. She might not have been mistress of her own fate, but at that time she had determined the fate of the kingdom, for the queen did whatever Emma told her, and the king, whatever the queen told him, at least where politics were concerned. She was only twenty-one when she had first arrived in Naples, dumped by her previous lover and passed on to his rich old uncle, but within a few years she could lay claim to being the most famous woman in Europe. It was said that young men on the Grand Tour did not consider it a success unless it had concluded with a visit to Lady Hamilton at the Palazzo Sessa—you could keep your Alps and your volcanoes.

And now . . .

He thought of that grieving figure in black crepe. Overweight and crippled by debts, viciously lampooned by the cartoonists, despised as a harlot by king and country, with an illegitimate child to maintain—two, perhaps—and a crumbling manor in Merton. What would become of her now? Nelson might have loved her, but he could not leave her a fortune, or very much money at all. Hardy had told Nathan that in his last letter he had bequeathed her to the nation. Much good that would do her, with George III on the throne and William Pitt in Downing Street.

These and similar thoughts occupied Nathan for most of the drive back to London. The day had fulfilled its early promise, but it was still January, and out in the countryside the frost lay heavy on ground and trees.

Nathan huddled in his boat cloak, his feet like blocks of ice in his Hessian boots, thinking of the golden days of Naples and the voluptuous beauty who had danced like a goddess in a muslin veil for the delectation of her guests at the Palazzo Sessa.

He joined his mother at breakfast.

'How was she?' she said.

He shrugged.

'Stupid question,' she said. 'Poor woman. Well, I hope she has kept his letters. They will fetch a pretty price in a year or so, when the nation has finished mourning and wants another sensation.'

'Honestly, Mother . . .' He shook his head.

'In fact, anything he touched would do. Nelson memorabilia will be worth its weight in gold. Does she have much in the way of a dinner service?'

'You can be monstrous cruel sometimes.'

'I am merely being practical. But if you are to talk to me about cruel, you would do well to think on what they did in Naples, the pair of them.'

'You know nothing about Naples.'

'I know a lot more about Naples than most people. Treat it like you would a rebel town in Ireland—that is what she said to Nelson, Queen whatever her name is. And they did. Men, women, and children butchered in the streets. Spitted on spikes. Thrown on bonfires. Talk about blood on their hands.'

'Nelson had nothing to do with what happened in Naples. Apart from that poor admiral he hanged. The rest was the mob. Catholic fanatics and royalists. Queen Carolina was a vindictive old cow, I will give you that. But what could Emma have done about it?'

'She encouraged her. Then she encouraged him.'

'Oh, for God's sake, Mother. I refuse to talk to you when you are in this kind of mood.'

'When am I not?' she said, reasonably enough. 'Has she any money at all?'

'I doubt it. I think she has the house, but . . . it was not the best of buys.'

There was silence for a while, broken only by the crunching of toast.

'I heard they brought his body back from Spain in a cask of brandy,' his mother resumed.

Oh God, he thought, here we go again. He shook his head.

'Everyone is talking of it,' she said. 'Is it not true?'

'How am I to know?' he retorted. 'It might be. It is a form of preservative, I believe.'

'Brandy?' She frowned consideringly. 'I would have thought vinegar was more the thing.'

'Well, I don't know, Mother, I am not a doctor.'

'Why did they not bury him at sea? Is that not what you usually do? Needle through the nose and a cannonball at their feet and all that.'

Nathan regarded her in something close to wonder. For someone who affected to despise the sea and all who sailed on her, she had picked up a surprising amount of naval lore over the years, though it was usually the more eccentric or macabre rituals that had stuck in her mind.

'They are saying he did not want that,' Nathan confided. 'That he instructed Hardy specifically on the subject even while he lay dying. "Do not let them throw me in the sea, Hardy," he is supposed to have said. He wanted a state funeral. Nothing less.'

'Men,' said his mother.

'What has it to do with men?' he demanded. 'Specifically?'

'Oh vanity, thy name is woman. Ha.'

'I do not know that one's sex has anything to do with it.' Nathan tried to think of a woman who had been honoured with a state funeral, but apart from Queen Elizabeth, no-one sprang readily to mind, and that was going back a bit.

'I heard the common sailors drank most of it,' said his mother, 'and when it was opened up, the body was found to be in an advanced state of decay.'

Nathan put his toast down. 'Good God, Mother, we are having breakfast.'

'Are they that desperate for drink in the king's navy? I suppose they are, the way they are treated.'

'It would be nothing to do with that. If it did happen, and I am not saying it did, it would be more as a form of respect.'

'Respect! Respect? To drink the brandy you've been pickled in?'

'To imbibe of his essence, his fighting spirit.'

'What?' She stared at him in that way she had, as if she was wondering just what kind of creature she had brought into the world, and could she give it back.

'For the same reason cannibals consume the bodies of their enemies,' he explained.

His mother shook her head again. 'You are all quite barking,' she said. 'I must say, I have never understood the power of superstition. Seafarers seem to be particularly prone to it. Your father would never venture out of doors if he saw a black cat in the yard. Or was it a hen?' She considered. 'I think it was a hen. And if you spilled a few grains of salt on the table—my goodness, you would think the four horsemen of the apocalypse had rode into the room. I asked him about it once, and he told me in all seriousness that in Leonardo's painting of the Last Supper—it was the only time I ever heard him mention art in all the time I knew him, even if he didn't know who painted it—Judas Iscariot is seen to knock over the salt cellar, and that henceforth, spilled salt has been a sign of treachery and lies. Poor man.'

Now Nathan was further confused. 'Judas Iscariot?'

'No—your father, you fool. He would oblige one to throw a handful of salt over one's shoulder—the left shoulder, I recall, because this is where he believed the Devil was sitting, and tossing salt in his eyes would blind him for long enough to make one's escape. Dear me. Well, perhaps it was only his head that was decayed.'

She saw that Nathan was struggling to keep up.

'Nelson's. In the cask. I assume he was standing up in it.'

'Do you think we could talk about something more appropriate?'

'Well, I do not know what is more appropriate on the day of the poor man's funeral.'

Sooner or later, Nathan thought, conversations with his mother degenerated into absurdity or disagreement, no matter how promisingly they began, and they rarely began promisingly.

'Why were you not invited, by the by?' she asked, fixing him with her eye.

'I *am* invited.'

'But not in the guard of honour with his other friends. What do they call them—the band of brothers?'

Again, he was surprised at her knowledge, but it had likely been in the newspapers. The whole nation was feasting on the details like a flock of vultures. (If you called vultures a flock. It was probably called a murder of vultures, but perhaps that was crows.) After lying in state in Greenwich for three days, it had been arranged for the coffin to be brought up the Thames in the royal barge and housed overnight at the Admiralty, then conveyed to Saint Paul's in some kind of hearse, and escorted by seven royal dukes, sixteen earls, thirty-two admirals, and over a hundred naval captains, together with the usual baggage of lesser nobles, politicians, and members of Nelson's family.

Although Nathan had been granted a seat in the stalls, as it were, he was not a member of this august assembly.

'No,' he conceded. 'No. I—they may not have known I was back in London.'

He scraped his chair back and tossed his napkin on the table before she could interrogate him further.

'I will just have time to change into my dress uniform,' he said, 'and then I must be on my way.'

He had kept the carriage waiting outside, but the streets were so congested with horse transport of one form or another that he abandoned it halfway down Holborn and continued on foot. Even then it was hard going, and it took him the best part of an hour to make his way through the crowds lining the route, arriving at the cathedral only a few minutes before the corpse.

Housed in the magnificent funeral bier designed as a replica of the *Victory*, it towered at the head of an immense procession like the effigy of a Catholic martyr on some saint's day in Italy, advancing slowly up Ludgate Hill towards its final resting place at Saint Paul's.

The funeral of Admiral Lord Nelson was always going to be a unique national occasion, but as he had remarked to the ape, Nathan could not help but think that the government was out to milk it for all it was worth, if only to distract from the truly awful news from Europe where Napoleon was sweeping all before him. There were thirty thousand troops either involved in the procession or guarding the route, he had read, far more than had been involved in battle against the French, even after twelve years of more or less continuous warfare. If they still had plans to invade England, now was the time to do it.

The troops were especially heavy on the approaches to the cathedral, assiduously checking invitations in case anyone unauthorised had managed to slip into the hallowed precincts. Nathan was obliged to show his pass three times before he was admitted to one of the stands that had been erected under the great dome for the several thousand spectators privileged enough to attend the ceremony.

He shuffled along the row and took his seat, nodding to the gentleman next to him. He looked about the vast interior, in search of a friendly face.

'Forgive me, sir, but are you not Captain Nathaniel Peake?'

Nathan observed his neighbour more closely. He wore the uniform of a colonel in one of the highland regiments, but if they had met before, Nathan was unable to recall the circumstances. He hoped they were not too disagreeable. He did not want to be challenged to a duel at Nelson's funeral.

'I am,' he replied with a polite smile. 'How do you do, sir. I am afraid I cannot quite place the circumstances of our acquaintance . . .'

'Madras, ninety-nine,' the officer informed him briskly. 'Montgomery. Seventy-seventh Foot.'

Nathan did a swift decode of names and numbers. Madras, 1799. That would be when Nelson had sent him to India after the Battle of the Nile to warn the British authorities there that Bonaparte was heading their way. Upon his arrival, he had been given command of a motley flotilla of sloops and gunboats assembled by the East India Company and known as the Bombay Marine. The 77th had been among the troops he had embarked at Madras for an attack on the French base in the Andaman Isles.

'Of course,' declared Nathan. 'You were with Wellesley.'

'I was a mere captain then,' said the colonel. 'But I led the grenadiers when we stormed the fort at Port Blair.'

Nathan regarded him with new respect. 'How could I forget?' said he. 'It was the bravest thing I ever saw.'

Whether this was true or not, it was certainly a memorable occasion.

Nathan had sailed out of Port Blair at the head of thirteen ships: six of his own, five captured from the French, and two East Indiamen he had rescued. But his career had been in decline ever since, and the East India Company had cheated him of his prize money, just because he had burned down one of their opium warehouses.

'So, you were promoted to colonel,' Nathan remarked, observing the star and crown at his shoulder. 'My congratulations, sir.'

'No small thanks to you, sir,' said the colonel. 'And General Wellesley, of course.'

'A general, is he now?' Nathan returned, though it was not altogether surprising given that he was the younger brother of the governor-general.

'And you, sir, I trust you had your just reward.' But his eyes reflected a hint of doubt, for he had clearly observed that Nathan had not advanced beyond the rank he had held in India.

He was saved from a reply by the solemn beating of a drum, and a hush fell over the congregation as the coffin entered.

It was in fact three coffins, according to the newspapers, one inside the other, like Chinese nesting dolls. The first was a simple pinewood affair carved from the mast of the French flagship *L'Orient*, which had blown up at the Battle of the Nile, and into which the admiral's body had been laid, according to his own instruction. But the master of ceremonies Sir Isaac Heard—or Garter King of Arms, to give him his proper title—had decided that it was not suitable for the magnificence of the occasion, and so it had been placed inside another coffin made of lead, to preserve it from decay, and then in another made of mahogany and draped with the Union Jack. Unfortunately, it was then discovered to be too large to go through the door leading down to the crypt, and so a hole had been excavated in the floor of the cathedral so that the coffin could be lowered at the end of the ceremony and left there until they made the door big enough.

All in all, there was an unfortunate element of farce to the whole procedure, Nathan reflected, from the moment the illustrious corpse had been placed in the cask of brandy. Or rum.

He watched as the vast swaying edifice was carried down the central aisle by twelve sturdy bluejackets from the *Victory*, followed by a long train of the great and the good. It took the best part of an hour to get them all into the cathedral and stowed away, but at last the Archbishop of Canterbury ascended the pulpit and the service began.

It lasted four hours—as long as it had taken Nelson to die; almost as long as the battle itself. Finally, the archbishop intoned the solemn final blessing, and the twelve bearers began to remove the Union Jack before lowering the coffin into the hole in the ground.

But to the astonishment of the entire congregation, instead of disposing of the colours in the required fashion, fold by fold, the sailors began to pull and tear at it with a considerable amount of violence. Not a word was said, but a great deal of effort went into it. Most used their bare hands, but one took out a penknife, and another made use of his teeth. For a moment Nathan thought it was part of the ceremony, a final dramatic piece of theatre devised by the master of ceremonies, like the ritual rending of one's garments in grief. However, the consternation of the archbishop and clergy suggested otherwise.

Nathan recalled what his mother had said at breakfast about the rising price of Nelson memorabilia. Obviously the sailors had come to the same conclusion. Despite the presence of so many admirals and generals and soldiers and marines, no-one attempted to stop them, and once they had secured their piece of cloth and stowed it about their persons, they resumed their stations on either side of the coffin and lowered it carefully into the hole.

Nelson would have loved it.

It took even longer to get them all out of the cathedral than it did to get them in.

Nathan was shuffling along with the herd when he felt a heavy hand clapped onto his shoulder and turned to see a familiar face from the past.

'Ben Hallowell!' he exclaimed.

Hallowell was one of the few senior officers he genuinely liked. There were a number of reasons for this, but perhaps it was mainly because they were the only senior officers in the service who could claim to be Americans, should they be inclined to do so, Nathan having been born in New York and Ben in Boston in the years before the Independence War.

'How the devil are you?' Hallowell greeted him, rather more loudly than he perhaps should have, given the location.

'All the better for seeing you,' Nathan replied. 'Even in the present circumstances.'

'What a farce!' Hallowell exclaimed. 'The only bit of Nelson was the last bit—the rest was all Sir Isaac Turd, Garter King of Arsewipes.'

Hallowell was a big man—as tall as Nathan and almost twice as broad in the beam, and he had a voice to match his frame. There were a number of shocked exhalations from those nearest to them. Even Nathan was a mite disconcerted, for they were not quite out of the nave.

'I guess we have you to thank for that,' he pointed out, for it was Hallowell who had presented Nelson with the simple pine-wood coffin that Sir Isaac Heard had felt obliged to encase in more magnificent apparel.

'Are you heading off somewhere?' Nathan enquired, 'or do you have time for a tipple?'

'I fear I have a prior engagement,' Hallowell confessed, looking embarrassed.

Nathan wondered if it was with the band of brothers.

'But, what of tomorrow?' said Hallowell quickly. 'Would you be free for dinner?'

Now it was Nathan who hesitated. 'Are you sure . . . ?' he began.

'Of course, I am sure. Dear God, man. In fact, apart from the pleasure of your company, there is something particular I wanted to say to you. That is, some intelligence that might . . . that you might find interesting. Now is neither the time nor place.'

'Very well, it would be my pleasure,' said Nathan, wonderingly. And so after agreeing on a suitable venue, he trudged off alone into the darkness.

It was not too dark, in fact, for a great many people were now making their way homeward, many with link boys or servants in attendance, and the road was filled with carriages whose lanterns provided an additional source of light. It was impossible to find a cab, of course, and even if he had, with the state of the roads it would have been quicker to walk. Though the night was cold, at least it was not raining, and it was a safe enough route back so far as footpads and other inconveniences of London life were concerned.

He arrived at Soho Square more footsore and weary than he should have been after a two-mile hike. But it had been a long day, with a considerable drain on his emotional resources, and he wanted nothing more than to stretch out his feet to the kitchen stove and console himself with a mug of spiced wine and whatever leftovers he could find in the larder.

But this was not quite true. He *did* want something more.

He stopped to think about it for a moment, and the more he thought about it, the more he wanted it, so he walked down Dean Street in the direction of Louise's house.

At the junction with Meard Street he paused, however, wondering if it was such a good idea, for he had told her he would not call on her that night, thinking that he might meet up with a few friends after the ceremony. She had been more than a little put out, in fact.

Before he could decide one way or another, a hackney carriage turned the corner at the opposite end of the street and stopped outside her address to discharge a gentleman wearing a bicorn hat and what appeared to be a boat cloak who, after paying off the jarvey, strode confidently up to the front door and tugged on the bell pull.

There was an interval of perhaps half a minute when both men stood at their stations, Nathan in the shadows at the end of the street, the other man outside the door.

Then something made the caller turn his head, and in the light of the flambeau beside the door Nathan recognised the features of his former commanding officer, Sir Sidney Smith.

The door opened, and without further ceremony, he stepped inside.

Nathan stood there for another minute or so, until a light appeared in an upstairs room, and then he turned away and walked back up Dean Street to his mother's house in Soho Square.

Chapter 7

The Efficacy of the Scapegoat

Ben Hallowell came quickly to the point.

'I hear you are in a spot of bother with their lordships,' he said as soon as they had taken their seats at the table and the first bottle had been broached.

'That is one way of putting it,' said Nathan. 'The way Old Cuddy put it, I was to be hanged, drawn, and quartered.'

'Surely not?' Hallowell looked startled. He was a man who tended to the literal. 'Well, I must say you are remarkably cool about it.'

'I am trying not to let it put me off my appetite,' said Nathan.

They had reserved a private room at the Spring Garden, a tavern in that part of London known as Sailortown. Bordering the Thames to the east of London Bridge, the area was devoted to the service and supply of the seafaring population.

Unlike the majority of local hostelries, the Spring Garden catered to a superior clientele of shipowners, merchants, and naval officers and had established a reputation for its gastronomy. Not content to rest on their laurels, they had recently introduced a new attraction in the form of a series of wax dummies, representing some of the more famous, or infamous, figures in society. These were not quite to the standard of the House of Wax in Paris, but most of them were at least recognisable, even if they owed more to Gillray than to Gainsborough or Reynolds. Through the windows of the little booth where they were seated Nathan could see passable imitations of Nelson and Napoleon, William Pitt and his chief political rival, Charles James Fox, and a bestial figure which the waiter assured him was the notorious werewolf Nicolas Damont, howling to the moon. Nathan was not sure if they worked as an attraction, but he was hopeful about the cuisine.

'So what exactly are they accusing you of?' Hallowell persisted when they had toasted absent friends. 'If that is not too importunate of me.'

'Not at all,' Nathan assured him, although it was not his favourite topic of discussion. 'I am to answer for my conduct at Trafalgar.'

'Ah. You mean the business of being with the French.'

One thing about Hallowell, he did not beat about the bush. It probably came from being American. An Englishman, if he had raised the matter at all, would have phrased it so obliquely it would have taken another Englishman to know what the hell he was talking about.

'Quite,' said Nathan.

Although Hallowell had not been at Trafalgar—he had been sent to escort a convoy into Gibraltar—he had almost certainly heard of Nathan's misfortune, if not the circumstances behind it. Nathan did his best to explain them, though Hallowell's deepening frown suggested he was testing his credulity, or possibly his concentration. It was not a good augury for his defence at the inquiry.

They were interrupted by the arrival of their waiters with the first course: a rich soup of boletus mushrooms heavily laced with brandy, accompanied by a basket of fresh white rolls and a bottle of Palo Cortado sherry. For some minutes they applied themselves to more serious matters, but Hallowell had his own views on the subject, and he was clearly not to be diverted.

'Every nation needs a scapegoat,' he declared. 'It is the prerequisite for an ordered society. Trafalgar was a great victory, no doubt about it, but what came next? Austershitz.'

Nathan was not sure he had got the name right, but he took the point. Within a few weeks of Trafalgar, Napoleon had smashed the combined armies of the Austrian and Russian emperors and left Britain without a single worthwhile ally in Europe.

'So now we've buried Nelson, what next?' Hallowell demanded. 'Old Three Bottles is up to his neck in bilgewater and people are starting to notice.'

Nathan was confused.

'Old Three Bottles?' he queried.

' 'Tis what they are calling our esteemed leader, Mr William Pitt—on account of the fact that he is now believed to be quaffing three bottles of port at one sitting. There is a story that . . .'

But the waiters were back with the main course. A substantial haunch of venison, a rabbit pie, and several kinds of bird, accompanied by two bottles of claret and the proprietress, Mrs Valencia Harding, to make sure everything was to their satisfaction.

They assured her that it was.

'What was I talking about?' enquired Captain Hallowell when she had gone.

'Old Three Bottles?'

'Ah, yes. Pitt. On his way out, I hear. Austershitz has done for him.'

It had done for a lot of people, Nathan reflected, including the thirty thousand Russian and Austrian corpses left on the battlefield, but he was yet to hear that Billy Pitt had played much of a part in it.

'Took him the best part of two years to get them up to scratch,' Hallowell pointed out, 'and the useless whoresons have thrown in the towel after the first round. And now he is totally buggered. Like the rest of us.'

Nathan had heard more sophisticated expositions of the strategic situation in Europe, but he supposed this was as good as any. He carved himself a large slice of venison philosophically.

'Did you hear about the map?' Hallowell asked.

Nathan had not heard about the map.

'You know that niece of his, keeps house for him?'

Nathan nodded cautiously. Lady Hester Stanhope was not known to him personally, but she did a lot more than keep house, according to his mother, having more brains than anyone in government, in her view, Pitt included.

'Well, story goes she has this map of Europe spread out on the table, wondering what to do next, and he comes back after a night at Brooks, or wherever else he goes these days, and says, "You can roll that up, petal, we will not be needing it these ten years or more."'

Nathan had heard a version of this story from several different sources in the last few days—that and the story of Nelson and the cask of brandy were going the rounds, so he supposed there was some truth in it, though he did not suppose for a moment that Lady Hester Stanhope had ever been called 'petal,' even by her esteemed uncle.

'Then he takes to his bed and has been there ever since,' said Hallowell. 'They are giving him no more than a few days, apparently.'

Nathan paused in the act of raising another glass. 'What—in government?'

'In life.'

'Go on.'

'Ran into Beatty yesterday. Liver, he says.'

Beatty had been Nelson's doctor on the *Victory*, which possibly gave him more knowledge of Pitt's liver than most men, but Nathan was inclined to be sceptical.

'Pitt does not have a liver,' he said. 'If he did, he would have been dead years ago.'

'I agree, he is not, in many respects, as most men, but he does have a liver, and it is shot to pieces. King sent his own doctor to take a look at him. Told Beatty he'd not see the week out.'

Nathan was shocked. Pitt had been in power for all but a year or two since he first went to sea as a thirteen-year-old midshipman. If he really was on his way out . . . Well, he supposed there would be consequences, though what they were he could not rightly say. He had not been the greatest war leader in the world, nothing like his father, but he was a still point in a turning world, or something like that.

'So if Pitt goes . . . ?'

'Fox,' said Hallowell.

'Never,' said Nathan.

'Put money on it. Fox and the Peace Party. You see if it ain't.'

'Can't see Farmer George putting up with that. He'd sooner move into the madhouse permanent and to hell with the lot of us.'

'Might have to. Then we would have the bloody son as prince regent, God help us, Georgy Porgy Puddin' an' Pie. With Fox as his chief minister, can you imagine? No wonder the Tories are running for the hills. That is why I say'—he frowned—'what was it I was saying?'

Nathan was still thinking about Prinny and Fox poncing around running the country.

'Oh aye—a scapegoat. Nation needs a scapegoat. Someone to blame for the shite we are in. And you, my friend, are it.'

'I beg your pardon?'

'Nothing personal. Don't matter who the scapegoat is, whether he is guilty or innocent, right or wrong, so long as he looks the part. Something is rotten in the state of Denmark, sir, and if we ain't got no more fireworks, bring on Hamlet.'

Nathan was even more confused.

'I am sorry—Hamlet, perhaps, I could understand, but why me?'

'Well, there you go. Why you? Well, apart from being on the ship that killed Nelson, you have the merit of being an outsider. As I say, nothing personal, but you have never really fitted in, do you know what I mean?'

'I am afraid not,' Nathan confessed.

'Well, for one thing, they think of you as an American, and if there is one thing they hate more than a Frog, it is a Yank. Rebels and traitors to a man. Cowards, too. I know, we were the ones who surrendered, but they are the cowards. Hide behind trees, you know. When I lost the *Swiftsure* there were those who put it about that I had no stomach for a fight. Odds of four to one, masts, rudder, and taffrail shot to buggery, but I'd only lost two men, d'you see? A real Englishman would have lost half the crew before he called it a day. Look at the *Revenge*.'

It was unusual for Hallowell to draw attention to the circumstances of his birth. He usually pretended to be Canadian, but was known throughout the service as 'the American captain' with a nod and a wink, and very likely a sneer. He had once had a man flogged for humming 'Yankee Doodle' in his hearing, but it made no difference. He had spent his formative years in Boston when it was probably the most troublesome colony in King George's dominions; in fact, his father had been commissioner of customs at the time of the infamous Boston Tea Party, and he and his entire family had been obliged to flee for their lives. First Nova Scotia, then England.

Nathan was inclined to think that Hallowell's theory was based on his own sense of grievance, rather than anything else. He had not advanced as far in the service as he felt he deserved, while lesser men had been promoted above him. But Nathan had never thought this applied to him.

'I am only half American,' he pointed out. 'And though I was born in New York, my father was a serving officer in the king's navy at the time. It is only my mother who considers herself to be American—despite spending more than half her life in London.'

'Ah yes, well, there you go, that is the other thing. Your mother.' Hallowell sighed heavily, shaking his head as he reached for his glass. 'A remarkable woman, and handsome, handsome as the day is long. But—well, what can I say?'

Nothing that had not been said many times before, Nathan reflected grimly. For all her many qualities, he had to admit that his mother was an embarrassment at times. Her public support for revolution, whether in America, France, or Britain, had not endeared her to those of a certain class and inclination. Certainly, it had not made his own life any easier. In Nathan's youth, her house in Saint James's had been a magnet not only for the Whig opposition and other even more disreputable characters, but also for the Prince of Wales and his entourage, making her as much an enemy of the king, at least in His Majesty's eyes, as the revolutionaries across the Channel, probably more so given that she lived only a few houses down from Saint James's Palace. But the war had played havoc with her finances, and her move to unfashionable Soho had done for her so far as the beau monde was concerned, which was at least one thing to be grateful for, at least in Nathan's mind.

'My mother's political influence is a thing of the past,' he said, though he was aware that she would dispute this with some vigour. 'Certainly, she is no threat to their lordships of the Admiralty.'

'So, what do you think it is, then?'

'Besides being on the ship that killed Nelson, you mean?'

'You think that is all there is to it?'

'Well, it is no small thing but . . . ' He hesitated, for these were dangerous waters. 'It has been put to me that it may have something to do with Sir Sidney Smith,' he said.

'Ah. The Swedish Knight. Well, you might have something there.' Hallowell was regarding him shrewdly.

'Why, what have you heard?'

'Nothing in particular. But you were under him for the best part of two years, was it not? I know it was not your fault, but . . .

well . . . guilt by association, as they say.' He shook his head over his glass before he knocked it back and reached for the bottle.

'I gather you are not among his admirers.'

'Oh, he did very well at Acre, I will not deny it, though I believe it was the Turks who did most of the fighting. But he has never been shy of blowing his own trumpet, and to come back dressed as a Turkish pasha and go swaggering about the salons of London, the way he did . . . Well, it did not win him many admirers, to be honest, apart from among the ladies. And then there was that business in Boulogne.'

Nathan remained silent. 'That business at Boulogne' was doubtless a reference to the abortive raid on the French invasion fleet that Bonaparte had assembled across the Channel. Smith had come up with the idea of attacking it with fireships and various submersibles known collectively as 'the infernal machines,' which he had persuaded the Admiralty would change the face of modern warfare. It had been an abject failure. Not a single French ship had been destroyed. Unfortunately for Nathan, he had been at the sharp end as Smith's second in command. He had spent a year in a French prison as a result.

'So, you think I am being made the scapegoat for the failings of Captain Sir Sidney Smith,' he reflected wearily.

'*Admiral* Sir Sidney Smith.'

'Excuse me?'

'Had you not heard? He has been promoted to rear admiral and is about to be sent off to the Mediterranean on some secret mission about which the Admiralty is being even more cagey than usual. He might already be on his way.'

Nathan frowned. It was good to hear he was headed out of the country; not so good that he had made it to admiral.

'I heard there was an attempt to haul him over the coals over Boulogne,' said Hallowell, 'and that other business he was involved in over Boney.' He was giving Nathan that look again, but Nathan merely raised a questioning brow.

'The kidnap plot,' said Hallowell. 'Did you not hear about that?'

Nathan shook his head.

In fact, he knew a lot more than he was prepared to reveal to Ben Hallowell, or anyone else outside his intimate acquaintance. Either Smith or someone close to him had come up with the idea of kidnapping Napoleon Bonaparte and incarcerating him in a medieval fortress on the island of Jersey. Nathan had been charged with landing the kidnappers on the Normandy coast, whence they had made their way to Paris. Almost all of them had been rounded up by the French police and subsequently disposed of, either legally, by way of a trial, or by other, more devious means.

It had been extensively covered in the British and French newspapers, though so far as Nathan was aware, Smith's part in the operation had not been disclosed. Nor Nathan's, for that matter.

'Well, he managed to talk his way out of that, too,' said Hallowell. 'You know what they say. If Thor was to hurl a thunderbolt at the rogue, he would step smartly aside and put some other poor booby in his place.'

'You are not suggesting that I . . .'

'Again, nothing personal, and I admit 'tis all hearsay, but what I *heard* is that when Smith was charged with incompetence or whatever it was—and I am not sure it ever came to a charge—he claimed that he was betrayed by a British officer with a role in both operations who divulged his plans to the enemy. A turncoat, in fact, who had undertaken a number of secret missions in France over the years and was a close associate of the Bonaparte family.'

He gazed evenly across the table at Nathan, and despite the amount of drink consumed, his eyes were entirely sober.

'Can you think of who he has in mind?'

Chapter 8

The Inquisitors

'We are here assembled to establish the reasons that persuaded Captain Nathaniel Peake to relinquish his post as captain of the frigate *Panther* on July 29th last and to determine whether the said Captain Peake has a case to answer on a charge of desertion and communicating with the enemy in time of war.'

The boardroom of the Admiralty on a cold, wet, wintry day in late January. A coal fire attempted a cheerful blaze in the Grinling Gibbons fireplace but had as little warmth in it as the three faces at the head of the long table.

One of them was the man who went by the title of First Secretary of the Admiralty, Mr Marsden, who despite his absence of naval rank was the most important of those present. It was he who had read out the commission's terms of reference. Flanking him were two admirals, Sir John Colpoys and Sir Roger Curtis, both of whom had last seen service some years ago. Nathan did not know either of them personally, but he knew *of* them, and what he knew he did not like.

Colpoys had long been regarded as a leader of that faction of the Admiralty that believed in the strict observance of discipline and the Articles of War in all circumstances, even if that meant losing a battle, or even the war itself, according to some. Any departure from them should and would be punished, as the

Articles indicated, with death. He had last seen action during the American War of Independence over a quarter of a century earlier, but the most noteworthy incident in his long career was during the naval mutiny of 1797 at Spithead, when the seamen of the Channel Fleet had refused to put to sea without an improvement in their pay and conditions. Fearful that his own crew would join the mutineers, though they had shown no signs of doing so, Colpoys had ordered them below deck and instructed his marines to batten down the hatches and fire on them if they tried to break out. When a few of them attempted to do this very thing, most of the marines had refused to obey the order, but those who did succeeded in killing several men before they were overwhelmed, at which point Colpoys and his officers were clapped in irons and came close to being hanged.

Shortly afterwards the Admiralty had agreed to the seamen's demands and the dispute had been settled without further bloodshed, but Colpoys was explicitly named by the men as an officer they would refuse to serve under in the future. He was removed from active service on the grounds of ill health and, so far as Nathan was aware, had not been to sea since, though this had not stopped him from being promoted to full admiral and given the honorary but lucrative post of treasurer of Greenwich Hospital.

Hardly less objectionable from Nathan's point of view was Rear Admiral Sir Roger Curtis, whose sole claim to fame was being flag captain to Lord Howe at the battle known as the Glorious First of June, which was fought some four hundred miles west of Ushant in the year '94. Curtis had assumed command of the fleet when his superior, then much advanced in years, had gone to have a lie-down. Not only had he failed to pursue the retreating French and intercept the grain convoy they were protecting, but he had then written a self-serving report to the Admiralty, which he prevailed upon Howe to sign, denouncing those captains who had been critical of his failings. These included the officer who later became Vice Admiral Collingwood, who had publicly accused him of being a deceitful, sneaking rogue whose fawning manners concealed a rapacity to seize all honours and profits that came his way. This in the hope of provoking him to a duel. It did not have the desired effect, nor had it prevented him from advancement, despite a notable lack of achievements since. He considered himself something of a lawyer, having acted as prosecutor in a number of prominent courts-martial, which had ruined the careers of many more capable officers than himself.

Nathan's only hope was that they would do whatever Marsden instructed them, for that was the kind of men they were, and Marsden was an unknown quantity. It was said that he had learned the art of inscrutability from Chinese mandarins during the quarter-century he had spent with the East India Company, which he had joined at the age of sixteen. He had served under drunkards, dilettantes, and despots, and that was just since his move to the Admiralty. He had been here since the start of the last war in '93. First lords came and went, but Marsden was a rock of stability. He somehow managed to have a life outside the service, as well, in the roles of linguist, historian, and Fellow of the Royal Society. In his spare time, he collected old coins.

Nathan was seated opposite Marsden at the far end of the table. He wore his best dress uniform minus his hat, which he had taken off himself, and his sword, which had been taken from him upon his entering the room by a captain of marines who now sat in a chair beside the door, lest he be tempted to make a bolt for it. Two of his marines stood on the far side in case he was obliged to call for assistance, and halfway down the table sat two Admiralty clerks who were taking verbatim notes of the proceedings for future reference.

'Be it understood that this is not a trial,' Marsden advised Nathan at the start of the proceedings, 'but a commission to establish the truth in so far as that can be ascertained. However, you should be aware that our conclusions will be passed on to a higher authority which may result in a court-martial or such action as may be determined. Is there anything you wish to say in relation to the terms of reference that I have just verified?'

Nathan objected to the use of the word 'relinquish,' spoken at the start of the proceedings, protesting that he had temporarily ceded command to his first lieutenant in the same way as a captain leading a boarding party or a cutting-out expedition. He had expected to return within a day or two, he said.

His objection was noted, Marsden replied coolly, before outlining what he described as the known facts of the case.

'Namely, that on July twelfth last, you did assume temporary command of the frigate *Panther*, of thirty-two guns, with orders to join the squadron commanded by Rear Admiral Calder, charged with the blockade of the Spanish ports of Vigo and Ferrol. You were subsequently engaged in the action of July twenty-second with the combined French and Spanish fleet off Cape Finisterre, after which the enemy sought safety in the port of Ferrol. The squadron then being scattered by storm, you were proceeding to the rendezvous off Ferrol when you encountered a French frigate, the *Perle*, of forty guns, which you engaged and captured, subsequently taking as prize an American merchant ship, the *Grampus*, which you had reason to believe had been in communication with the *Perle* before the engagement. Is this correct?'

Nathan agreed that it was.

'Will you please tell the commission in your own words what happened next?'

Nathan gave them a shortened version of what he had told Collingwood and Hallowell. The shorter the better, he had decided.

'I determined to take the *Grampus* into Ferrol in the guise of her American captain and give false intelligence of our strength to prevent them from coming out and continuing with their journey to Brest.'

'Why would you wish to do that?' Colpoys demanded, once it became clear this was the only explanation they were going to get.

'Because it seemed advisable to delay them long enough for Admiral Calder's squadron to regroup and to receive reinforcements.'

'So, what was this false intelligence that you proposed to give the French?' Curtis wanted to know.

'That I had observed a large British fleet of some twenty-five to thirty ships off the coast to the north, and that one of them was the *Victory*.'

A swift exchange of glances between the two admirals.

'Why did you name the *Victory* in particular?' said Colpoys.

'Because that was the flagship of Lord Nelson, and I knew that Villeneuve feared him before any other British admiral.'

'How did you know that?'

'It was common knowledge in the service since the Battle of the Nile, when Villeneuve fled from the encounter in Aboukir Bay.'

'But Villeneuve came out anyway, did he not?' Curtis put to him accusingly.

'Yes. But he took the fleet south, instead of north.'

'And why does that matter?'

Nathan glanced at Marsden to see if he shared his surprise at the question, but he was as inscrutable as ever.

'You will recall that Villeneuve had hoped to lure Nelson to the West Indies in his pursuit, and then leave him there while he returned across the Atlantic to join with the French fleet at Brest.'

The two faces gazed stonily down the table at him.

'They believed this would give them sufficient forces to overwhelm our defences and escort the invasion fleet across the Channel. I concluded that if Villeneuve was under the impression that Nelson had come back and was ready for him, he would abort the plan.'

'And how did you know of this plan at the time?' Curtis demanded.

'From information I had received after taking the *Perle*.'

'You did not consider that our forces were already sufficient to give a good account of themselves?'

'It seemed advisable to avoid the risk. I thought it imperative to prevent Villeneuve from uniting with the French forces at Brest before we could assemble a fleet large enough to stop him.'

'This seems a great deal for a mere captain to take upon himself,' Colpoys declared with a snort of derision. 'Or did you think you knew better than your superiors?'

'You are aware that communicating with the enemy at a time of war is a crime punishable by death?' put in Colpoys.

Nathan was saved from having to answer either of these questions by another from Marsden: 'Even if we accept this to be a worthy stratagem, why did you consider it necessary to put yourself forward as the bearer of this intelligence, instead of sending a less senior officer?'

This was possibly more difficult to justify and obliged Nathan to reveal an aspect of his previous career that he would rather have kept to himself, though he was in no doubt that Marsden knew as much about it as anyone at Admiralty.

'Only that I speak fluent French and am probably more accomplished in the art of subterfuge,' he replied, 'having played the part of an American sea captain on previous occasions when it was deemed necessary to misguide or otherwise confound the enemy.'

There was a significant exchange of glances between the two admirals, who were unlikely to have been informed of this, but may have heard rumours.

'What previous occasions were these?' demanded Curtis. 'And whose orders were you under at the time?'

'I regret that would be to betray a confidence,' Nathan replied.

He was sorely tempted to give the name of Earl Saint Vincent, who had been first lord before Barham, or Sir Sidney Smith, who had been his commander in Jersey, or even the king's chief minister, who had twice sent him to Paris on missions of this nature. But though he might have derived some satisfaction from these revelations, he was too much of a confidential agent to give way to the temptation. Not yet, at least.

'Captain Peake, I do not think you have grasped the seriousness of your situation.' Colpoys had his voice under control, but only just. 'If the commission is to decide on this matter, we must be informed of all the facts. So, I will you ask you again: On these previous occasions you mention, when you were ordered to communicate with the enemy, *whose orders were you under*?'

This time Nathan met Marsden's eye and an unspoken message passed between them. Or at least, Nathan hoped it did. But before he could react one way or another, there was a knock upon the door. A further exchange of glances between the commissioners, who had presumably given instructions that they were not to be disturbed, but Marsden nodded to the marine officer, who opened it to admit a man wearing the sober garb and countenance of one of the Admiralty clerks.

Marsden excused himself and advanced across the room to meet the interloper. A few quiet words were exchanged, and a look of what might almost have been shock or dismay crossed the first secretary's normally impassive features. He returned to the table and a private converse ensued with his two colleagues, which appeared to have an even greater effect upon them. Colpoys uttered an expletive and put his head in his hands. Curtis blew out his cheeks and shook his head.

What in God's name was it? Had the king died? Had he suffered another fit of madness and done something so unspeakable it required his immediate incarceration? Or had the French invaded after all?

Marsden raised his voice to address those lesser creatures who remained in ignorance.

'I am afraid I have received an intelligence that makes it necessary for us to adjourn this inquiry,' he said. 'I apologise for the inconvenience.' He looked down the table to Nathan. 'You will be informed of a future date if and when we are to resume.'

Nathan took this to mean he was dismissed. He stood up, bowed towards the head of the table without response, recovered his sword from the marine captain, who looked entirely at a loss, and left the room before anyone changed their minds.

It was the porter at the front door who gave him the news on his way out of the building.

'Old Three Bottles done croaked it,' he said.

Nathan needed a moment to decipher this intelligence.

'Billy Pitt,' the porter supplied helpfully. 'Cashed in 'is chips, downed 'is last Madeira, poor sod. End of an era, i'nt it? D'you need a cab, sir, or is you walking?'

Chapter 9

The New Broom

Eras, in Nathan's limited experience, did not normally end with a straight line. They tended to be a lot hazier than that, like a blurred horizon shrouding an uncertain future, with the strong possibility of gales.

The death of Pitt certainly had an end-of-era feel about it, for he had been the king's chief minister for all but three of the last twenty-one years and had led the opposition in Europe to what had seemed at times to be the relentless march of revolution. But despite his mother's jubilation, there were no immediate signs of it marching through the streets of London. The king was not led in chains to the Tower, Parliament was not instantly dissolved and replaced by an assembly of the people, and the only person he saw dancing in a Phrygian cap was her, and that in the privacy of her own home—mostly, he suspected, to annoy him. Those of a more sober disposition, as he coolly informed her, mourned the passing of a great statesman and a rock of stability in a sea of chaos. To which she made a characteristically vulgar retort.

Her celebrations were short-lived, however, for it was duly announced that the king had offered the seals of office to Pitt's cousin, Lord Grenville, an appointment which so inflamed his mother's sensibilities that she was obliged to take to her writing desk to communicate with a series of fellow dissidents, aided by constant replenishments of the inkwell and the restorative glass of gin and lime at her elbow.

When Nathan entered the room at the close of day to enquire after her well-being, he was regaled with an account of Grenville's iniquities in not only supporting Pitt through the Years of Repression, as she described them, but in suspending *habeas corpus* when he was Home Secretary so that he could lock up whomsoever he liked without the inconvenience and uncertainty of a trial. There was nothing for it, she announced, but to take to the streets.

'There will be heads on spikes,' she darkly informed Nathan, adding the slogan that had been so popular in Paris at the time of the Revolution—'*À la lanterne!*'—which had invariably preceded the incursion upon the streets of a violent mob intent on hanging anyone they did not like the look of from the nearest streetlamp.

The streets in the vicinity of Soho Square remaining tranquil, however, Nathan felt sufficiently relaxed to spend the night with Louise, returning shortly before noon to find his mother at breakfast and in a better frame of mind. The *Morning Chronicle* had reported that Grenville had agreed to lead the government only on condition that Charles James Fox was appointed Foreign Secretary.

'Why would he do that if he is as much of a reactionary as you say he is?' Nathan demanded as he helped himself to a large plate of bacon, eggs, and sausage.

'Because he needs his support in Parliament in order to command a majority,' his mother answered assuredly, 'or else he must advise the king to call an election.'

'And what did he have to say to the prospect of having Fox in government—the king, that is, given that by your own account he would have had him executed for treason at least thirty years ago? Or did the *Morning Chronicle* not advance an opinion on the matter?'

In truth, Nathan was not very much interested, having other things on his mind, and only asked to provoke, but his mother entertained him with a summary of the king's reply, delivered in a faux German accent, which was entirely unfair, as the king spoke better English than she did.

'"Verdammt to dein Parliament und confound dein elections," says he. "Ve haf none of zis in Hanover, und if 'twas down to me, vud haf none of it in England, Gott in Himmel!"'

His mother persisted in the belief that King George had always wished to rule England—and America, too, when he still had it—in the same despotic manner he and his forebears had ruled their provinces in Germany, and could only be prevented from doing so by the threat of armed rebellion.

Nathan opened his mouth to utter his usual weary rebuke, but she was in full flow.

'Grenville, however, pointed out to His Majesty that Hanover was presently occupied by French troops, and that there was not the slightest prospect of getting rid of them without Parliament providing the funds. So, your precious king put a saucepan on his head and went running around Saint James's Park, charging at trees.'

His mother could never resist a jibe at the king's mysterious malady, which had led him to sporadic irregularities of behaviour. It was true that he had once stopped the carriage in Hyde Park and addressed a tree as the King of Prussia, but Nathan was inclined to think this was done in conscious parody, King George having oft remarked that talking to the King of Prussia was very like talking to a tree.

'And were you party to this conversation,' he enquired coldly, 'or did you have someone taking notes?'

His mother sniffed to indicate superior insight. 'It will all become clear in the next day or two,' she insisted, 'and you will see that I am right—as usual.'

Astonishingly, on this occasion, she was. Not only was it announced that Mr Fox had been appointed foreign secretary, with the king's apparent consent, but several of his supporters in

Parliament had been given lesser appointments in the new Ministry, including his closest ally, Lord Howick, as first lord of the Admiralty. Howick, it turned out, was another of his mother's old friends, though by no means as old as Fox, and hopefully not as intimate, being not much older than Nathan.

'You must write to him immediately to demand your complete exoneration on all charges,' she instructed him, adding, when he made a face, 'and if you do not, then I will.'

Rather than succumb to this humiliation, after a day or two of further badgering Nathan did write to the new first lord, requesting that he might either face a court-martial or be restored to his command of the frigate *Panther*, presently idling in Gibraltar for want of her captain. Rather to his surprise he received a reply the very next day, inviting him to a personal interview at the Admiralty.

Despite his mother's enthusiasm, Nathan did not expect much of the encounter. At best, the inquiry might be delayed by some weeks, and he might not be hanged until Louise had delivered of her child, but he doubted if Howick was quite as radical as his mother claimed, especially when she admitted she had not met him for some years.

Superficially, at least, nothing had changed since his last visit. No cracks had appeared in the elegant frontage of Admiralty House, the weather was as wet and miserable as it usually was in London at this time of year, the same porter greeted him at the door with a gloomy 'Back again?,' and the same languid captain of marines, or someone very like him—they all looked much the same to Nathan—escorted him up the stairs for his appointment with destiny.

But destiny, for once, was wearing a smile on its face.

'Well, well, Captain Peake! I am delighted to resume our acquaintance, but I do not suppose you remember me . . .'

Lord Howick, all smiles and bonhomie, not quite coming from behind his desk but at least standing up and waving him to a chair. With him, however, to keep a check on his exuberance, was Mr Marsden, who greeted Nathan with a cool nod.

'It must have been some years since,' Nathan agreed, not having the faintest recollection of ever having met the man. His mother had described him as handsome and witty, but Nathan's first impression was of a rather horsey face, with a long, straight nose, thin lips, and a high forehead, like most of his breed. As to his wit, he would have to wait and see, but now was probably not the time or place.

'Your mother's house in Saint James's,' the first lord reminded him, 'on the eve of the last war. She was hosting a leaving party for the French ambassador and his staff.'

This sounded very likely, but Nathan's mind remained a blank.

'Talleyrand was there, and we established a connection that has endured to this day, surprisingly perhaps, given the circumstances have been somewhat difficult at times.'

This might pass for wit, Nathan supposed, Talleyrand being the French foreign secretary and the two countries having been at war more or less ever since. He remembered Talleyrand of course, for he had been his mother's houseguest at the time, having fallen foul of the ruling faction in Paris and been obliged to flee for his life.

'You were lately returned from an encounter in the Baie de Seine and brought back a cannonball, the first that was fired at us, I believe—in that war, at least. Your mother had it on display.'

This jolted Nathan's memory.

He had been master and commander of the sloop *Nereus* and in pursuit of an English smuggler when a French battery had fired on him from the mouth of the Seine. He had brought back the cannonball to show the Admiralty by way of evidence, but his mother had appropriated it for the amusement of her guests. It was still used as a doorstop in the house at Soho.

But he still could not place Lord Howick.

'I was then plain Mr Grey,' his lordship went on. 'I do not suppose you would remember a Mr Grey among such esteemed company. But I was a great admirer of your mother—her politics, that is,' he added, lest it be taken the wrong way. 'It took great courage in those days to acclaim the positive achievements of the Revolution. She is in good health, I trust.'

'Excellent, my lord,' Nathan confirmed, 'for the time of year.'

In fact, he had serious concerns over the amount of drink she was consuming lately and had issued a mild remonstrance over breakfast, receiving a stream of abuse in return, but he did not consider it necessary to reveal this to his lordship. Before their conversation had degenerated into the usual exchange of pleasantries, she had given him her particular insight into Howick's character and politics, including the information that he was a passionate abolitionist, an advocate of parliamentary reform, and the father of seven children, one of whom was the result of a scandalous liaison in his debauched youth with the Duchess of Devonshire.

Observing the man now sitting across the desk from him, Nathan could not imagine him ever being debauched, even in youth, but he was prepared to give him the benefit of the doubt.

'Well, here you see us!' Howick beamed and spread his arms in self-parody. 'The new broom. So, let us get down to business.' He fitted a pair of spectacles on the bridge of his long nose and peered down at the documents laid before him. The smile faded and he heaved a heavy sigh.

Nathan braced himself. He did not find the sigh encouraging. It hinted at a man preparing himself for an unpleasant duty. Nor did he like the look of the paperwork. There was altogether too much of it, and he assumed it all referred to him.

'This "inquiry," as it is called, into your conduct before the Battle of Trafalgar . . .'

He shot Nathan a look. Nathan inclined his head in polite interest.

'Are you aware of the reason for it?'

Nathan frowned. 'The reason, my lord?'

'For the inquiry.'

'Ah, the inquiry. Not really, my lord, no.'

'No. Nor am I.'

Nathan studiously avoided looking at Marsden.

Lord Howick had returned his attention to the paperwork. He turned over a page or two.

'I have your justification for entering the port of Ferrol and your subsequent capture and imprisonment about the *Redoutable*. It does, on the surface, appear reckless. However, I have also read Admiral Villeneuve's account of the battle and the events leading up to it.' He looked up. 'You may be aware that the admiral is presently being held prisoner in England until a suitable exchange can be arranged?'

Nathan was. He had seen him at Nelson's funeral, in fact, looking morose, as well he might. Once his exchange had been agreed, he would have to return to Paris to face the wrath of his emperor.

'Well, he gives the strong impression that the false intelligence you conveyed to him in Ferrol was crucial in persuading him to turn south and proceed to Cadiz in defiance of Bonaparte's orders.'

He glanced towards Marsden, as if to invite a comment, but the official was scratching his chin thoughtfully, his own eye apparently occupied in admiring the contours of the Grinling Gibbons fireplace.

'We will not be making this public, of course,' continued Howick, 'lest it prove of use to the enemy in their own analysis of the Trafalgar campaign, but you may rest assured that there will be no more talk of an inquiry.'

Nathan tried not to show his satisfaction, much less jubilation, lest Marsden remember and hold it against him. First lords came and went; first secretaries remained forever, or at least until death removed them to less nautical spheres of influence.

He contented himself with a respectful 'Thank you, my lord' and asked if he was now at liberty to return to his duties.

'Of course, of course. However . . .'

The vagueness of his tone, combined with that qualifying word alerted Nathan to the strong possibility that he may not be out of the woods yet.

'The *Panther*, I understand, is presently at Gibraltar attached to the Mediterranean fleet.'

'I believe so, my lord.'

He glanced towards Marsden, who gave a slight nod, apparently in confirmation.

'And ready for sea?'

'So far as I am aware, my lord.'

'And yourself?'

If Nathan truly wished to remain in London for the birth, and he did, now was the time to put in a request for leave.

'Of course, my lord.'

He regretted it immediately, but it was too late now. He might have a reputation for independent action, but he invariably did what his superiors asked of him. Duty and obedience had been drilled into him as a young midshipman—from birth, in fact, given his father's predilection for running his family and his farm like the crew of a ship. King George commands, and I obey.

A small, mocking voice in his head begged to differ, but he shoved it back where it came from.

'You may have heard the rumours that the French Atlantic fleet has broken out of Brest.'

Nathan shot a quick glance at Marsden. Had they not received his report, or did Howick not know about it?

Marsden's face was as inscrutable as ever.

'I had heard something to that effect.' Nathan chose his word with care. 'But not all the details. I confess I was surprised that they had evaded our blockading fleet.'

'Ah yes, well, it appears that the blockade was lifted on the orders of my predecessor. I am informed that he imagined the French would be so dispirited after Trafalgar, so low on morale, that it was safe to withdraw the fleet to the shelter of Cawsand Bay, to give the crews a rest from forever beating up and down off Ushant. Unfortunately, this became known to the enemy, and out they duly came.'

'Do we know how many?' Nathan had counted eight, but he was aware that there may have been more.

'We think perhaps eleven or twelve ships of the line.'

So, his initial report must have been confirmed—and expanded.

'And do we know where they are now?'

'Unfortunately not. There is conflicting information.' He turned to the first secretary.

'We think they may have divided into two squadrons,' Marsden replied. 'One heading for the South Atlantic, the other for the Caribbean, or possibly further north.'

'The obvious target is the trade routes,' Howick proposed. 'But they may have other objectives in mind. We have sent two squadrons in pursuit, one under Sir Richard Strachan, the other under Sir John Warren, totalling thirteen ships of the line—but first we have to find them.'

Which would mean sending every available frigate and sloop that could be spared from other duties closer to home. Including *Panther*.

The prospect of beating twenty million square miles of the South Atlantic in search of a few French ships which may or may not be there did not fill Nathan with any great enthusiasm, but he supposed it was better than his previous expectations.

'Well, I am at your service, my lord.'

'Very good.' But Howick's tone was vague. He was looking down at the paperwork, apparently lost in thought.

Nathan took this as an indication that the interview was over. He glanced at Marsden in hopes of a more positive response. But Marsden too was looking thoughtful.

Nathan wondered if he should just get up and go.

But then Howick spoke again.

'The fact is, Peake, we have a more specific mission in mind for you that will, I think, make better use of your talents, but the foreign secretary has expressed a wish to speak to you personally about it before we go into further detail.'

'The foreign secretary, my lord?'

He sounded like an idiot, but he was quite taken aback. What had the foreign secretary to do with the disposition of frigates, or frigate captains, for that matter? Unless it was another of those missions that had gotten him into so much trouble in the past—with his own side at least as much as the enemy.

'He has made a carriage available to convey you to his house at Chertsey.'

'What—now, my lord?'

A tilt of the long chin, a twitch of the brow, a nose provided for the express purpose of looking down it—Charles Grey might be the most liberal of those yet to hold the office of first lord of the Admiralty, but he was, above all else, an aristocrat.

'If that is not too inconvenient for you?'

Chapter 10

The Intrepid Fox

Whilst Nathan had a reasonable knowledge of most seas in the world and could tell you the location of most of the major seaports, if you so desired—or even if you did not—he was considerably less informed concerning the geography of his own country.

Chertsey included.

He might have expected the foreign secretary to be in the foreign office, which was in Cleveland Row, just behind Horse Guards, a few minutes' walk from Admiralty House. But perhaps he did not go into the office much. Nathan trawled through the various snippets of information his mother had supplied in the last few days, while he was half listening at best, and dimly recalled her saying something about Fox living in a house that one of his wife's previous lovers had given her in the Surrey countryside, as a reward for services rendered.

This seemed to be their most likely destination, a view that was confirmed for him when the coach crossed the Thames at Putney Bridge and continued through a landscape of trees, fields, and sheep—he even saw someone in a smock who could well have been a shepherd—all of which suggested the county of Surrey. Whether Chertsey was in Surrey was another matter, of course, but it could not be much further afield, if Fox was to make regular appearances in Parliament.

He gave himself up to contemplation of what the foreign secretary might wish to discuss with him.

He knew a lot more about Fox than he did about most politicians. This was largely due to his mother, of course, but he had been sufficiently intrigued over the last few days to read up on him in the newspapers. He was invariably caricatured by those sympathetic to the king and his ministers as a burly ruffian with unshaven jowls and a big nose who had the reputation of being a drunkard, a gambler, and a womaniser with no respect for authority, tradition, morality, religion, or anything else that in their view held the country together. Ironically, despite being descended from an illegitimate son of Charles the Second and the scion of one of the wealthiest families in England, he had made a name for himself as the champion of liberty against the tyranny of kings and emperors. He had supported the American rebels in the War of Independence and the French revolutionaries in Paris; he was known to favour the abolition of slavery, the reform of Parliament, and the emancipation of Catholics and Jews, all of which were strongly opposed by the king and his supporters in the Tory party; and most infamously, he had sought to have the king declared insane and the Prince of Wales installed as regent in his place.

And to compound all of these abominations, he was in favour of peace with France.

It was this that troubled Nathan the most—not because he was much opposed to peace with France, but because it was the most likely reason for his summons to the residence of the foreign secretary. He was aware that upon his appointment, Fox would have had access to a great many state secrets, including the missions that Nathan had undertaken in the French Republic at the behest of William Pitt. In fact, it was quite possible that he had read Nathan's confidential reports to Pitt and the Admiralty concerning his dealings with the Bonaparte family over the years, and though Nathan had omitted certain details of his own conduct that might be regarded as reprehensible, it was not unlikely that Fox had read intelligence reports from other sources that were neither as favourable, nor as discreet.

He looked out of the window—more fields, more sheep, more shepherds—but then they passed through a small village and began to climb a hill that brought them, at length, to a modest country house. Whilst by no means grand, it was pretty enough and well appointed, with a sweeping view of the Surrey countryside—not at all the environment Nathan had associated with the new foreign minister, but a perfect bucolic retreat from the snares and follies of political life.

'My dear boy! Forgive me for dragging you into the wilds of Surrey, but I am practically an invalid these days, and Mrs Fox will not let me leave the house, even if the king himself demands an audience—though that, I believe, is unlikely.'

The voice still had a flavour of the great orator who had dominated the House of Commons for so long, but Nathan was shocked by the change in his appearance, even from the caricatures that were his only reference point of late. He had expected the years and the drink to have taken their toll, but not quite to this extent. Fox appeared to have shrunken in on himself, the jowls still unshaven but looser and more liverish, his nose redder and more prominent, his eyes bloodshot and with more than a hint of yellow. He looked less like the intrepid Fox and more like a weary bloodhound that has long since tired of the chase.

He was seated in the library, close to the fire, with a turban wrapped around his head and a blanket around his lower regions. A great many papers covered the floor at his feet and for some distance around, and there was an inkwell and a battery of quills on a table by his side in case he should be moved to sign them or scrawl some appropriately caustic comment in the margins. There was also a bottle of brandy, Nathan noted, and a glass half full, or half empty, depending on one's disposition.

'Step into the light, sir,' he said, 'so I can see you properly.'

Nathan did not know if he meant the light from the windows or from the fire, but he compromised by advancing into the centre of the room and standing there, hat in hand, much as he had thirty years ago when he had first been introduced to the great man in his mother's drawing room—a nervous young midshipman back from his first voyage and wishing he was still on it.

'By God, sir, I said step into the light, not block it entirely.'

Nathan retreated a step or two, but apparently this was Fox's idea of raillery.

'I imagined you'd've growed some since we last met, but not a yard or more. What do they feed you in the navy? Grey says we must increase the rations, but if this is the result, we should be cutting 'em. You must be a terror to the ladies, not to speak of the French. How many have you killed since I last saw you?'

'Very few ladies,' Nathan protested. 'More Frenchmen than I would have wished, had they not been trying to kill me.'

'Well said, sir, well said!' Fox went so far as to beat his hand upon the arm of the chair in an excess of enthusiasm before he was overtaken by a fit of coughing. When sufficiently recovered, he invited him to take a seat, if he could find anywhere that did not have papers upon it. 'This is Carteret, by the by, one of my principal secretaries.' He indicated a gentleman Nathan had not yet noticed, seated at a proper desk on the far side of the room with more papers, considerably better organised. He was younger than Nathan by a few years, and well groomed, with an air of promise, doubtless carefully cultivated.

They exchanged bows.

'And Venables will arrange some refreshment.' This to the servant who had brought Nathan hither and now stood at the door awaiting further instruction. 'We will take it in the dining room and bring our work with us. In the meantime, my dear, can we offer you a drink. Wine, brandy, beer? Rum? You sailors drink rum, do you not? I believe we have rum.'

Nathan settled for a dry sherry, which seemed to disappoint him, but Venables departed in search of that commodity, and he found an armchair with only a few papers upon it which, upon instruction, he removed to the floor.

'Now then, you have seen Grey? Well, of course you have, that is why you are here. So, he will have told you about the situation we face in the Atlantic and certain deployments that have been made in response?'

Nathan confirmed that this was the case.

'Yes, well, we do not know what purposes the French have in mind—an attack on our commerce is one, of course, but there may be others, and one that concerns us is the possibility of them bringing pressure upon the United States.'

Nathan indicated polite interest, though it had not been among his own concerns of late.

'Having helped them boot the British out, the French had hoped for certain advantages in the future. They may have envisaged something of a client state—a French protectorate, even. I think it is fair to say this hope has not been realised. But you probably know more about that than I do.'

This might simply have been a reference to his mother's views on the subject, but it was possible that Fox had seen the reports on Nathan's dealings with the Americans in the past, particularly during the Barbary Wars and the conflict in Saint-Domingue. For the present, however, he decided his best response was silence and a gently raised brow.

'What you will probably not know, however, and I must ask you to keep it confidential for the time being, is that we are presently engaged in talks with the Americans with a view to expanding the trading links between our two countries. If they go as well as I hope, we will seek to expand them into other areas—notably, the possibility of establishing joint naval patrols to curtail the trade in African slaves across the Atlantic.'

He gave a bark of laughter which narrowly avoided developing into another coughing fit.

'That was a shock, eh? Eh, Carteret?' He threw a glance in the direction of his aide. 'I wager we will see that look on a lot of faces before long. If all goes according to plan. Well, sir, let me inform you that we are preparing a bill to prohibit the trade throughout the British Empire.'

This time Nathan did not have to feign surprise. For once, he thought, his mother might have been right, for whilst this was not as revolutionary a measure as storming the Bastille, it was a step in that direction.

'I trust you would not oppose such an initiative?'

Nathan found his voice. 'On the contrary, sir, but I am not a member of Parliament.'

Fox frowned. 'You anticipate a degree of opposition?'

'Well, I believe there might be a few dissenting voices, sir, given the level of investment in the trade.'

'Ha!' Fox seemed delighted. 'There you are, Carteret, we will make a diplomat of him yet. By God, sir, the wealth and power of England is built on the abominable business. Yes, there will be opposition, but I believe that shame, and yes, even honour, will outweigh greed for once, and it will be law before the end of the year. And what is more, a similar measure has been introduced in the American Congress with the approval of President Jefferson.'

This was an even greater surprise. It would be untrue to say that Jefferson was one of his mother's heroes, for she did not have heroes, but she tended to speak of him more generously than of other American politicians since the end of the Independence War. He had been the representative of the new republic in Paris at the time of the storming of the Bastille and had spoken in favour of the ideals, if not the methods, of the French Revolution. But Jefferson had one great black mark against him, not only for her, but for all the dissidents and radicals and revolutionists of her acquaintance, for he was a slave owner from Virginia, and the planters of the southern states were as dependent on slave labour as the British planters of the West Indies, and they were at least as strong in Congress as the West Indies lobby in Parliament.

'It is said that his hand was forced for fear of breaking up the Union,' Fox went on, 'for the northern states are strong for abolition, but I do not think this does him justice. Jefferson has long been a champion of liberty, and I believe he could no longer resist the demands of his friends and his conscience. However, if both Parliament and Congress pass a law to prohibit the Atlantic slave trade, it will be necessary to police it, and part of your mission will be to pave the way for cooperation between our two navies.'

Nathan was startled. 'My—my mission?'

'Oh, did I not say? We have it in mind to send you to Washington.'

'To Washington?'

He knew he must sound like an idiot, or one of those exotic birds given to mimicry, but his mind was sufficiently stunned to render it incapable of anything more cerebral.

'The capital. Of the United States.'

Nathan was perfectly aware of what Washington was, and where. The mystery was in his being sent there. It was not even upon the sea.

'You will be part of a diplomatic mission that will include our friend Carteret here.'

Our friend Carteret smiled apologetically.

Nathan's brain reconnected with his tongue.

'But, sir, I am not a diplomat,' he protested.

'Nonsense, sir. You forget that I have read the reports. You are more of a diplomat than most diplomats that I have encountered, certainly under the previous administration—flatterers, rogues, and deceivers to a man, in thrall to royalty and their lackeys.'

This elicited a delicate cough from Carteret, which Fox ignored.

'You have the facility to deal with royalists and republicans alike without revealing to either party whether you favour one or t'other, added to which you have that rare advantage among Britons of being favoured by President Jefferson.'

Nathan confessed he was unaware of any such distinction, and begged to be informed of what inclined the foreign secretary to this opinion, never having met the president nor, to his knowledge, done anything to earn his approbation.

'On the contrary, sir, I believe that at one stage in your illustrious career you shared a prison cell with his very good friend, Mr Thomas Paine, who has impressed the president with your services on his behalf, including your success in saving him from the guillotine.'

How could he have known that? Nathan was aware that the foreign secretary must have read the confidential reports from when he had been a secret agent in Paris during the time of the Terror, but his rescue of Thomas Paine had not appeared in any of them, partly because it had been more inadvertent than not, but mainly because Paine had fled England to avoid being hanged for treason.

'Oh come, sir, it is not uncommon for a senior naval officer to assume the duties of a diplomat,' Fox persisted. 'As your friend Sir Sidney Smith has demonstrated on a number of occasions.'

Nathan changed the subject slightly.

'You said something of cooperation between our two navies,' he said.

'I did. The slave ships will not be stopped by laws alone. It will be essential to establish naval patrols off the coast of Africa and the eastern seaboard of North America, for which agreements will be necessary, and, it is to be hoped, we will have the participation of the United States navy.'

'But . . . the American navy—'

'Consists of six frigates and a few gunboats,' Fox finished for him. 'Whereas we have—how many ships of the line is it, at the last count? If you do not know, I am sure Carteret does.'

'One hundred and six ships of the line,' Carteret supplied smoothly, 'and ninety-five frigates of thirty-two guns or more . . .'

Nathan glanced in his direction once more, for this was impressive. He could not have given the figures himself, nothing like so exact.

'As many as that.' Fox raised a brow. 'No wonder we pay so much in taxes. So yes, you are quite correct. If there is such an agreement, it will be largely symbolic, but that is not to be despised. A single frigate, even a sloop of war, joined with one of our own patrols would send a significant message to the slave traders, the southern states, and I dare say, the French. But here is Venables with news of our provisions, so let us continue this in the dining room, if you do not mind lending me your arm.'

It was a delicate operation, but once accomplished and fortified with another bumper of brandy, the foreign minister resumed his narrative.

'One other thing you should know. It has been necessary, for various reasons that we need not discuss here, to recall the British envoy in Washington. Mr Carteret will assume that role, with your support.'

So far as Nathan was concerned, this was none of his business, but he did point out one practical consideration.

'I hope you are aware of the accommodation available in a thirty-two-gun frigate,' he remarked to Carteret. 'You may end up sharing with the midshipmen.'

'Oh, Carteret might like that,' Fox remarked, 'but what is this about a thirty-two-gun frigate? Has Grey not informed you of the nature of your command?'

'He said I would resume command of the *Panther* in Gibraltar,' Nathan replied warily. He would be sorry to lose the *Panther*, if this was what they had in mind, though his tenure as captain had been brief.

'It must have slipped his mind, else he thought I should have the pleasure of telling you myself. We agreed on a seventy-four, did we not, Carteret, and a few smaller ships besides?'

'The *Scipio* of seventy-four guns, the frigate *Panther* of thirty-two, and two sloops of war whose names escape me for the moment, I am afraid, but Captain Peake is, I believe, acquainted with them both.'

'A squadron?'

It seemed there was no end to the surprises Fox had in store for him. At least this was a pleasant one.

'I believe that is the correct nautical term, or is it a flotilla—Mr Carteret?'

Mr Carteret believed a squadron would be more correct, though he was not an expert on the matter. They both looked to Nathan expectantly, but he was obliged once more to resort to repetition. 'The *Scipio*?'

'French prize, taken by Admiral Strachan at Cape Ortegal,' Carteret supplied. 'Seventy-four guns. But for further information I am afraid you must consult your colleagues at the Admiralty.'

Surprisingly, Fox possessed additional information on the subject, though it was not of a nature to impress the average seafarer.

'Named after the Roman general Scipio, I understand. The main architect of the victory over Carthage. He was named Africanus in honour of his conquest, it is believed, rather than that he was an African, but it is an interesting thought in the circumstances, do you not agree?'

Nathan was more concerned with how much damage the ship had sustained at Ortegal, and what she had in the way of a crew.

'And I am to command her?' he said, just to be sure.

'You will be rated commodore, I believe, and given the nature of your duties in Washington, I would advise that you have a captain to serve under you.'

'Of my own choice?' He was pushing his luck, but now was the time.

'That, I am afraid, is not for me to decide. But if there is anyone you have in mind, have a private word with Carteret, and we will see what we can do.'

'And the crew?'

'The crew?' Fox appeared baffled. He looked to his aide once more. 'Does it not come with a crew?'

'The original crew would have been French,' Carteret pointed out.

'Oh, that would not do at all.'

'But an exchange was arranged for a number of British seamen who were imprisoned in Spain.'

'There you are, my boy, you have a crew,' declared Fox, though it was clear the subject did not especially interest him. 'But these are mere details. What I must impress upon you is the importance of your mission in Washington. According to the intelligence we have received, the federal government is facing a number of crises at present which may very well prove critical. Not to mince matters, they may threaten the very existence of the United States as it is presently composed. This may be welcomed by a number of people in this country, but not by me, or indeed, by anyone of influence in the present government. You are to make it known to President Jefferson and his associates that they may count on our full support.' He paused for a moment's reflection. 'This is, I dare say it, a unique opportunity to repair our relations with our friends across the Atlantic and to establish agreements not only in the matter of trade and politics, but a harmony that will, I trust, outlive us all.'

His eyes had misted over, and it was clear to Nathan that not only was this an issue very close to his heart, but that it was something he very much wished to achieve in his own lifetime, and that there was not a great deal of it left.

'Look upon it as the force of fate,' he advised Nathan with a smile. 'Shakespeare, you know, used the sea as a metaphor in that respect. The force that put one's enemies in one's power and brought peace and harmony in the final scene.'

Nathan did not know. His mother was always quoting Shakespeare at him and it had not, hitherto, proved beneficial.

'I am honoured by your confidence, sir,' he declared, 'but despite what you have said, my experience of diplomacy is extremely limited, and I fear that in many ways, I will be all at sea and . . . and . . .'

There was another metaphor there somewhere, something to do with rocks and shipwrecks, but it evaded him.

'Which is why we have assembled a team to advise you,' Fox assured him smoothly. 'As well as Mr Carteret here, there will be two American gentlemen who will act as your guides and whose standing in Washington will assure you of a better welcome than you might otherwise expect. One of them is by way of being both a naval officer and a lawyer—I think we can call him that, Carteret, can we not?'

There was a glimmer of mischief in his rheumy eye, but Nathan could think of no obvious reason for it.

'And the other gentleman?'

'Oh, I believe he is another old acquaintance of yours. His name is Imlay. Gilbert Imlay.'

CHAPTER 11

The American Agent

OF COURSE. HE MIGHT HAVE KNOWN. IN A STRANGE, INEXPLICABLE way he *had* known, even as he put the question to the foreign secretary. The name insinuated itself into the rhythmic drumming of the horses' hooves, the rattle of the iron-shod wheels on the paved turnpike leading back to London.

Imlay, Imlay, Imlay . . .

He had hoped never to hear that name again, let alone have any further dealings with the man who bore it. For if there was a rival to Sir Sidney Smith in the role of nemesis in his life, it was surely Gilbert Imlay.

He had looked up the meaning of *nemesis* once, in some ancient volume of Greek myths in his father's library in Windover House, and he had read that it meant, among other things, the inescapable means of one's downfall, the divine agent of retribution for the hubris of challenging the gods.

All of which rather flattered the rogue. For there was nothing divine about Imlay, and if Nathan had ever inadvertently challenged the gods, he believed he was deserving of a more just, a more worthy avenger. For Imlay was a deceitful scoundrel who pretended to be all things to all men and cloaked his treachery in a facade of friendship.

They had first met in Paris during the time of the Terror, where Nathan had been sent by William Pitt on the first of several covert operations in the guise of the American seafarer Nathaniel Turner, and was in the process of being strung up to a lamppost for neglecting to wear the red-white-and-blue cockade that showed his support for the Revolution. Imlay had intervened to explain that his neglect of this vital accessory was not from opposition to its principles, but from ignorance, being a native of Massachusetts.

He was a good talker, Imlay. He could talk his way out of most things, and he had at times exerted himself in the interests of others, provided it was also in the interests of himself—and Imlay's interests always came first.

But that knowledge came later.

At the time Nathan knew him as a friend and ally—an American writer living in Paris who had been persuaded by Pitt to act as one of his agents in the war against the new French republic. Later, he discovered that Imlay was also working for the French, and the Americans, and very likely for the Spaniards and the Austrians and the Prussians and anyone else willing or under pressure to pay for his services.

It was almost impossible to know whose coin he was taking at any particular moment in time. He was a true entrepreneur in the commerce of human conflict. He had once had the nerve, and perhaps the self-delusion, to describe himself as an honest broker, happy to oblige anyone in need of his expertise and with the means to pay the asking price. In the years before Nathan had met him, he had been, by his own account, a sailor, a soldier, a spy, an explorer of the American frontier, and a writer of both fact and fiction. In the years since, he had been a blockade runner, a soap merchant, a shipowner, a gunrunner, and the confidential agent of at least four mutually hostile governments. And now what? An adviser on a mission of peace and understanding. Times must be hard.

The man's origins were something of a mystery. Nathan had heard from various sources, not necessarily to be relied upon, that he was born in New Jersey when it was still a crown colony and that his family had been respectable merchants and shipowners. In those pre-Revolutionary days he and his brother had taken to smuggling rum and molasses out of Jamaica and other Caribbean islands and transporting them to Boston and other markets on mainland America, which was probably as respectable an occupation as any other in the British Empire in those days.

There were varying accounts of his career during the Independence War. Some said he had been paymaster of the New Jersey militia before absconding with the pay. Others, that he was a spy for the British. But one man who was in a better position to know than most had told Nathan that Imlay was one of a select band of gentlemen, rogues, ruffians, and adventurers known as 'Washington's Boys,' paid from a secret fund available to the rebel commander in chief for services deemed too murky and disreputable to be openly considered, let alone approved by members of the Continental Congress. However, Imlay's duplicity extended into his personal life, and Nathan had concluded that he was one of those amoral individuals who are all things to all men—and women, particularly women—and who when confronted with their perfidy will appear bemused, even aggrieved that one should think ill of them.

On that first occasion in Paris, he had been living with the English writer Mary Wollstonecraft, author of *A Vindication of the Rights of Woman* and a close friend of Nathan's mother. She was there to write about the Revolution for an English journal, but when France and England went to war she found herself in danger of arrest, and Imlay had offered to marry her to give her the protection of American citizenship. Or so he always claimed.

Mary, however, was in love with him and believed Imlay to be in love with her. Their marriage was conducted by his friend the American ambassador, who was said—by Imlay—to have the same legal rights as a captain in a ship at sea. This later proved not to be true. By then, however, Mary was carrying his child. The next time Nathan met her, over a year later, she and the child were living with his mother in London, and Imlay with an actress in Charlotte Street. And yet Imlay invariably managed to talk his way back into favour—with his women, his employers, even with Nathan, who had been persuaded to join him in running guns to the rebel slaves of Saint-Domingue during the short-lived peace with France.

That had ended badly, too, and come close to ending Nathan's life, but he had at least got a ship out of it, sailing off in a captured French corvette called the *Falaise*, which Imlay had purchased with American government funds but registered in Nathan's name, in the hope of blaming him, and the British, for the entire operation. Nathan had hired her out to the navy and commanded her for the best part of two years before he was given the *Panther*.

Nathan had not included everything in his reports, but there was enough for Fox to know what manner of man they were dealing with. Fox must have thought Imlay's standing with the Americans was worth taking the risk. The greater question was why Imlay had agreed to work with Nathan again after the last experience.

It was useless to speculate, of course. He turned his mind to other less complex subjects, if only by comparison. First thing in the morning he was to meet with Marsden at the Admiralty to discuss the details of his promotion and his squadron. He wondered if Marsden had approved the decision, or even if he knew about it. Well, he would soon find out.

Then there was Louise. His new appointment meant that he would soon be leaving her again. The thought made him unspeakably wretched, and yet he had always known it was going to happen. If he had not been sent to sea, it could only be because he had been condemned to a worse fate.

But what would she make of it?

There had been times when he was assured of her love for him, as certain as of his love for her. But then, he had thought that in Jersey, and she had left without warning, leaving him a brief note of farewell. And later, at Malmaison, she had refused to come with him to England. She said she owed it to the empress, and that it would have felt like a betrayal.

But he suspected the real reason was her loyalty to Smith.

He knew for sure she had been one of his secret agents in the past. What he still did not know was whether she had also been his lover.

He was haunted by that vision of him in the light of her doorway in Soho. If it *was* him, and not an apparition brought on by his own suspicions. The trouble was, he could not trust his own judgement in this, for it was polluted with jealousy, a vice he loathed in himself. It combined vanity with insecurity, the assumption of ownership with a terrible vulnerability, and he would not tolerate it, any more than he could abide the idea of a woman as his own exclusive property.

Really?

A familiar sardonic voice in his head.

He marshalled his arguments against it.

If you love a woman like Louise, you have to accept that she is never going to be your exclusive possession, not without destroying the very thing in her that you love. Her spirit, her independence. She must have the freedom to choose.

Even if she chooses another man?

No.

No, he knew he could never accept that. From vanity probably, but there was something else he found more difficult to put into words. You could only use the word 'love,' even if it was a selfish love. A love that implied possession.

So, what are you to do? Lock her up in a country house like all the other officers' wives, with a brood of children and a few servants to keep an eye on her while you sail away to the far corners of the world, free to do as you please whilst pleading your duty to King George, God bless him.

No, I would never want a woman who would be content with that.

Really? Examine your heart. Is this not exactly what you want?

He thought about it. A woman tamed, content to dwindle into a wife, as his mother's friend Sheridan had put it in one of his plays—or was that someone else? Some theatrical nonsense his mother had dragged him to, any rate.

And that was another thing. His mother. He could not pretend that her own easy ways with men, and morals, did not disturb him deeply. He loved his mother. He admired and respected her, at any rate. But he did not want to marry a woman like her.

And this gave rise to another, even more disturbing thought: Was Louise like his mother?

It was not the first time this had occurred to him, but he had always rejected the thought. There were similarities, sure, but his mother despised morality as the shackles imposed on women by men to further their own interests, their own controls. Whereas Louise . . .

Well, Louise was different. She had been through a lot, far more than his mother ever had. Her life in Paris during the Terror must have been truly monstrous. Her own mother had died on the guillotine, a victim of the very things Nathan most despised and feared in himself—the fear of an independent woman, the need for control, for total, unquestioning loyalty and servitude. And Louise had been confined in the Carmes, awaiting her own execution. Then, when she was released into the care of her father, he had been brutally murdered, nailed to a cross, and she had joined the rebels. What had that been like? How could he even begin to judge her? Much less seek to control her.

And yet . . .

He knew himself well enough to acknowledge that if he ever discovered that Louise had another lover, he would want nothing more to do with her. Not because he thought she was a whore—or even that he despised whores. But he would not be able to live with it, or her. He would not want her anymore.

And so he went round and round in circles.

The coach was back in London, turning into Piccadilly and through Haymarket to Leicester Square. It was dark now, and the women of the night were out in all their finery. And on to Soho. Darker here, only shadows at the sides of the road, but he could hear the cries of the watchmen and the bellmen—and the street sellers, still at their labour . . .

Knives to grind, bellows to mend.

A light here, hang out your light, see your horns be clear and bright. Look to your fires and your candles.

Come buy my ground ivy, here's feverfew, gillyflowers, and rue.

Look to your locks, good people, lock out the thief who comes in the night.

Lock up your wives and daughters . . .

Chapter 12

The Bull and the Bullring

'So, when are you to leave?'

The question appeared to be directed at the creature emerging from the tree trunk in the centre of the drawing room.

Louise had been working on it when he arrived, and though she had greeted him with a kiss, involving a slight turn of the head, and the offer of refreshment, he had the impression that she would rather have been left to continue working on it for some while longer, free from interruption.

She had placed four large candles in black iron stands, like those on the altar of a church, at intervals in a semicircle about it, and inevitably this reminded him of the first time he had seen her in the chapel on Jersey with her angel. The 'bump,' however, was now impossible to disguise, even in the loosest of garments. She had, by her own reckoning, five or six weeks to go.

'I am not sure,' he replied, though he was not sure if she was listening, or even expected an answer. 'I will probably find out tomorrow, when I have an appointment at the Admiralty, but I expect it will be within the next few days—or so.'

He had been instructed by Fox to keep the nature of his mission to himself, apart from those at the Admiralty who had a need to know. He had told Louise only that he was no longer obliged to answer to an inquiry and had been ordered to resume his command in Gibraltar.

She reached out and moved one of the candles slightly as if to shed more light on a particular feature. He felt a surge of what might have been irritation but suppressed it.

'Do you . . .' He stopped himself. He had been going to say, do you mind? 'Will you be all right?' he said instead.

She looked at him then. A quick, sharp glance. Withering? He could not be sure. The flickering light of the candles illumined more of the dryad than of her.

'Why should I not be?' she enquired.

He was reluctant to point out that childbirth was an extremely risky business. She probably knew this already.

He had attempted to discuss the risks with his mother but had received a predictable response.

'Pray do not lose any sleep over it,' she had advised him. 'It is what we women are born for, is it not?'

It was, of course, a delicate subject. Several of her closest friends had died in childbirth, including poor Mary Wollstonecraft, who had contracted an infection within a few days of giving birth to her second child. His mother always maintained that she herself had been extremely lucky to have survived the ordeal—meaning his own birth—and that the shock and pain were 'unimaginable.' Certainly, it seemed to have deterred her from ever doing it again.

He assured himself that Louise was a fit and healthy young woman who had survived greater perils than the delivery of a child, though admittedly it was difficult to calculate the odds. At twenty-five she was probably older than the average for a first child, but by no means ancient, and she had found an experienced doctor—yet another French exile living in Soho—who did not object to the unfashionable practice of obstetrics.

However, his mother did not consider this to be an advantage. She was inclined to put more trust in Louise's maid, Bella, or her own maid, Izzy, both of whom had assisted in a number of deliveries and were prepared to help with Louise, too, should she require it.

'It is a peculiarity of childbirth that more women appear to die under the supervision of a man, than not,' she had informed Nathan. 'And more die at hospital than at home. Why do you think that is?'

He knew he was being provoked and batted the question back to her. 'Why do you?'

'Oh, I expect we have been designed wrong,' she said with arched brow.

He had attempted to get more sense out of Izzy, and even Bella, but they had either dodged his questions or replied with baffling technicalities that he suspected were deliberately designed to confuse him.

Louise was even worse, so that eventually he had given up asking. He knew he would not have been allowed to attend the birth, even if he was able to do so, but he felt extremely guilty that he would not even be in the country.

'I have no choice,' he said to her now. 'I am under orders.'

'Of course you are,' she said, though still without looking at him. 'The king commands, and you obey.'

He took this as a criticism and considered it unfair.

'None of us is entirely free to do as we wish,' he pontificated. 'Such freedoms as we have we owe to'—he searched desperately for the right words—'to our willingness to fight for them.'

'Well, off you go and fight for them,' Louise advised him generously.

It was probably not the best time to have this kind of a conversation, he thought. He was still reeling from his encounter with Fox. It had made him dull and stupid, inclined to be pompous.

He lapsed into an unhappy silence.

'You do not have to defend yourself to me,' she assured him after a few moments tap, tap, tapping away with her hammer.

'I have always accepted that you must do your duty. How could I not?'

He shook his head sadly. 'Why does it have to be like this?'

'What?' She gazed across the room at him. 'You mean, between you and me?'

He had not meant that, no, but perhaps it was something worth raising. Another time, maybe.

'No. I mean, why is there always something that compels us to do the opposite of what we truly want to do with our lives?'

'Oh.' She seemed to be thinking about it. 'Perhaps I am not the right person to ask,' she offered at length.

'Because you would never do that?'

'What?'

'What you do not want to do.'

This was unkind, and probably unwise. But it was in his mind that she had put duty before love on several occasions where he was concerned. Or if not duty, then something else, or some-*one* else.

She did not reply.

He watched her for a moment as she sat there apparently lost in her creation. For all the intimacies there had been between them, she was almost as impenetrable to him now as when he had first seen her in the chapel on Jersey.

But if he knew more, if he knew her as well as he knew himself, would it not break the spell, destroy the enchantment, bludgeon the love in an excess of knowledge?

'Why does the bull enter the bullring?' she said suddenly.

She looked at him then, with what appeared to be genuine inquiry. In the glow of the candles, with that inquisitive frown, she seemed like an innocent child, puzzled by some profound mystery.

'Why does the bull enter the bullring?' he repeated flatly.

What did that have to do with anything? Another provocation, or obfuscation, designed to confuse or divert. He knew nothing of bullfights. It was a sport of the ancient Greeks now popular in Spain, he had heard, and parts of southern France. Perhaps she meant it to be an analogy of his own situation. He was the bull. The fighting bull. A brute animal, bred for conflict, led to its inevitable slaughter.

'Because it has no choice,' he replied.

'This is probably true,' she agreed thoughtfully. 'And the bullfighter?'

She was probably trying to trap him into saying the wrong thing, but he said it anyway.

'Well, he does not really have a choice either. He has to prove his manhood, to show he is not afraid, that he has balls.'

'Ah.' Enlightenment. 'Then it is the balls.'

He grinned and shook his head. He did not know why he grinned. Perhaps because he could not imagine having this conversation with anyone else.

'Then if the bull did not have balls,' she went on slowly, 'and the bullfighter did not have balls, neither of them would have to get in the ring.'

'This is probably true,' he said, in echo of her earlier reply.

'Have you ever thought . . .'

'No,' he said. 'Never.'

Early next morning he set off for the Admiralty for his meeting with Mr Marsden.

He was alone in his office on the first floor, his manner courteous but distant. He did, however, offer coffee.

'So, I take it that you have been fully briefed by the foreign minister,' Marsden began, 'and will be anxious to be on your way.'

There was a slight note of sarcasm in his tone, Nathan thought, but he let it pass.

'I have been told the nature of my mission,' he confirmed, 'but little in the way of practical information.'

'Such as?' His tone implied polite interest rather than a willingness to remedy this deficiency.

'Well, such as the ships under my command, the state they are in, whether they are crewed or provisioned, even where they . . .'

'I trust you will find all that out when you get to Gibraltar,' Marsden advised him blandly. 'I have no more information than you have at present. Probably a great deal less.'

If this were true, they were in a worse state at the Admiralty than even their most severe critics imagined.

'And how am I to get to Gibraltar?' Nathan pressed. 'Or am I to make my own way?'

He expected Marsden to confirm this was what was expected of him, but surprisingly, transport had been arranged.

'Well, normally, of course, we would send you by the Falmouth packet, or even a sloop of war, if there was one going that way, but in the circumstances, berths have been secured for you and your entourage on an East Indiaman due to leave Deptford in the next few days.'

Nathan's face remained expressionless, but his mind was considerably exercised, for this made no sense to him at all. Whereas a post chaise would have conveyed him 'and his entourage' to Falmouth within forty hours, forty-eight at most, a fast packet could have him in Gibraltar six or seven days later. With contrary winds and tides, an East Indiaman might take up to a fortnight to reach the western end of the English Channel before it had even begun the journey to the south. What 'circumstances' could Marsden possibly mean? Whatever they were, they had not formed part of the foreign secretary's briefing.

'And when I arrive in Gibraltar, what then?' Nathan persisted. 'Am I to report to Admiral Lord Collingwood, or what?'

'I understand you will be under Admiralty orders, which means you will be answerable to the first lord, but . . .' Marsden almost shrugged as if to say that this did not amount to very much. He probably knew, or at least believed, that the first lord was under the thumb of Fox and incapable of doing anything without his approval.

'Then perhaps Lord Howick would wish to advise me on the disposition of my squadron,' Nathan proposed.

Marsden stiffened. 'The first lord has rather more important matters to deal with at present,' he informed him coldly. 'However, the lieutenant governor of Gibraltar has been advised of your appointment. I imagine he has everything under control.' Then after a small pause: 'You are aware that he is brother to the new foreign secretary.'

Nathan was not so aware. His last stay in Gibraltar had been brief, and he was no more acquainted with the lieutenant governor than that notable was with him. However, the family connection might work to his advantage, he supposed. He hoped something did.

This reminded him of Imlay.

'And what of the Americans?' he asked.

'The Americans?' Marsden appeared puzzled.

'I was informed that I would have two Americans as my advisers on the mission and that they were presently in London.'

'Ah. Yes. *Those* Americans. Not my department, I am happy to say. However, you will have plenty of time to become acquainted with them on the voyage to Gibraltar.'

'Mr Imlay and I are already acquainted,' Nathan informed him, though Marsden must know that, and a lot more besides. He was assured that his dealings with Imlay over the years would have been filed away in the archives, along with all the other information that might be used against him someday.

'I need have no further contact with him before we embark,' Nathan said, 'provided he is ready to depart at a moment's notice.'

Marsden made no comment.

'And the other gentleman?'

'Ah yes. The Hebrew gentleman.'

Nathan frowned. Was this significant?

'Again, he does not come within my jurisdiction, so to speak. I can make enquiry, of course. But what is it you wish to know?'

'Well—I assume he, too, is in London and knows what is expected of him?'

'Oh, yes, he is in London, and my understanding is that he will be made available to you whenever he is required.'

There was a strong hint of irony in his tone, and again, Nathan had the impression that there was some mystery here, even that he was being made game of, but other than demanding that the two men be summoned for his immediate inspection, he was unsure how to proceed. He was determined to get something out of Marsden, however, before he left the building.

'And this East Indiaman we are to take to Gibraltar—where is she at present?'

He would not have been surprised to hear she was in India, or currently making her stately way across the south Atlantic and due to arrive in London sometime before the summer.

'The *True Briton*,' Marsden supplied after consulting a paper. 'Presently berthed in Deptford and preparing to sail within the next day or two. A cabin has been reserved for you and the other gentlemen. Now, if that is all . . .'

Nathan had the distinct impression that Marsden had washed his hands of him. He was leaving him to the Foxes and the Greys of this world. He was their boy, and he could make the best or the worst of their acquaintance. Either way, the first secretary would not be losing any sleep over it.

Which was all very well, but a little more clarity, even some definition, would have been helpful. He could only hope that the situation would be somewhat less ambiguous when he arrived in Gibraltar, but he fully expected to turn up on the Rock and find that neither Collingwood nor the lieutenant governor knew anything about his promotion, his squadron, or his mission to America. It was quite possible that the squadron did not exist, except in the foreign secretary's fond imaginings.

He took a cab back to Soho and found there was a message waiting for him. It was from Imlay, and as strange as it was unexpected. He proposed a meeting at the Anchor tavern on the Thames at Bankside, a notoriously dissolute area of the waterfront, at ten o'clock that evening.

A postscript, underlined, advised him not to wear his uniform, and to dress down.

Chapter 13

The Liberty of the Clink

The Anchor was on the south bank of the river a little to the west of London Bridge, in an area once owned by the bishops of Winchester, and famous in Shakespeare's day for its theatres and its brothels. The theatres had long since moved north, and if the brothels were still here, they had seen better days.

Nathan wore a greatcoat over the shabbiest suit he could find among the clothes left at his mother's house. He had a pistol in his pocket, a dirk in his boot, and carried a stout walking stick.

The tavern itself was not so bad. It was attached to a large brewery of the same name—known for this reason as the 'brewery tap'—and the air in the vicinity was heavy with the smell of malt, which was possibly an improvement on the stench of the river.

He found Imlay with some difficulty in the crowded interior. He had taken a private nook off one of the bars.

'Captain Peake—or is it Turner?' He rose ponderously from the table, beaming at his own wit, for he had known Nathan by both names, but his eyes betrayed an element of uncertainty or embarrassment.

Nathan sat down opposite him without speaking and gazed at him in silence for a moment, to see if it would disconcert him any. He had decided not to mention the circumstances of their last encounter in Saint-Domingue unless Imlay did. He was fairly sure the American had betrayed him to the French, but he had no evidence for this, and it would be more entertaining to see if Imlay embarked on an explanation. It was over three years ago now; perhaps the exact circumstances had slipped his mind.

Imlay had put on a good deal of weight in the intervening years. Nathan would scarce have known him from the handsome rake he had met in Paris during the Terror. He would be in his early fifties now. It was not possible to judge from his appearance how well he was doing. He had presumably, like Nathan, dressed down for the occasion.

There was a bottle of Madeira on the table and two glasses. Imlay filled up the one that had been empty and topped up his own.

'Let us drink to your elevation,' he said. 'And the success of our mission.'

So, he knew about Nathan's promotion. But then when it came to Nathan's darker forms of employment, Imlay often knew more than anyone else involved. Nathan had noted the reference to 'our' mission. It was like Imlay to claim credit for a venture in which he was barely implicated—until it started to go wrong, of course, when you would not see him for dust. Nonetheless, it would have been ungracious not to raise his glass.

'Is this a regular rendezvous of yours when you are in London?' Nathan quizzed him, glancing back through the windows of their private enclave into the large public bar beyond. The clientele was predominantly male, as was to be expected, but there was a goodly representation of the opposite sex, which, judging from their appearance, might be categorised as 'ladies of the night.' Although most of them and their potential customers were dressed in some style, it was a style that failed to convince of its authenticity, those of a certain class and inclination tending, when out on the razzle, to attire themselves in the cast-off clothing of the quality picked up from the numerous street markets and slop shops of the city. There was little to tell a common prostitute from the Duchess of Devonshire in the low lights of a tavern, or indeed, a footpad from Charles James Fox.

'First time I have been here,' Imlay confessed. 'They call it the Liberty of the Clink, for reasons that have not yet been adequately explained to me, for I believe the Clink was a prison maintained by the Bishop of Winchester in former times. As for this establishment, I am advised that it is one of the oldest taverns in the city. It was from here that Samuel Pepys watched the Fire of London, and in more recent years, Dr Johnson was among its more esteemed customers. He was a friend of Lord Thrale, you may recall.'

Nathan did not recall any such thing, nor its relevance to their present location, but apparently he had been the brewer.

Imlay was nervous, Nathan gathered, and when Imlay was nervous, he had a habit of rattling on. He had also become rather theatrical since they had last met, even plummy, like some minor author whose bon mots and general air of consequence would help detract from his lack of literary recognition. He reminded himself not to underestimate the man, however. He might come across as a fool, but he was as dangerous a fool as any Nathan had encountered.

'So, why are we here?' Nathan asked.

'We are to meet an associate of mine,' Imlay informed him. 'Well, not here, precisely. On the river. But we have a little while before we must brave the cold and damp.'

'On the river?'

'The riverside, that is. But only a short walk from here.'

'Is it not a little late for an assignation on the waterfront? Especially in this area. You do know of its reputation?'

'Where is your sense of adventure, sir? All will be made clear, I promise you. But how are you, my friend? You were at Trafalgar, I believe?'

'I was.' Nathan wondered if Imlay knew he had been on the wrong side. He probably did. 'And you? How long have you been back in London?'

'I have but recently arrived.'

Nathan wondered if this was true, but though deceit came as naturally to Imlay as breathing, there seemed no necessity to lie in this instance.

'I was sent on a diplomatic mission, as the foreign secretary may have informed you, but now I have been instructed to return with you to the States and guide you through the swamps and cesspits of Washington.'

'I am sorry. That must be something of a demotion for you.'

'Not at all, not at all. It is yet another opportunity to bring our two countries together in the course of peace—and of course, abolition.'

'I did not know you were hot in the cause of abolition.' Nor peace for that matter, Nathan reflected. 'Was it upon the road to Damascus, or of longer genesis?'

'Oh, I have always abhorred slavery,' Imlay insisted. 'I consider it an affront to the laws of God and man. Why else would I have been running guns to the rebels of Saint-Domingue?'

The bare-faced effrontery of the man never ceased to astonish, even after so many years of acquaintance. Nathan waited for him to say more, but that was it, apparently, as far as Saint-Domingue was concerned.

'So, who is this associate of yours we are to meet?' he demanded.

'Ah, I had meant to keep it as a surprise, but as you ask, his name is Levy—Lieutenant Daniel Levy—and he is the third member of our team. Or should I say, fourth? For I believe Fox is sending one of his young cubs to keep an eye on us.'

Nathan would never have described Carteret as a young cub, despite his comparative youth, but he let it pass.

'And why are we meeting him here, as opposed to the American consulate—or are you not welcome there?'

Imlay smiled agreeably. 'There is a need for discretion,' he confessed, 'but pray curb your impatience. All will be revealed.'

Nathan's suspicions were now thoroughly aroused. It did not take much where Imlay was concerned.

'I am sorry,' he said, 'but that is not good enough. You say he is an associate of yours. Was he involved in these trade talks, or what?'

Imlay sighed. 'Did Fox tell you nothing of this?'

'All he said was that you would be accompanying me on the mission to Washington along with another gentleman who is both a naval officer and a lawyer. I assume this is Levy?'

'Indeed. He served aboard the USS *Constitution* in the Barbary Wars, but has for some time been located in Washington as an adviser to the president. Largely, I think, on account of his legal training.'

'And what is he doing in England?'

'That is . . . complicated. But he was lately imprisoned on a charge of espionage.' Imlay noted Nathan's concern. 'An entirely spurious charge, brought by our enemies in the British establishment. Returning him safely to Washington will bring our mission off to an excellent start.'

'So, he has been released?'

'You could say that, yes.'

'But why in the middle of the night?'

'Is it that late?' Imlay glanced at the clock on the wall above the bar. 'My goodness, we had better be getting on.'

'Imlay . . .'

But Imlay was already on his feet and calling for the reckoning.

Chapter 14

Fireworks!

It was noticeably colder than when Nathan had arrived at the inn. There was no-one about, and even the river looked empty, for London Bridge was an impenetrable barrier for most vessels of over a few tons burthen, and there were few smaller boats about at this time of night. Imlay strode ahead, his heavy build further accentuated by a coat of many capes and a large bicorn hat worn athwart in the manner of Napoleon, possibly the only man in London to chance comparison. He was rattling on about something or other, not in the least important—anything to avoid telling Nathan what their true purpose was, Nathan imagined. He wished he would pipe down. Imlay was an incitement to violence at the best of times, and this was far from being that. There were possibly more footpads and their like in the Liberty of the Clink than any other district of London save the Saint Giles rookery. He had checked his pistol before leaving the security of the inn. Known as a Toby, it was specially designed for a gentleman's pocket and was equipped with a small metal cap that fitted over the firing pan so it could be carried fully primed and loaded, with less risk of an accidental discharge.

They had crossed a rickety footbridge over a narrow wharf that stank like a cesspit, and now they were skirting a churchyard. Nathan noted the church steeple against the night sky. It was impossible to see much else. It was as much as he could do to keep his feet on the path ahead of him.

'Do you know the name of this church?' Imlay enquired.

Nathan confessed that he did not. 'Why—are you lost?' he demanded. It would not have surprised him.

But Imlay wished only to show off his knowledge of London. He had spent a lot of time here, of course, during his marriage to Mary Wollstonecraft—though not, in fact, with her. The actress in Charlotte Street had not been the first of his liaisons, nor the last.

'It is Saint Mary's Overy. Some people think it is Saint Mary's Ovaries, but that is a nonsense. Not even the Papists in the Middle Ages would have called a church after the Virgin's private parts. It is short for Saint Mary's Over the River, to distinguish it from all the other Saint Marys in London. Even so, an odd name for a church, is it not?'

Nathan had nothing to offer on the subject. He was too busy putting one foot carefully in front of the other and hoping he did not step in something disgusting.

They crossed under one of the arches of London Bridge, close to the water's edge. The darkness was almost impenetrable here, but Nathan sensed the presence of humanity, could smell it, too, and once he almost tripped over it. He could not see them, but he knew there would be recumbent figures stretched out on either side of the archway, gathering their rags about them on the damp riverbed, sleeping or dead. There were rats, too, hoping to find a corpse or two, or to take a bite out of something living that was too weak to fight back.

They emerged from under the shadows of the bridge and were confronted with the vast forest of masts and yards that was the Pool of London. From here to Rotherhithe the river was dense with shipping, from East Indiamen with the spoils of the East to humble colliers bringing coals from Newcastle. It was almost full tide, and Nathan could see the oily blackness of the water in the lights of the ships, like a great worm writhing its way inland. He could smell it, too, now they were clear of the brewery.

Imlay stopped suddenly enough for Nathan to almost run into the back of him, and there in the spill of light from a brazier he saw two burly figures on the narrow path along the river. He reached in his pocket for his pistol.

Imlay stayed his hand. 'They are ours,' he said. 'Right, lads?'

A muttered response and they stepped back into the shadows to let Imlay warm himself at the brazier.

'Now what?' said Nathan.

'We wait,' said Imlay.

'For what?'

'Our man.'

Nathan assumed he must be arriving by boat, but from where? He gazed out over the black water. Across the river, outlined against the paler sky, Nathan could just make out the spires of two or three churches. No names were supplied by his helpful guide. Further east was the monument to the Fire of London, then the bulk of the Customs House—and then the even greater bulk of the Tower.

A sudden thought came to him, as alarming as it was absurd. He tried to form a question that would not appear quite as foolish as the one in his head, but he was distracted by the sound of a bell from the nearby church, and then many more, mostly from north of the river. The bells of London ringing out the end of one day and the start of another.

'We have heard the chimes at midnight,' declared Imlay, in his new role as Falstaff. It might have been ironic.

The last of them had barely died away when, almost as if it were a signal, a rocket burst in the night sky across the river, directly north of the Tower, briefly illuminating its turrets and battlements. There followed another, and another.

Imlay raised his head to the sky. In the light of the exploding rockets and the starbursts, Nathan saw that he was beaming like a child.

'I love fireworks,' he said. 'Are you not glad you came?'

Nathan declined to reply, but his mind was much exercised.

Why fireworks in February? It was not Guy Fawkes, nor Hallowe'en, New Year, or Christmas. The king's birthday? But that was in June. Besides, they were never so late at night. In the silence between explosions, he could hear dogs barking, and he could have sworn, the distant roaring of a lion.

It would be one of the lions in the Tower, he thought, for it was a menagerie as well as a royal palace. It was where the kings and queens of England kept their exotic pets, and their most dangerous enemies, including, on occasion, their wives, for it was also a royal prison. Anne Boleyn, Catherine Howard, Sir Thomas More, Sir Walter Raleigh . . . They and many others had been lodged at the Tower of London before they lost their heads to the executioner on Tower Hill. It was like a roll call of English nobility and foreign spies . . .

The thought was like a thunderclap, which did, in fact, coincide with one of the real ones from across the river.

'He cannot be in the Tower!' he exclaimed.

'I fear so,' said Imlay. 'I believe it has always been a prison for those accounted a particular danger to the state, and presumably they would not wish him to mix with the common felons at Newgate.

Oh, yes, he is in London, and will be made available to you whenever he is required.

Nathan had thought it an odd choice of phrase at the time. It was obviously Marsden's idea of a joke.

He peered across the river towards the battlements of the Tower, but his eyes were dazzled by the flashes of light in the sky, and between flashes it seemed doubly dark.

'The thing about fireworks,' said Imlay, 'is that I defy anyone not to look up at the sky.'

He was looking up at it himself with a beatific smile on his face. But with one last glorious golden explosion it came to an end, and the sky returned to the preserve of the stars.

'Show the signal,' Imlay instructed his hirelings, one of whom produced a lantern and began to wave it to and fro at the water's edge. A minute or so went by. The lions still roared from across the river and closer to hand the dogs still barked. Then Nathan heard the splash of oars, and a boat emerged from the darkness and ground on the thin strip of mud—all that was left of the foreshore this close to high tide.

There were four men in it: two at the oars, one on the tiller, and another in the bow, huddled in a cloak and clutching a bottle. One of Imlay's men helped him ashore, and he stumbled towards the fire.

'Lieutenant Levy.' Imlay executed a noble bow. 'Welcome to the Liberty of the Clink.'

One of his hirelings stepped forward with a large towel and a bundle of what turned out to be dry clothing.

'Give me a moment,' said Levy, in as much as he could say anything through his chattering teeth. 'Or do we not have a moment?'

'It would be wise not to tarry,' said Imlay.

'Very well.' He took off the cloak and passed it to one of the men. Under it, Nathan saw, he wore a shirt and breeches. They were soaking wet. Suspicion had now hardened into certainty. He took Imlay firmly by the arm and marched him a little way into the darkness.

'What the fuck is going on here?' he demanded.

Imlay recoiled. 'My dear sir. If you are to be a diplomat, I really feel . . .'

Nathan pointed at the shivering figure by the brazier. 'How did he get here?'

'You truly wish to know?'

'I do.'

'Very well, though it would probably be better for you if you did not.' He kept his voice low so it would not carry to the men about the brazier. 'It has all been arranged at the highest level,

I do assure you. He was escorted by one of the guards from the cell where he has been confined for the past six weeks to one of the towers overlooking the river. The Cradle Tower, I believe. A rope was provided with a weighted end which was cast across the outer walls. This was secured by our friends in the boat, and Mr Levy made his way down it, hand over hand, until he was able to drop into the river. As neat an operation as you could wish for, I believe.'

'You are telling me that we have just assisted in breaking a prisoner out of the Tower of London?'

'In a manner of speaking, though as I say—'

'And the Tower guards were a party to this?'

'Not all of them, by any means, but sufficient to ensure its successful conclusion, yes.'

'And the fireworks?'

'To distract those that were *not* a party to it. A stroke of genius, I think, though I say it myself.'

'So this was all your idea?'

'I was not the originator, but I say, in all modesty, that some of the more subtle ideas—'

'But why?'

'*Why?*'

'Why was he not released in the normal manner?'

'Ah, you must ask that of your Mr Fox next time you meet with him.'

'Fox is not here. You are.'

'Well, I cannot speak for Mr Fox, but I gather it would have been an embarrassment to free the gentleman without a trial. Questions might have been asked in Parliament. The government might have fallen.'

It was difficult to know if he was serious or not.

'Dear God.'

'God was indeed on our side,' Imlay murmured, with fake reverence.

'And why was it necessary to bring me here?'

'I am afraid that was at my insistence. We could not have the Americans take the entire credit for the operation. I felt that your presence would be a guarantee of discretion if things did not go according to plan.'

Nathan could have hit him. It would not have helped Anglo-American relations, but it would have helped ease his frustration. Any satisfaction he would have derived would have been fleeting, however.

He looked back at the man by the fire. He was now wearing breeches and a frock coat and being helped into a pair of boots by one of Imlay's hired hands. His hair hung lankly about his face, and Nathan could see little of his features, but he had the impression he was fairly young.

'So, what are we to do with him now?' he demanded.

'We are to deliver him to the *True Briton* at Deptford where he will remain aboard until we embark for Gibraltar,' declared Imlay. 'Which hopefully will occur on the next ebbing of the tide.'

Chapter 15

The Prisoner of the Tower

The tide came and went, and the *True Briton* stayed as firmly attached to Deptford Wharf as a barnacle to a rock. Not all of Imlay's formidable powers of persuasion could shift her an inch, nor would they change the fact that the next high tide would be in the middle of the night, when movement through the crowded waters of the Thames was difficult to say the least for anything larger than a wherry.

Nathan sat with his feet dangling from the mizzentop, munching upon an apple and watching with no little pleasure as Inlay remonstrated with the ship's master, Captain Elisha Thomas. Captain Thomas was a large man with side whiskers, a face as brown and solid as Indian teak, and an expression as rigidly opposed to compromise as the prophet for whom he was presumably named. In other circumstances, Nathan might have been disposed to wish Captain Thomas to the Devil, but despite the precariousness of his own position as the unwitting assistant in a jailbreak, he could not but warm towards him for putting Imlay so firmly in his place.

Nathan was now clear in his mind why Imlay had chosen this form of transport over one of the Falmouth packets. The East India Company was a law unto itself, and besides, it would be well-nigh impossible to search every ship moored in the Pool of

London in search of the fugitive, whereas setting up roadblocks on the major roads out of London was by no means unfeasible.

However, it was clear Imlay had not taken Captain Thomas into his reckoning. For every argument that Imlay advanced, he had an answer. The *True Briton* was scheduled to join a convoy assembling in the Downs, Thomas said, and would not leave until the end of the week at the earliest.

But there was no reason why they should not wait in the Downs, rather than Deptford, Imlay argued.

Ah, but there were many reasons, Captain Thomas retorted. There were stores to get in, including a quantity of powder and shot from the arsenal at Woolwich. He was still waiting for several of his officers to join him, including the ship's doctor. And he was under orders to embark a detachment of soldiers for the private armies of the East India Company, which was presently on its way from Colchester, and whose arrival was not anticipated before nightfall. All India might be lost without them, the captain implied. Besides which, there were a number of civilian passengers whose berths had been reserved months in advance and who had yet to come aboard.

Nathan suspected that the most powerful of these considerations was the latter, for he knew from his own experience as a passenger of an East Indiaman that their fares were paid directly to the captain. Had he been as anxious to depart as Imlay, he might have suggested making up the lost revenue—though Imlay would likely have baulked at the expense—but he was torn between the necessity of leaving London before the inevitable hue and cry and his desire to see Louise at least one last time.

He had sent one of Imlay's men to Soho with letters for both her and his mother alerting them to his sudden departure, which he put down to 'reasons beyond his control,' which was true enough. In the note to his mother, he had attached a list of belongings which he had begged her to have one of the servants assemble for him and bring out to Deptford as soon as possible.

In fact, he was seriously considering the risk of a visit to Soho himself.

The only sign that the escape had been discovered was the sound of a cannon fired from the Tower early that morning, but there had been no further alarms, and neither Captain Thomas nor any of his officers seemed to know anything about it, though Nathan's enquiries had been necessarily discreet. Levy's cabin had been reserved under the name Spencer, indicating that the escape had been planned well in advance, and Imlay assured Nathan that Levy would stay there at least until the ship left London. He took his meals in the cabin, and a washbasin and chamber pot had been provided for his convenience.

This was the only information Imlay had imparted since they came aboard. He refused to discuss the matter further on the grounds that they might be overheard, and it was impossible to persuade him to climb into the rigging, which was the only place they could be private. Nathan considered writing to Howick, or even Fox, to express his concern about the events of the previous night, but he found it impossible to put them into words, and besides, he had a notion that it would be foolish to commit anything to writing.

Instead, he wrote to Louise, warning her of his intention to skip ship and spend the night with her. In other circumstances he might just have turned up at her door, but he did not care to do so without warning. It was not that he seriously considered running into Sir Sidney Smith, but he was in no doubt that she was keeping something from him, and he was torn between wanting to know what it was and shutting it from his mind.

He had no sooner sent the message off, however, than the soldiers arrived, along with an extensive baggage train. This coincided with a delivery of several dairy cows, a small herd of goats, two pigs, and a great number of geese, ducks, and chickens as provisions for the voyage to India. In the ensuing chaos, Nathan took the opportunity to lead Imlay forcibly to the stern rail and demand a more complete explanation of Levy's escape from the Tower.

'I have told you all I know,' Imlay protested. 'You were there—you saw as much as I did.'

'But what was he doing in the Tower in the first place? What was the specific charge against him, and why would the government, or certain individuals in the government, conspire in his escape?'

Imlay wriggled and writhed in his usual manner, but when Nathan showed every intention of pitching him overboard or taking himself off to the Admiralty to confront Lord Howick, he finally unburdened himself. Or at least told a story that was as believable as any other Nathan had heard from him in the past.

'You will recall that I told you about the current negotiations with the British government?'

'What of them?'

'Well, one of the chief obstacles to agreement is the illegal seizure of American seamen and their impressment into the king's navy.'

This was not a surprise. Desperate to man their ships, the navy had resorted to stopping American vessels on the high seas and taking some of their best hands on the spurious grounds that they were still subject to King George. He had not resorted to the practice himself, but he knew plenty of naval officers who had, and he had benefited from it himself at times. His last ship but one had been mostly crewed by Americans, and he was quite certain that none of them had volunteered.

'There are those in government, notably Fox and Grey, who agree that this must be stopped,' Imlay continued. 'Unfortunately, there are also those who argue that without the Americans, the navy would be unable to continue at its present levels.'

'But what has this to do with Levy?' Nathan demanded.

Imlay's expression was pained. This usually preceded one of those rare moments when he was obliged to tell the truth.

'The fact is that Lieutenant Levy was dispatched to England on an official mission to oppose this practice in the courts,' he admitted. 'He has a list of high-ranking naval officers who are among the worst offenders and whom he proposed to sue privately for their illegal detention of United States citizens.'

Nathan pursed his lips in a silent whistle. This would have caused considerable agitation in certain circles. At least half the commanding officers in the service might have been involved.

'Fearing the consequences of this, the previous ministry accused him of spying,' Imlay explained. 'He would have been locked up for months, years even, while they made a case against him.'

'But now Pitt is gone, and Fox is running the show,' Nathan pointed out. 'And he is all for us wearing feathers in our caps and singing "Yankee Doodle."'

'Well, if you believe that, good luck to you. But they are singing the same old songs in Parliament and the ministry needs their support. Besides, there are those who believe they can set a trap for Fox—lure him into defending Levy, and reveal that he is more bothered about keeping Thomas Jefferson happy than his own king and country. They have never forgiven him for cheering on the king's enemies when we were fighting for our independence. They hate him worse than the French.'

This was probably true.

'Jefferson would never make an agreement with Britain while Levy is rotting in the Tower of London,' Imlay went on. 'And as for your mission to Washington—you would be wearing feathers then for sure, along with a quantity of tar, and they would run you out of town on a rail.'

This, according to Nathan's father, being the standard procedure for supporters of the king during the Independence War. His mother was much in favour of the practice.

'But surely they could have come up with some other means of securing Levy's release,' Nathan argued. 'I mean, some legal means, without having to spring him out of jail.'

'Fox has enough on his mind at present, and as you probably know, he is not in the best of health. Arranging Levy's escape seemed a daring way of resolving the matter. Intrepid, one might say.' Imlay smiled at his own wit. 'Please excuse me, as I really must speak with Captain Thomas. Now that he has got his red-coats aboard, and his other animals, I really do not see any reason why he cannot sail for the Downs upon the next tide.'

Nathan watched him march off down the deck as if he meant business. The irresistible force against the immovable object.

This time, however, he managed to shift the captain a little. He agreed to Imlay's request to moor the vessel in mid-river so as to be ready for a swift departure on the morning tide.

Nathan considered whether to take the risk of returning to Soho in the meantime, but whilst he was anguishing over this, a large carriage drew up on the quayside piled high with luggage. As it drew to a halt, a footman leapt from the back, down came the steps—and out stepped Louise and his mother.

Chapter 16

The Fugitives

'What can you mean—that you are coming with me?'

Nathan looked from his mother to Louise and back again. It was the situation he had feared most: these two formidable women presenting a united front against him, and not even in the privacy of their own home, but in the public arena of a London dockside before an assembly of interested spectators whose sentiments, judging from the vulgar remarks that reached his ears, were entirely on the side of his female antagonists. Apparently, they had formed the opinion that he was the villain of this particular piece of theatre: a degenerate scoundrel attempting to evade the responsibilities of marriage and fatherhood, apprehended in the act of escape by the long arm of justice in the form of two determined women.

He had not failed to notice that they were accompanied by Branoc and Bella, his mother's factotum, Izzy, and the footman, Francis, and that even while he remonstrated with his mother, they were in the process of unloading the luggage.

'Please leave that where it is,' he instructed them. 'Have you seen the condition she is in?' he demanded of his mother. 'And you would expose her to the perils of a sea voyage?'

This unleashed a torrent of abuse in French from Louise expressive of her resentment at being spoken of as if she was not there or had no opinion on the matter or voice to express it.

'Do you think I would have exposed myself to *this*'—she indicated the dock, the ship, and Nathan himself with an imperious sweep of the arm—'if there was the least possibility of doing anything else?'

'But it could be a month before we reach Gibraltar,' Nathan protested feebly, 'and to go into labour aboard ship . . .'

'Better than in Newgate,' said she.

'Newgate?' He repeated stupidly. 'Why would you—'

'Because I am in imminent danger of being arrested as a French spy.'

Whilst he attempted to comprehend this intelligence, his mother requested that they continue their converse in less public surroundings, 'before we let the whole of Deptford know what is afoot.'

Nathan was still staring at Louise in despair whilst she gazed out over the crowded anchorage of the Thames with an expression of glacial contempt. He was torn between wanting to wrap her in his arms, murmuring assurances of comfort and support, and condemning her for whatever indiscretions had brought her to such a pass. He leaned towards the latter. All his suspicions, all the fears that had first been aroused in Jersey, had returned with a vengeance, though in all the time he had known her they had never entirely gone away.

'Nathan,' his mother urged him quietly.

'What?' he turned upon her. 'What do you expect me to do? Please tell me, because I am damned if I know.'

'Well, to begin with, we could continue this conversation in the privacy of your cabin,' she replied calmly. 'I assume you have one.'

'There is no privacy in my cabin,' he countered. 'There is no privacy anywhere aboard a ship. Unless you would care to climb into the rigging with me.'

'Your cabin will do,' she insisted firmly.

Nathan strode towards the gangway, but as soon as he set foot upon it, he was recalled to a sense of propriety, even common decency, and turned back to take Louise by the arm. She swiped it away with a backhand swing of her own, hitched up her skirts, and began to ascend the sloping bridge to the entry port.

He conducted them to his cabin where they could at least be free of onlookers if not listeners, for the bulkhead was no more than a temporary partition of canvas and slats. They strove for a degree of privacy, however, by speaking French. The two women sat on the narrow bunk while Nathan remained standing, his head in uncomfortable proximity to the overhead deck beams.

'So, what have you been up to, to be in danger of arrest?' he began, and then, observing her expression, 'I am sorry—what are you *accused* of being up to?'

She regarded him without reply, but with narrowed eyes as if he was a species of rat or reptile.

His mother replied for her. 'They have arrested a number of French exiles in Soho and accused them of spying for Napoleon.' Her voice was redolent of an ingrained scepticism and deep-rooted contempt for whoever 'they' were. 'A nest of spies, the newspapers are calling them. Louise is one of the names on their list.'

'How do you know that?' Nathan demanded, still looking at Louise. 'Have they published it?' A shrug. He was provoked. 'Does this have anything to do with Sir Sidney Smith?' he demanded.

Louise stood up.

'Let us go,' she said to his mother. 'I told you we should not have come.'

Nathan directed a mute appeal to his mother.

'Louise,' she said quietly, reaching out a hand, but Louise stood there, rigid, like the statue of the avenging angel, a silent fury. 'He is an idiot,' his mother announced. 'But we cannot go back.'

'It is so dangerous,' Nathan pleaded. 'In her condition.'

'Not as dangerous as to stay.'

'What are the charges against her? If we knew that, then—'

'We have no notion,' his mother replied. 'But you may rely upon it, they will be whatever they wish them to be.'

His mother's faith in the integrity of British justice had never been strong.

He released another lengthy sigh. As if Levy was not enough. He now had two fugitives on his hands, both under a charge of spying.

'Why are *you* here?' he addressed his mother.

'You think I would let her go through this alone.'

'She is not alone. However, it is a thousand miles to Gibraltar, and even if there are no untoward events en route'—perhaps not a diplomatic way to describe the birth of her child, but it could also be applied to the possibility of attack by French ships of war, or any number of other things that might happen to a ship at sea—'Gibraltar is under British rule,' he pointed out, 'and subject to British law. She could be arrested there as readily as in London.'

'How could they know where she has gone? And besides . . . ' His mother looked hesitantly at Louise as if she did not wish to betray a confidence.

Louise sat down again as if suddenly deflated. 'There is someone I must find,' she murmured, as much to herself as Nathan. 'Someone who will speak in my defence.'

'In Gibraltar? Who do you know in Gibraltar?'

She declined to reply, but he recalled what Hallowell had said about Smith being sent to the Mediterranean on a secret mission. It was one of those times when he felt he did not know her at all—did not know who or what she was.

He might have said something which would very probably have made matters worse, but he was distracted by a new urgency in the usual sounds of the ship—voices raised in command, a drumming of feet on the deck timbers above his head.

'I will go and speak to the captain,' he declared coldly.

It was apparent to him as soon as he came on deck that they were preparing for departure. The gangway was still in place, but several of the ship's boats were in the water, and he could see they were about to take her in tow.

He found Captain Thomas on the quarterdeck and begged for a word.

'I am engaged at present,' he answered curtly, 'as you can surely see for yourself.'

'Forgive me, but I must speak with you before we cast off.'

'We are only casting off, sir, because your friend Mr Imlay has required us to do so. If you have any objection, I suggest you take it up with him.'

It was on the tip of Nathan's tongue to inform him that Mr Imlay was not his friend and did not command here, but it was probably more prudent to leave this in doubt, given the presence of Lieutenant Levy aboard ship. So far as he was aware, Captain Thomas had no knowledge of their present mission or the nature of their relationship—only that Nathan was a British naval captain sent to join the Mediterranean fleet, that Imlay and his associate were Americans about their own impenetrable business, and that all three of them had chosen, for reasons best known to themselves, to travel to Gibraltar on an East Indiaman instead of by the Falmouth packet.

'Surely you cannot hope to tow her much beyond Greenwich before the tide turns,' he pointed out. 'And the wind, I perceive, is blowing from across the river.'

'Thank you, sir, for that intelligence,' the captain replied tartly. 'Mr Imlay, however, has insisted that we stand out into the river to be prepared for a swift departure upon the next tide—and as he appears to have the ear of my superiors . . .'

This was news to Nathan. He raised a brow but did not challenge the assumption. It might well be true. Imlay had a way of 'having the ear' of people in power, though it was a mystery how he contrived it—and whether they ever got their ears back.

'So, I would suggest you assist your visitors ashore before they are put to the inconvenience of boarding a wherry.'

'That is why I wished to speak with you, sir.' Nathan adopted the more respectful tone he utilised in conversation with admirals and apes. 'For if you have room for them, they would like to come with us.'

The bushy brows rose sharply. 'What?'

'To Gibraltar.'

'I see.' It was obvious that he did not.

'And what are they to you, sir, if I may respectfully enquire?'

'My wife, sir, and my mother. The others are their servants.'

Further explanation might be necessary, he thought, though humiliating.

'My wife is very distressed by the necessity of my departure for Gibraltar, and I have become concerned for her health. She is, as you may have perceived, with child, and—'

'A ship is no place for a lady in her condition, as I am sure you are aware. How long before—'

'Two months,' Nathan lied. It was closer to one.

'And you would take the risk?'

'Well, I believe it is my wife who is taking the risk, sir, but yes, neither she nor my mother will be denied.'

The captain regarded him for a moment, doubtless despising him as 'a crouching vassal to a tyrant wife,' as Burns had put it, though he would probably not despise the money he would make from the transaction.

'You had better speak to the purser,' he instructed Nathan stonily. 'And now, if you will forgive me, sir, I must give my attention to the ship.'

The purser would not settle for less than eight hundred guineas, a preposterous sum, as Nathan informed him, but he argued that it would deprive 'the company' of five fare-paying passengers for the entire passage to India. Nathan agreed to give him a draft upon his bank. It would make a large dent in his savings, but he hoped to be receiving a considerable influx from the prize money due for his capture of the *Perle* when his agent finally agreed a price with the Admiralty.

On his way back to his cabin, he ran into Imlay, who was looking unusually agitated.

'What is this about your wife?' he enquired abruptly.

With some reluctance, Nathan told him a version of the story he had told the captain.

'I did not know you were married,' said he, with a frown that might be considered disapproving.

'No? And is there anything else about my personal situation you would care to know?' Nathan asked him. His supplications to the ship's master had made him sensitive.

'Only in as much as it could affect our mission. I understand she is with child. Would you put her to the risk of a sea voyage?'

'Confound it, sir, what is it to you?' Nathan was strongly opposed to instruction from Imlay, whose own record as a husband and a father was hardly exemplary. It was on the tip of his tongue to remind him of this, but he managed to restrain himself.

He had yet to tell his mother Imlay was aboard the ship and associated with him in his present venture. She was likely to take it badly, for Mary Wollstonecraft had been a close friend, and she was unlikely to be as restrained as he was where Imlay was concerned.

They spent the night moored in mid-river, halfway between Deptford and the Isle of Dogs.

At first light Nathan awoke to the unmistakeable sounds of a ship preparing to make way. He dressed hurriedly, and went up on deck to find that they were moving slowly downriver, assisted by a single staysail, with the ship's boats in attendance. The wind was light and northerly, but the tide was with them, and they were gliding smoothly through the crowded anchorage with very little effort by the men at the oars. Greenwich slipped past on their starboard bow, looking like an oil painting in the early morning mist, with the seamen's hospital on the waterfront and the royal observatory up on the hill above. Nathan thought he could smell the sea, but with the wind from the north and the tide on the ebb, it was probably in his mind only.

'At last,' said a voice in his ear. Imlay, of course. He had the nerve to clap him on the shoulder as if they were old comrades sharing a moment of togetherness. 'And so begins another chapter in our adventures.'

Imlay could never forget he had once been an author, nor would he let anyone else. He did not stand high in the league of literary achievement, but Nathan could not but wish that he had persisted in that career; it would have saved him a great deal of personal inconvenience over the years.

'How is your friend, Mr Levy?' he asked, for he had not seen him since they first came aboard.

'Sleeping, I would suppose, but he will be as glad as I to find we are finally leaving England.'

Nathan was framing another question in his mind concerning their mysterious passenger when he recollected another of his recent acquaintance.

'But we are without Carteret!' he exclaimed. With everything else that had occurred, he had quite forgotten the fourth member of their team. And the most important, so far as Nathan was concerned, for not only was he their conduit to Fox, he was meant to be taking over as the representative of King George in Washington.

'He will join us at Falmouth,' said Imlay smoothly. 'He will travel poste closer to the time and we will collect him in passing, as it were.'

Nathan was left to ponder this intelligence, not so much its import as the fact that Imlay had known this when he had not. How could this be—unless he was in direct contact with the British foreign office, even with Fox or Carteret personally?

Better not to ask, he decided. It would all sort itself out when they reached Gibraltar, when, assured of his own command, he could put Imlay in his place, which as far as he was concerned, was in the chain locker.

At this moment, there was another question that demanded his attention.

'How much does Captain Thomas know of our business?' he ventured, dropping his voice.

'Nothing,' replied Imlay shortly.

'He cannot know *nothing*,' Nathan objected. 'How did you explain Levy's arrival in the middle of the night?'

'I was not required to.'

'Really?' Nathan thought about this. 'He appears to think you have the ear of his employers,' he said.

'This is true.'

'That this is what he thinks, or that you do?'

'I do.'

'On the board of the East India Company? How is that?'

Imlay looked smug, or shifty, or both. 'Let us say I have been able to do them a small service from time to time.'

This should not have been a surprise when Nathan thought about it, the board of the East India Company being as notoriously corrupt and mercenary as Imlay himself.

'So why does he think we are travelling with him to Gibraltar—instead of by the packet?' he persisted.

'He has not questioned it. In your case, he probably thinks you prefer the comfort and convenience of a large cabin and a well-endowed table.'

Nathan did not rise to this.

'And in your case—and Mr Levy's?'

'They may be under the impression that we are lawyers representing the United States government, and that we have been engaged to report on the facilities available on the passage to India.'

Nathan shook his head. As was invariably the case in his dealings with Imlay, he had the sensation of wading ever more deeply into a bog.

'And now if I have satisfied your curiosity, I believe I will retire below deck and see if there is any breakfast to be had,' Imlay declared. 'Will you join me, or are you happy enough to stay here and bid a fond good-bye to London?'

Nathan remained on deck with his thoughts.

They were not at all uplifting. It appeared that Imlay was intent on taking over this entire enterprise, but perhaps he had been running it from the start. Nathan's own role was that of the ignorant stooge who was too dim-witted and inconsequential to be kept apprised of every turn of events. It did not escape his attention, however, that if Carteret could travel poste to Falmouth, he might easily have done so himself. In fact, it had probably been in his power to insist upon this. But then Louise would have been at the mercy of whatever authority was in pursuit of her.

Even so, he concluded, it was time he began to assert himself.

He stayed up on deck for the next hour or so, until they reached the Woolwich Arsenal where they were due to take on powder and shot, but then his hunger got the better of him and he went below in search of breakfast.

Chapter 17

The *True Briton*

For the next twenty-four hours the *True Briton* continued her leisurely progress downriver. Had he not been in the company of Gilbert Imlay and two fugitives from justice, Nathan might have felt quite relaxed. He had not had the opportunity to observe the countryside on either side of the Thames before, or the extraordinary amount of shipping passing to and from the capital. Had he brought a sketchbook with him, or even better, his paints and brushes, he thought he might have attempted something in the artistic line.

This was a side of him that was too often repressed, he thought. The Renaissance man who could turn his hand to music, art, the study of the cosmos . . . When the war ended, if it ever did, he could embark on the Grand Tour with Louise. He would sketch and paint and play the flute. She would work on her latest sculpture. But given that she would need at least one tree or a large rock, they might be better off hiring a yacht and going on a cruise.

A pipe dream at best. It did not even require a great deal of self-knowledge to know it would never happen. He was not equipped for passive observation. He was restless enough when he was in command of a ship of war; being a passenger on an East Indiaman was far worse.

And their progress was so very, very slow.

This was partly because the wind had shifted slightly to the north-east, so that they could not use the sails and were reliant entirely upon the oarsmen in the ship's boats who struggled with the incoming tide, but also because the number of ships coming in the opposite direction was so great, it frequently obliged them to drop anchor and wait for a patch of clear water. By nightfall they were no further west than Gravesend, where the captain determined to moor.

In all this time, Nathan saw nothing of Lieutenant Levy. Imlay said he came up for air only at night and avoided speaking to anyone for fear of being recognised. The journals had carried news of the 'daring escape' from the Tower of London and the authorities had put up wanted posters, he said, with a description. Justices of the peace and parish constables were on the alert in every parish, he said. Nathan had no means of knowing if this was true; it might be that Imlay thought it would make him more malleable.

He did see a fair bit of Louise—usually but not always with his mother—and although she remained tense, she at least spoke to him. She would not enlarge on her reasons for leaving London, however, and he knew better than to pursue the matter, though it weighed heavily upon him.

When they passed Sheerness and felt the first impact of the North Sea, the two women retired below with their servants, and refused all attempts to persuade them back on deck. They would feel much better if they fixed their eyes upon the horizon, he advised them, or even tried a bite of food, but he received a predictable reaction from his mother, who said that she had heard from a more reliable source that the only remedy for seasickness was to remain horizontal and this she was determined to do, she said, until she felt better, or died, and that in her present condition, she did not mind which.

Deprived of the role of comfort and counsel and at something of a loose end, Nathan decided to embark on a thorough inspection of the ship. She was relatively new to the company fleet, he had learned, and appeared to be as well-maintained, if not quite as spick and span, as a ship of the king's navy. He paced her out at a hundred and eighty feet from stem to stern, and forty feet in the beam, not much smaller than a seventy-four-gun ship of the line. In fact, she carried thirty guns, a mix of twelve- and eighteen-pounders, which also appeared to be in pristine condition, so much so, in fact, that he wondered if they had ever been fired in anger, or even in practice.

But though she had about the same number of officers and petty officers as a seventy-four, and an impressive number of cooks and stewards, she had barely a fifth the number of seamen—sufficient to make sail, but not to man the guns, at least not simultaneously—or even deal with a prolonged period of bad weather. Which was possibly one of the reasons why an inordinate number of East Indiamen disappeared without trace. The smallness of the crew did, however, make more space available for carrying passengers and thereby increase the profits available to the captain. The seamen—all seventy-eight of them—were crammed into a space measuring forty-fix feet by forty on the lower deck, just forward of the mainmast, a space that on this voyage they were obliged to share with the hundred or so soldiers taken aboard at Deptford.

Otherwise, Nathan found little to carp at, though of course it would not have stopped him had he found anyone to carp to. His main concern was the time it took to cover the relatively short distance to the Downs, where they were to join their convoy. He could understand why it took so long to navigate the Thames when they were mostly under tow, but even on the open sea and with the wind steady on the larboard quarter, he estimated that they were making little more than two knots.

Lacking a more useful occupation, he spent most of his time eating. Meals—at least for the more privileged passengers—were served in a large, well-furnished cabin under the poop deck, known by the ship's company as the roundhouse, or cuddy. They consisted of a substantial breakfast that was available from seven to ten; dinner, served at two in the afternoon and involving at least six courses; and a light supper with as much drink as you wanted until you were ready for bed. The cost was included in the fare. Nathan knew from his previous experience that some captains kept a poor table, being reluctant to let the expense eat too much into their profits, but he was glad to find that this was not the case aboard the *True Briton*, at least, not this close to London, where there was no shortage of fresh meat and vegetables.

But if the food and drink was varied and plentiful, the company was not. Besides Imlay, there were just the two East India Company officers—a captain who was on his second tour of duty, and a much younger second lieutenant who could barely have been out of the schoolroom. Nathan knew that officers in the company service were regarded as socially inferior to those in the regular army—at least by those in the regular army—and though he had no opinion on this one way or another, he was hard pushed to keep the conversation going. The officers themselves were both Irish, and of course Protestant, but one was from Dublin, the other, Cork, and they had little to say to each other, let alone Nathan and Imlay, with whom they were desperately ill at ease, Imlay possibly because he was an American and something of an enigma, Nathan because he was so much their superior in rank.

There were two other passengers, apparently, but they, too, were suffering from seasickness and chose to remain in their cabins. More were expected to join them at Deal and Falmouth, apparently.

Once clear of the Isle of Sheppey they were able to cast off the tow and bring the boats back on board, but they did not reach their rendezvous in the Downs until shortly after noon on the third day. As usual there were several hundred ships moored in the wide channel between the Kent coast and the Goodwin

Sands, including the ships of their own convoy. This comprised eight merchantmen of various sizes, and their escort: *Bellatrix*, an ancient fourth-rate of fifty guns, and *Myrmidon*, a sixteen-gun sloop of war, neither of which left Nathan with an enhanced sense of security. The merchant ships included two more East Indiamen, however, and two of the Levant Company, all heavily armed, so that with their chequered gunports they more resembled a naval squadron than a convoy, and Nathan had little fear of being attacked. He was more concerned with the time it would take to reach Gibraltar, for the speed of the convoy was, of course, no greater than that of its slowest member. They were, in any case, obliged to wait for two days off Deal for the last member of the convoy to join them. Nathan took the opportunity to stock up with supplies from the various bumboats that offered their services, despite the usual exorbitant Deal prices, for he was reluctant to depend on Captain Thomas's largesse all the way to Gibraltar.

They were joined here by two more passengers, both in the service of the Honourable Company, and by the ship's doctor, who had missed the boat at Deptford and travelled to Deal by the mail coach. He was a Highland Scot by the name of Munro, and a welcome addition from Nathan's point of view, for besides emerging as well-travelled and cultivated, it turned out he had been in the king's navy for many years before accepting a post at Aberdeen University and then, for some mysterious reason, signing on for the *True Briton*. This suggested a scandal of some sort, at least to Nathan, for if he missed the sea and a life of adventure, why had he not re-joined the service? But it was not a question he could ask. They had both served in the Caribbean and the Med, and Munro had been on the *Canopus* at the Nile and then the *Queen Charlotte* when she was the flagship of Lord Keith, so they had plenty of other things to talk about.

They talked so much, in fact, that they remained at the table long after the other guests had left, and Nathan finally took the opportunity to ask him about his work in Aberdeen. He was glad that he had, for, unusually in a naval surgeon, Dr Munro turned out to have a special interest in obstetrics.

'I would not have thought you encountered much in the way of childbirth aboard a ship of the king's navy,' Nathan supposed.

The doctor acknowledged this with a smile but explained, rather embarrassedly, that he had developed a personal interest in the subject after his wife had died in childbirth.

Nathan expressed his regret and apologised for intruding upon a personal matter.

'Not at all. I was of course devastated at the time, but it is some years since it occurred. I came to terms with it, as one must, but'—he hesitated—'well, sometime later, during the year of peace, I attended a number of lectures in London which suggested that many such deaths can easily be avoided. This is scarcely a subject for the dinner table, or one that can possibly interest a serving officer in His Majesty's navy.' He laughed awkwardly.

'We have finished dinner,' Nathan pointed out, 'and believe me, sir, I am very interested.'

The doctor regarded him doubtfully, but Nathan's expression encouraged him to continue.

'I obtained a job as physician at the Dispensary in Aberdeen, where I continued research on my own account, and what I discovered was frankly astounding.' He looked about as if afraid that he might be overheard, but they had been so long at the table, even the servants had abandoned them.

Nathan urged him to go on.

'The fact is, and this is well attested, it is generally accepted that in the case of an assisted birth—assisted, that is, by a doctor or a midwife—the death rate is at best one in six. Of the mother. It is much higher for the child, and we often lose both, commonly of a blood infection following the birth. However, according to my own research, of a hundred women who gave birth at home, in Aberdeen and the surrounding area, only two had died, and only twelve of the babies.'

He saw that Nathan remained attentive.

'Over the next three years I pursued my research further afield, and the results were similar. In an assisted birth, between fifteen and twenty per cent of the mothers usually died of an infection within days or weeks of the birth. A home birth, without professional help—almost all survived. Two deaths in a hundred was the worst I ever came across.'

'But that is incredible!' Nathan exclaimed. 'What could possibly be the reason?'

'Dirty hands.'

'What?'

'I discovered that the women—the *untrained* women, among those we might call the Great Unwashed—are in fact accustomed to washing their hands assiduously when they undertake some delicate domestic task, such as baking bread or making a pie, or inserting their hands into a woman's private parts. When I asked why, I was told, rather shamefacedly, it was because their hands were normally so filthy, they did not care to leave a mark on another woman's "furnishings," by which I assume they meant something rather more intimate than an easy chair. It had become a kind of folklore among them, like an herbal remedy. Soap and water.

'This was not the case with the professionals—the doctors or nurses who assist a birth in hospital, or in the homes of the more affluent. When I suggested that my own colleagues might consider taking such a precaution, they were outraged. To suggest that they were as dirty as a mere kitchen wench, let alone that they had killed untold numbers of their patients . . . I was promptly run out of town, as the Americans would say, and was lucky to avoid being horsewhipped. I took service with John Company and have been with them ever since.'

'So, if you were to attend a birth now, you would take these precautions yourself?' Nathan asked him.

'Of course, though the occasion is unlikely to occur at present, ha ha.'

Nathan thought of telling him about Louise's condition, but decided it was advisable to consult with her beforehand, and when he did so, she declared herself perfectly content with Bella and Izzy, and that she had no intention of being poked around with by a drunken sea surgeon who had probably killed far more patients than he had saved. Although Nathan would normally have concurred with this, he assured her that Dr Munro was very different from the usual run of naval surgeons, and well worth consulting, but she was not to be convinced, and he did not pursue the matter.

On their second day in the Downs, the sea being reasonably calm, the two women ventured on deck, though they clung determinedly to the rail on the lee quarter, and the sharpness of the wind drove them below again after scarcely half an hour. Nathan did his best to entertain them during this period, but Louise appeared distracted, and his mother gave him to understand that if he said anything about the sea, or indeed, ships in general, she would not be answerable for the consequences. Other than that, however, she appeared to be in reasonable spirits, which she ascribed to a concoction Bella had made for them to settle the stomach and whose main ingredients were laudanum and brandy, with a grating of fresh ginger.

'I cannot recommend it too highly,' she told Nathan, 'though I think she could be less generous with the ginger.'

'I believe ginger is an excellent antiemetic,' he told her with the diffident air of the expert, 'but I would advise taking it with weak tea, and no milk.'

'Yes, well, you know what you can do with your advice,' his mother informed him briskly. 'Speaking personally, I intend to remain on the brandy and laudanum as long as we remain on this shitting shitheap of a ship, so you can take your weak tea and apply it to whatever part of your anatomy you think it will do most good.'

'I am sure I can find you suitable accommodation in Deal if you so wish, Mother,' Nathan assured her, with as much dignity as he could contrive. 'If you found the journey from London difficult, I cannot imagine what you will make of the Bay of Biscay, which is notoriously—'

'I warn you . . .' She blew out her cheeks.

'No, but seriously, Mother, in Louise's condition . . . If she is prepared to live quietly in Deal, I am persuaded there is no more chance of the authorities finding her here than in Gibraltar—probably less.'

But if he had thought that after a few days at sea Louise might be prepared to take her chances with the officers of the law, he was much mistaken. She had made up her mind to go to Gibraltar, she said, and clear her name.

'What is in Gibraltar that you will not find in England?' he demanded. 'Or should I say, who?'

But she would not answer, only shaking her head.

'You are speaking of your friend, Captain Smith.'

This at least earned a response.

'He is not my friend,' she retorted sharply, 'but he is in a position to help me in this matter.'

'How?'

'You know I cannot say that.'

He did, but he could not help himself.

'Why can you not write to him?'

'Because the letter may be read by others, if it even reaches him, which is doubtful. I need to see him face-to-face.'

'How do you know he is in Gibraltar?' he persisted. 'Has he communicated with you since you were in London?'

She shook her head, but he was unclear whether it was in denial, or a refusal to discuss the matter further.

He thought about this later, in the solitude of his cabin, divided from her by a thin partition of canvas and timber and a wide gulf of doubt and suspicion. The world of intelligence was as full of deceits and betrayals as relations between men and women in his experience, and so far as Louise was concerned, the two things were inextricably mixed—in his own mind, at least.

The wind remaining in the north-east, they made slow but steady progress down the Channel. Both Louise and his mother recovered sufficiently to come up on deck from time to time to take the air, and even a little food, though they avoided the long-drawn-out dinners in the cuddy. The convoy kept within sight of the English coast for most of the journey westward, and they passed the white cliffs of the Seven Sisters where he had spent much of his childhood before he went to sea. He could even make out the strand at Cuckmere Haven where he used to go shrimping, and the brow of Seaford Head where he had been lookout for the 'free traders' on the nights when there was a delivery from France. Later, when he was in his early twenties, he had returned to the same stretch of coast as master and commander of the brig *Nereus*, charged with supporting the king's revenue men in their war against these same companions of his youth.

It seemed to him now, gazing towards the haze of white cliffs, that so much of his life had involved divided loyalties of one form or another. First there had been the divide between his father and his mother, then the smugglers and the king's navy, and then the dangerous liaisons he had been obliged to make on his secret trips to France in the guise of the American sea captain and shipowner, Nathaniel Turner. He felt a sense of conflicting loyalties now, torn between his duty to king and country—or at least Fox and Grey—and his love for Louise, for if she did turn out to be a French spy, what was he to do? Betray her, or betray his country? He had already compromised his mission by taking her with him to Gibraltar.

He was accompanying her on one of her rare excursions on deck when they were joined by Dr Munro, and Nathan was obliged to make the necessary introductions, referring to her, as he had since she came aboard, as his wife. Although she wore her cloak, he had either diagnosed her condition or had been told of it by the captain, for the conversation quickly turned to how she was coping. It soon became clear that Louise had formed a favourable impression of him, for when the doctor diffidently offered his support should she need it, she consented to let him examine her in the privacy of her cabin. She later informed Nathan, with a note of satisfaction, that he had pronounced her in excellent health and foresaw no obvious difficulties.

When Nathan was able to have a discreet conversation with him, however, he put it rather differently.

'I said there would be no obvious difficulty *in the right conditions*,' he said. 'By which I did *not* mean on a ship at sea. I allow I am not aware of all the circumstances that have led to her embarking on this journey, but I must advise that she is put ashore at the earliest possible opportunity, and certainly when we reach Falmouth.'

Nathan admitted that this might be difficult. 'I am hopeful that the situation will not occur, but would it be so very dangerous for her to have the baby aboard ship?' he ventured.

'With respect, I am astonished that you should put such a question,' the doctor replied. 'The process of childbirth is always dangerous, but on a platform as unstable as a ship at sea, it could be fatal. Only consider if there should be a storm, which you and I know is not unlikely in the Bay of Biscay.'

Nathan promised he would renew his entreaties when they reached Falmouth, though he had little hope of success, and it was clear that the doctor could not understand why he could not exert his natural and legal authority as a husband and expectant father.

They moored off Falmouth on the evening of the fifth day after leaving the Downs, which was a lot quicker than Nathan had expected, but he had no more luck in persuading Louise to go ashore than he had during previous conversations on the subject. She was determined to continue to Gibraltar, and if he would not let her stay with him, then she would take the Falmouth packet, she said. If she was unfortunate enough to go into labour whilst at sea, she would rely on the competence of Bella and his mother and the advice of Dr Munro to pull her through, but she did not expect this to occur for a few more weeks, by which time she trusted they would be safely arrived in Gibraltar.

He was prevented from further discussion of the subject by the arrival of a boat from the shore with more passengers, including Carteret, who appeared no more comfortable on water than Louise or his mother, even in the shelter of the Carrick Roads. In fact, the wind had freshened somewhat and shifted westward, causing the ship to roll somewhat even in the sheltered anchorage. When Nathan asked the first mate if he had time to go ashore and purchase some more supplies, he was told they were about to resume their journey, the convoy commander fearing that a further shift in the wind might cause them to become embayed.

Nathan went below to check on the condition of his charges, but being instructed in both cases to Go Away, or words to that effect, he spent the rest of the day in the cuddy partaking of a solitary dinner, the rest of the passengers, even Imlay, having opted to remain in their cabins. Dinner was not easy, even for one as well practised as he at eating at a table that rose and fell by several feet, and unless restrained, the dishes slid from side to side like skaters taking an uncertain glide across a frozen lake. By the time he emerged, it was clear that they were facing the prospect of a storm.

When he checked on Louise, however, he found her sleeping peacefully enough in her cot, with Bella next to her in a hammock she had slung from a pair of large nails driven into the deck beams. His mother, too, was asleep, and Nathan suspected the maid's tincture had been applied even more generously than usual. He felt somewhat uneasy about this, but lacking an alternative remedy, he left them to their slumbers and slept soundly enough himself in the adjoining cabin, waking at first light with the instant knowledge that the weather had taken a turn for the worse.

He emerged on deck to find the wind had shifted even further to the west and increased in intensity, so that it was now blowing a near gale, and he was obliged to avail himself of one of the lifelines that had been rigged across the upper deck. They had reduced sail to a single reefed forecourse and flying jib, and though she was rolling badly in the long Atlantic rollers, they appeared to be holding a course to the south-west, about as close to the wind as possible. From what he could see of the other ships in the convoy, which was not a lot, they were under similar restraints, for they would be wary of the rocks of Cape Ushant, which could not be far off their larboard bow. He could see the swathed figure of what must surely be the captain at the con, and he was considering risking a snub by joining him there when another figure clawed itself up the lifeline to his side and revealed itself on further inspection to be Louise's servant, Branoc, who delivered the information that Nathan had dreaded.

Chapter 18

The Consequence of Love

He reached the lower deck to find his mother emerging from Louise's cabin. He had never seen her looking so ill or scared. He hoped it was the storm and not Louise.

She managed to speak, but at first he could make no sense of it.

'She needs more room,' she said.

For a moment he thought she meant in the uterus.

'Can you not do something with the walls?' she said.

Then she was sick all over him.

Nathan steered her back to her own cabin and lowered her gently to the bunk. By then he had gathered she meant clearing the decks for action. This he could do. The cabins were divided by thin wood and canvas partitions, and it took Branoc and himself only a matter of minutes to demolish the one between Louise's cabin and his own. It was only then that he saw the doctor was in attendance, kneeling down at one end of the bunk with Bella while Izzy was occupied with the other end.

Louise looked pale and frightened, her face covered with a sheen of sweat which Izzy was wiping gently with a cloth. At a rough calculation, the cabin was moving through a thirty-degree arc. They had hung three storm lamps from the deck timbers and their yellow light threw grotesque shapes on the canvas as if they were engaged in some demonic shadow theatre. Instead of music, there was an ominous groaning of timbers.

Louise saw him standing there, and he took her hand and told her he loved her. She said she loved him but appeared distracted. This he could understand.

He exchanged a glance with the doctor, which was meant to be questioning, but received no response. He was peering under the sheet that covered the lower part of her body while Bella held a light as close as she dared.

Izzy glared and made a gesture with her head which was unmistakeable.

'Is there nothing I can do?' Nathan pleaded.

'Nothing,' said Izzy. 'Go away. See if your mother needs anything.'

He kissed Louise again. 'Good luck,' he said and let go of her hand.

He found sanctuary in the gunroom and fortified himself with a bottle of cognac, which did nothing to ease the sense of helplessness and fear and self-recrimination. He should never have agreed to take her with him. He should have put her ashore at Deal or Falmouth, drugged her if necessary, and had her carried there against her will. Anything but subject her to the perils of childbirth in a storm off Ushant.

He knew little of the mechanics involved. He knew there were things called contractions but was not quite sure what they were. He did not know if throwing up as a result of seasickness would be a help or a hindrance. It was possible, he supposed, that it might force the child out more quickly, but of course it usually involved an expulsion from a different orifice.

Then there was the presence of the doctor. Was this a good sign or not? Were there complications that had finally compelled Louise, or his mother, to seek his professional assistance, and if so, what were they?

This, he thought, is the consequence of love. Something so magical, so uplifting of the spirit, could never end well.

Twice he returned to the cabin but did not get past the door.

On the second trip he heard a heartrending scream from within. Then, pressing his ear to the door, a stream of obscenities in French. He was inclined to find this encouraging. He almost went in despite the interdiction against a male presence other than the doctor. But what could he have done? He would only have been in the way.

You could hold her hand, he thought. *You could be the object of her vitriol, for if anyone deserves it, you do.*

But instead, he went back to the gunroom and the cognac.

Shortly into the first watch, a little after eight in the evening by a normal person's reckoning, Izzy appeared. She looked like the Angel of Death. He stared at her, unable to form the words, knowing what she had come to tell him.

But he was wrong.

'You have a baby son,' she said.

'And Louise?' It was all he cared about at that precise moment.

'As well as can be expected—under the circumstances.'

'But will she live?' he persisted.

'Oh God, I do not know. It is too early to say.'

He supposed it was the best he could hope for. Under the circumstances.

When they finally let him into the cabin, Louise was lying back on the bunk with her eyes closed, the babe at her breast. He looked to the doctor for reassurance. The doctor rolled his eyes and blew out his cheeks.

He saw that Louise was looking at him, her expression, one might say, thoughtful. He knelt down beside her and would have laid his head on her breast if the baby had not already been there.

He kissed the back of the creature's neck and then Louise's cheek. She felt very hot.

'You look like you have just done ten rounds with the Game Chicken,' he said.

Once, after making love, he had given her an account of this gentleman's championship bout with Jem Belcher, or at least until she had stuffed the best part of a pillow in his mouth, but she must have taken in the name at least, for she gave a tired smile.

'Did you put money on me?' she said.

Her voice was feeble, but he was encouraged to think that with proper care, she might live.

'Is there anything I can do?' he asked.

'I will let you know,' she said, 'if I think of something.'

'Does the motion bother you?'

The cabin was still moving through its remorseless arc, the shadows dancing.

'Why, can you stop it?' she asked.

The babe opened its eyes and looked at him from its sideways perspective. It did not appear especially reassured by what it saw. It began to howl. Louise put its mouth back to her breast.

'Have you got a name for it?' he asked, to cover his confusion.

'Izzy thinks Storm might be nice,' she said.

He stared at her in disbelief.

She began to laugh, but not for long. 'Oh, that hurt,' she said.

The baby lost the nipple and resumed its howl.

'You do not mean it?' he begged, when peace was restored.

'No. I thought a good Breton name, like Ewen. Ewen Nathaniel. How does that sound to you?'

'Better than Storm,' he said.

The day after the birth the storm had died down considerably, and the convoy rendezvoused off Pointe du Van to resume its journey to the south. To Nathan's surprise, both mother and child survived their immediate ordeal, though he was braced for a relapse. After a few days, however, Louise felt well enough to express a wish to take the air.

'On deck?' He was startled.

'Is there anywhere else to go?'

He agreed there was not.

'And is there a reason why I should not?'

He could probably think of a few if put to it.

'With the baby?'

'Well, I am not going to leave him here,' she said. 'But you had better carry him.'

He had never carried a baby before, even on land. He held him tightly to his chest but remembered to keep one hand for the ship. It was a very strange sensation, not only the feeling of a child clutched to his chest, but the feelings he held inside him.

From the moment of the child's birth, he had felt possessed of something that must be love but was alike to reverence for both mother and child, combined with an increased sense of responsibility. But at the same time, he was conscious of a dark shadow in his soul, or more properly, his mind, which he mostly kept suppressed, but which he knew would engulf him if he ever allowed it to surface.

He could not forget that the reason Louise was here was because she was in search of another man—a man he distrusted for many good reasons, and some that were probably more suspect. For Smith was a man of at least as many contradictions as himself, a man who, no matter how deserving of admiration for what he had achieved at Acre, displayed a lamentable duplicity, and an apparently irresistible urge to dominate, to prove himself superior to all other men. And there was a terrible suspicion in Nathan's mind that the real reason Louise was travelling in pursuit of him was not because she needed him to speak for her, to save her from prison or gallows, but because she loved him, and he was the true father of her child.

He never discussed this with Louise. He could barely acknowledge it to himself.

And so they sailed on—along the fringe of the Atlantic, along the coasts of France and Spain. They sailed upon a passive sea under a clear sky driven by a mild westerly breeze, shifting only a point here and there to north or south. They sailed past Cape Finisterre and Cape Saint Vincent, where Nathan had fought in two of the great naval battles of the war, and then Trafalgar, the greatest of them all. It seemed odd that there was nothing to mark them, such as a buoy with a tolling bell, but how could there be, so far out to sea? The sea that had buried so many thousand dead drew an indifferent shroud over their memory, the waves rolled on regardless.

And so finally, on the morning of the thirteenth day after leaving Falmouth, they came to Gibraltar.

Chapter 19

The Fox on the Rock

'Good God, sir, you took your time!' the lieutenant governor exclaimed when Commodore Peake was ushered into his presence. 'We have been expecting you these last few weeks or more.'

General Henry Fox was as portly as his elder brother and as intemperate in his manner, but at least he had a healthy glow about him, and it did not look entirely due to the drink. He had lost every battle he had ever fought in, but it was said that the British would not leave the Rock until the apes did, so perhaps it was safe for a while.

Nathan explained that he had come from England in an East Indiaman and that progress had been frustratingly slow.

'Well, what did you expect, man?' Fox complained. 'Why did you not take the packet like anyone with half a brain?'

This was not a good start.

Nathan blamed the decision on the foreign office and said he just did what he was told to do.

'Ah. Well, there you go. So do I, sir, so do I, and look where it has got me.'

Fox seemed to think this was a lot more amusing than Nathan did, but at least it broke the ice. 'Well, I suppose it gave us time to get your squadron ready for you. Did you see them when you were coming in?'

Nathan had not, having been obliged to hold the baby and strictly forbidden from taking the creature aloft. He did not mention this problem to the lieutenant governor.

'Well, there they be. Take a look.' Fox waved a plump hand in the direction of the telescope overlooking the bay. 'Just beyond the new mole,' he said, as Nathan released the clamp. 'In line ahead, pointing towards Algeciras.'

Nathan found them soon enough, there being surprisingly few ships of war out in the bay. He spotted *Panther* immediately at the rear of the line, sails hung out to dry, as usual; her sails always seemed to be hung out to dry, as if Simpson wished them to be as bleached as his beloved decks. How he had coped with the shambles the *Perle* had made of them was anyone's guess; possibly he had other things on his mind, lying in the cockpit waiting for the surgeon to saw off his arm. Then a pair of sloops, and with great delight Nathan recognised them as the *Falaise* and the *Aurore*, his own ships as he thought them, for the *Falaise* was the French corvette he had appropriated after his adventures in Saint-Dominique and subsequently hired out to the service, and the *Aurore* was her sister ship that they had taken prize off the coast of Normandy when they were landing agents for Sir Sidney Smith.

And beyond them, at the head of the line, was the *Scipio.*

Nathan could not read the name from his present vantage, but he knew it was her, and for the first time he comprehended that what the foreign secretary had told him in Chertsey was not a fantasy conjured out of the bottom of a bottle.

He could have looked at her all day, but he was conscious of the lieutenant governor's presence behind him, and his head was full of questions.

'Does she have a captain yet,' he said, 'and a crew?'

'She does indeed. Almost fully crewed from the prisoners that were released by the Dons, all prime seamen I am told, you are lucky to have 'em . . .'

'And her captain?'

'I am coming to that, sir, hold your horses! We have given you Tully from the *Aurore*, as you requested. Fox wrote to me most particular on the subject, said it would free you up for your diplomatic duties, though Old Cuddy was none too happy about it. Too big a step so far as he was concerned, but that's the way it is these days—every bugger wants to run afore they can walk, and the rest of us have to take the consequence.'

This was a gross slander on Tully, who was more capable of commanding a seventy-four in Nathan's view than two-thirds of the men on the Captain's List, if not more, but it did not spoil his pleasure in his friend's promotion. For the first time since he had been given the news of his own, he thought there was a chance that he might not disgrace himself.

But there were other questions that needed answering.

'I did not see *Euryalus* in the harbour,' he said. 'Nor much else in the way of a fleet. Is the admiral not here?'

He was wondering, in fact, if he had gone off across the Atlantic in pursuit of the French fleet, but apparently not.

'You have missed him by a clear fortnight at least,' the lieutenant governor informed him. 'He has shifted his flag to the *Ville de Paris* and buggered off to Port Mahon with the rest of the fleet, to support our operations in Sicily.'

Nathan raised a brow, not being conversant with 'our operations in Sicily,' but was not gratified with any further intelligence on the subject. Nor did he ask.

'However, being apprised of your mission, we have made every effort to assemble your squadron and put it in a suitable state of readiness,' Fox assured him. 'The *Scipio* is not far short of a full complement, though the crew may be a little rusty after languishing in a Spanish prison for a year or more. You heard we got them for the men we took at Trafalgar?'

Nathan indicated that he had.

'Aye, well, I've given you a hundred of my marines to help knock 'em into shape. And all four ships have been provisioned for a three-month cruise, so I doubt you will have much to complain about, despite your late arrival.'

Nathan expressed a proper gratitude, though he did wonder how much knocking into shape would be necessary.

'And the officers?' he queried. 'Were they also in prison?'

'The officers? Good Lord, no.' As if the very idea of putting an English officer in prison was unimaginable, even for rogues like the French and the Spanish. 'They were on parole one place or another, squiring the local señoras and counting off their rosaries. Besides, the admiral has given you some of his own people. Those he felt deserving of promotion and the like. I am sure the ship's purser will be able to give you what further information you require on that score.'

'And the other captains? I am sorry to press you, sir, but I am anxious to get it all up here.' He tapped his skull.

Fox was consulting a paper on his desk.

'Simpson on the *Panther*, Blake on the *Aurore*, and Curtis on the *Falaise*. I trust that is satisfactory to you, sir?'

That would be putting it a bit strong, but things could have been worse. Simpson had been his first lieutenant and probably deserved his promotion, though Nathan would never warm to him personally, and Blake had been Tully's first all the time he had commanded *Aurore*. He did not know Curtis at all, but it was the same name as the rear admiral who had been on his board of inquiry, which might merit further inquiry, though there was nothing he could do about it now.

'Oh, and then there are the Americans,' said Fox.

'The Americans?'

Did he mean Levy and Imlay?

'We have given you a score or so,' Fox went on. 'All prime topmen, I understand, though you will have to give them back, of course, when you get there.'

He saw that Nathan was at a loss.

'You do know about this?'

Nathan confessed he did not.

'Oh, dear God, did my brother not tell you? There is altogether too much of this. Spends the best part of his life trying to get into office and when he does, he is in his dotage, or his cups—I don't know if 'tis one or the other, or both. You can forget the intrepid Fox, 'tis more like the inebriate Fox.'

He thought this very droll and went off on one of his whooping chortles, very like Nathan's friend, the ape. In fact, he was widely known as Fox on the Rock to distinguish him from his more famous brother, and perhaps it rankled. Nathan thought the brothers had quite a bit in common, but there was obviously a strong fraternal rivalry.

'These American topmen,' Nathan reminded him. 'You say I have to give them back?'

'Right. Yes. Fox was most particular about it, with all the kerfuffle they are making over it in Washington.'

'Kerfuffle?'

'About the way you fellows go about taking their best seamen away from them. Boarding their ships without a by-your-leave and hauling off whoever takes your fancy.'

'Ah.' A little daylight crept into the cave. 'You mean, pressing them into service.'

'What the devil do you think I mean?'

'I beg your pardon, sir, but this is the first I have heard of it.'

'What, pressing Yankee seamen? Where have you been the last few years, besides floating about in an East Indiaman?'

'I meant having to give them back, sir.'

'Ah. Yes. That was my brother's idea, or one of his underlings. Gesture of goodwill and so forth. Only, you are to keep it under your hat. Don't want to give the impression 'tis government policy, or we will have a mutiny on our hands, and they will all be admirals. You must keep it to yourself and those who have a need to know, which is to say, the diplomatic corps you are carrying about with you. And your captain, I suppose.'

'And I am to take them with me to America?'

'Confound it, sir! What have I been talking to you about for the past ten minutes or more?'

'I beg your pardon, sir, I am a bit fogged about the ears today. And there are twenty of them, you say?'

'Give or take a couple. Old Cuddy scraped them together from all over the fleet. Two or three here and there, so they would not be missed. He don't like impressment any more than the Yanks do. You can work them on the passage, same as they are crew, but they are not to be entered on the muster roll. We want no questions in Parliament, Fox says.'

'And did he say what I am to do with them when we get there?'

'Not that I remember. No, I do not believe he did. His man will know, or the American fellow you have with you.'

'So, they both know about this?'

'They do, sir, they do indeed. Even if you do not. Now, is there anything else you need to know?'

There was quite a lot, but the lieutenant governor was probably not the man to ask. Besides, Nathan was anxious to assume his new command and see for himself. He supposed it would all fall into place once they were at sea; it usually did.

Then he remembered the French.

'Oh, there was just one thing, sir. I was wondering if you had any word of the French fleet.'

Fox looked at him. 'What French fleet?' He looked wary, as if he was dealing with someone who was as befogged as he said he was.

'The one that broke out of Brest, sir, before Christmas. We ran into them in *Panther* on the way back to England, and I thought it best to send her back here with Simpson to let you know of it.'

'Ah. That was you, was it? I see.' Nathan could almost see the cogs turning. 'Now then, what happened about that?'

Nathan gave him a moment.

'Ah yes, it all comes back to me now. It appears your fellow, what was his name—Simple?'

'Simpson, sir.'

'Simpson. Ran into that daft prick, Duckshoot, off Cadiz and told him about it, and without so much as a by-your-leave he gives up on the blockade and takes off after them. Collingwood wants him broke.'

'Duckshoot?'

There was not much that Nathan understood in the lieutenant governor's last statement, but 'that daft prick Duckshoot' was probably the most open to instruction.

'Rear Admiral Sir John Duckworth, to give him his proper title, though not for much longer, I suspect. Duckshoot, I call him, on account of he'll shoot at anything that moves in the hope it turns out to be French. Or Spanish, at a pinch. He was supposed to join Nelson at Trafalgar but got there too late. Story goes he was waiting in Portsmouth for his band to turn up. Got his own band, the prick. Won't go anywhere without them. Sails into Gib, bold as brass, when 'tis all over and done with, and Cuddy sends him off to keep an eye on what's left of the Dons in Cadiz. I expect he thought even Duckshoot was capable of that.

'Then *Panther* comes up with this tale of the Frogs slipping out of Brest and off he goes, haring off in pursuit, band playing "See the Conquering Hero Comes," no doubt. Lot more glory in a battle than a blockade, d'you see. Not that he's caught them yet. You should hear Collingwood on the subject. Apoplectic ain't in it.'

Nathan absorbed this information as best he could. What it amounted to was another inglorious cockup, which should not have surprised him in the least.

'So—they are still looking for them?' he said.

'Oh, yes, they are all still looking for 'em.' Fox obviously thought this was most amusing. 'Duckworth and all the other ponces they sent out from England—Strachan, Warren, Cochrane . . . probably half a dozen more since I last heard. Chasing about the Atlantic like a pack of hounds on heat, baying after anything that moves. I hope you really did see them, young man, and they really are out there, or they will be chasing after you when they get back.'

'Not only did I see them, we exchanged broadsides with them,' Nathan assured him. 'But talking of admirals, sir, I had heard that Sir Sidney Smith was in Gibraltar.' He kept his tone casual.

Another frown. 'The Swedish Knight? What of it? Friend of yours, is he?'

'No, sir, but I did serve under him for a while, and I had heard he was headed this way.'

'Did you, indeed. Well, he has been and gone, sir, been and gone. Like all of 'em. Away on this business in Sicily. If 'tis not the Atlantic, 'tis Sicily. While I sit on the Rock like one of the damned apes. And now if that is all, I have military matters to deal with, and must leave you fellows to your own element. Good luck to you in America, if you ever get that far. If the French don't get you, very likely Old Duckshoot will.'

Chapter 20

The Broad Pennant

The lieutenant governor had made his own pinnace available so the commodore could arrive in style—'Can't have you going out there in a bumboat,' he had declared—so it was all gleaming brass and varnish, with a dozen bluejackets at the oars and a Union Jack at the stern, and all he lacked was a brass band like Old Duckshoot's.

To reach *Scipio* they had to pass down the length of the squadron, and Nathan had the crew row close enough for him to make out some of the figures on the decks. The first person of note he saw was Simpson on the quarterdeck of *Panther*, with sufficient gold lace about him to conclude that he had wasted no time in visiting his tailor when he was made post, though perhaps he already had the uniform stored away in his cabin. For all Nathan's aversion to the man, it probably made sense to promote him, at least to Collingwood. He was competent enough, and you would never have to fear he would act on his own initiative.

Simpson spotted his new commodore at about the same time and they exchanged formal bows, only a little ironic in Nathan's case. Then the ship was full of her people, lining the deck and in the rigging, and by God, they were waving their hats and cheering.

Nathan was much moved. He waved back like the king.

And so it went, on down the short line of ships. He had not known he was so popular.

At length they reached the *Scipio*. He had known a little about her when the foreign secretary had first given him the news at Chertsey, but since then he had read a lot more. Everything he could lay his hands on, in fact, or that people more informed could tell him.

She had been built at Lorient in 1898 to a design by Jacques-Noël Sané, who was possibly the greatest naval engineer in France. On paper at least, she might be supposed to be one of the most complete warships of any navy in the world—packing a punch powerful enough to defeat a ship of much the same size, but fast and manoeuvrable enough to evade anything larger. For all of that, she had suffered a miserable introduction to the French navy. She had been at Finisterre when the combined French and Spanish fleet had fled in the face of an inferior enemy, then Trafalgar.

There was still some confusion over what Villeneuve had intended at Trafalgar. Certainly, there had been massive confusion between him and his commanders, both French and Spanish. *Scipio* had been one of six French ships in the vanguard of the enemy fleet, but Nelson's line of attack had put them downwind of the main conflict, and they had spent an inordinately long time beating back to the assistance of their beleaguered comrades. As a result, the battle had been won and lost before they had even come close enough to fire a shot, and they had fled the scene. Two weeks later the *Scipio* and three other ships had been tracked down off Cape Ortegal by a squadron under Admiral Strachan, and after a running battle lasting several hours, all four had been taken prize.

From his present vantage close to the water, Nathan could see no sign of the damage she must have sustained, but a lick of paint could hide a multitude of sins, and he was anxious to inspect her at closer quarters.

Up the side ladder he went to the rising wail of the boatswain's call, stepping onto the deck to the shout of 'Hats off!' and confronting a great expanse of red, white, and blue—the officers in their dress uniforms, the crew in their blue jackets and sennet hats, and the marines . . . He had never seen so many marines on one ship! Well, he had, of course, he must have, but never on a ship under his command. There must have been at least a hundred of them. Six hundred men in all, if the lieutenant governor was to be trusted.

And stepping forward to greet him, the best sight of all.

'Captain,' said the commodore.

'Sir,' said the captain.

Tully, looking much the same as when Nathan had last seen him almost two years earlier, when they had attacked the invasion fleet in Boulogne with Fulton's submarines, save that the single epaulette he had worn on his left shoulder had been switched to the right. This was a small distinction that might have passed unnoticed outside the service, but meant the world within it, for it was the insignia of a post captain—a captain with less than three years' seniority, at the very bottom of the list, but on a ladder that, provided he lived long enough and did not entirely disgrace himself, would take him to admiral someday.

'You got my message, then?' Nathan said, gazing about him with as casual a look as he could contrive, trying to keep his face straight.

'We did, indeed, sir,' said Tully, who was probably having the same difficulty, for they were neither of them very good at maintaining their dignity when it was most called for. 'Perhaps you would permit me to introduce you to your new officers.'

More of them, too, than he had ever had before, and far more names than he could remember, though he tried. Seven commissioned officers, including a captain of marines, eight or nine midshipmen ranging in age from small boys of twelve or thirteen to hulking great brutes of nineteen and twenty, a sailing master and two master's mates, purser, surgeon and chaplain, captain's clerk, schoolmaster—schoolmaster; where did they all come from?—master at arms, gunner, boatswain, carpenter, and sailmaker, a dozen or so petty officers, and among them, head and shoulders taller than the rest and a broad beam on his face . . .

'Mr Banjo,' said Nathan, his own face cracking open at last.

'I thought you would like to have your coxswain aboard,' said Tully at his shoulder, 'and Captain Simpson was good enough to release him from *Panther*.'

'Perhaps, Mr Banjo, you would be good enough to join me below in a little while and we will discuss your duties,' said Nathan, with an appearance of formality.

It would be considered favouritism, but to hell with it. Banjo and Tully were the only friends he had left, and he had a feeling he would need both more than ever in the next few months or more.

And yet, for all that, and for all his personal problems, and the demons that would never leave off tormenting him, he felt a sensation of what might almost be called happiness as he looked about his new command: the hands in their divisions, the yards squared, canvas neatly furled, every line and stay and hawser in its place, the decks spotless, and the guns . . .

He gave himself a moment or two for a contemplation of the guns, aware that every eye upon the ship was upon him, for Tully would have had the entire crew working on them every day since he had assumed his command, either practising with them out on the bay or getting them in a fit state for the commodore's inspection. The long twin rows of eighteen-pounders on the upper gundeck—they would be thirty-six pounders on the deck below—the dull matte black of the breeches and muzzles, the carriage wheels oiled with cook's slush and the brass fittings gleaming like gold in the southern sun, the powder and shot, rammers, spongers, and all the other accoutrements neatly laid out ready for action—reminding him, as if he needed reminding, that her prime purpose was to take her place in the line of battle. She could be a lone predator, too, of course. She was as fast as a frigate, faster than the *Panther* in all probability—she had the sleek, elegant lines of most French seventy-fours and could carry an immense spread of canvas—but in the final resort she was a floating gun platform, designed for a fleet action or a blockade. And it was worth remembering that thus far she had failed in the two actions in which she had taken part.

'What was the damage after Ortegal?' he asked Tully.

'Superficial,' said Tully. 'Nothing that could not be patched up in the dockyard here. Most of it aloft.'

They both looked up at the rigging. Nothing noticeably out of place now, though it must have been much knocked about in the chase at Ortegal.

'We were waiting for your permission, sir, to break out the broad pennant.'

It took a moment to sink in. But of course. The commodore's broad pennant.

He turned and regarded Tully with a bemused smile.

'Was it lying around?'

'We had it made specially.'

'Well, what can I say?' said Nathan, though he was more than a little embarrassed, 'as we have a breeze.'

It flopped about for a moment or two, before a welcome gust of wind caught it and caused it to stream out for its entire length, which must have been at least twenty yards—was it twenty-one that Pepys had laid down when he came up with the notion two centuries before? Surely excessive; it would have looked ridiculous if it had hung limply down to the deck. But there was another great cheer from the men and a collective waving of hats, and he heard the distant echo from the other ships of the squadron.

'This is a joke, surely?' he said quietly to Tully.

'Whenever you are ready,' said Tully, 'I will show you to your quarters.'

And so to the great cabin, at least twice, possibly three times larger than on the *Panther*, all polished brass and honeyed oak, the sailcloth on the deck, painted with a chessboard of yellow and black—the Nelson check—his table and chairs, his writing desk, his cot, his, his, his . . . and a great expanse of stern window with a blaze of southern sunlight and the dancing motes of its reflections from the sea thrown upon the white bulkheads and the spaces between the deck timbers.

'Well,' said Nathan as he tossed his hat on the table and threw himself down in one of the several armchairs, 'we have had worse.'

'No servants yet,' said Tully. 'I was waiting to see if you had brought any with you.'

'No,' said Nathan. 'Not a one.'

He was very bad at retaining servants, not that he had ever had many. But now he thought about it . . . 'Do we not have Kidd?'

Kidd had been his steward on the *Falaise*.

'I imagine he is still aboard the *Falaise*,' said Tully with a slight lift of the brow. 'I will send for him if you wish.'

Nathan gave him a look.

They had rescued Kidd from a hanging for desertion, and Nathan had foolishly appointed him his steward on the basis of a dubious claim that he had worked in that capacity for another captain. He had cause to regret his naiveté over the next two years or so, and he would have had to be a lot more desperate than he was to have him back.

'There are a number of men among the crew who would serve at a pinch,' said Tully. 'I have asked the purser to prepare a list. And in the meantime'—he lifted a bottle from a leather bucket packed with ice from the Sierras and kept in straw and darkness in the orlop for such an occasion—'a glass of champagne to celebrate your promotion?'

And surely this was the biggest joke of all, for they had both been told from an early age that they were born to hang.

They had met in '92, in the months before the last war, when Nathan was master and commander of the sloop *Nereid*, supporting the revenue in their war against the smugglers. There was irony in this, for they had both put in shifts with the free traders—Nathan, as a lookout on the Cuckmere, and Tully, a full-time moonlighter from the age of fifteen, dropping off cargoes all along the English coast from Kent to Dorset.

He was an odd mix, Tully, son of a Guernsey seigneur's daughter, and one of the most notorious smugglers in the region, born out of wedlock and brought up by his aristocratic grandparents until he ran away to sea on one of his father's boats. He had been skipper of his own lugger by the time he was twenty but was taken by a navy patrol off Poole and given the choice between the king's service and a noose. He had risen to master's mate by the time Nathan joined *Nereid*, but even then, both of them would have said he was far more likely to hang than make post.

'So'—Nathan raised his glass—'to your promotion . . . and mine, I suppose.'

'You do not sound too pleased about it,' said Tully.

'I will tell you in a moment what it involves, and you may not be too pleased either, but in the meantime, tell me about the crew.'

For the next few minutes or more they discussed the subject that interested them both, for it could make the difference between life and death for the pair of them over the course of their present commission.

'The officers are from several ships in the fleet,' said Tully, 'as I expect you know.'

'Any good?'

'I think so. We have had far worse.'

They spoke in Guernésiais, the French patois of Guernsey, which Tully had taught Nathan during the idle months of their passage back from India, and which they utilised as a private language whenever they felt it necessary, for it was a fair bet that no-one who had not been born and bred on the island would understand a word.

'Coleman, the first, was with Cuddy on the *Royal Sovereign*,' he began. 'Tyne man, as you might expect. Solid, competent, nobody's fool, been at sea since he was seven . . .'

'Seven? Blimey O'Reilly, what as?'

'Captain's servant on the *Martin*, sloop.'

'Doing what?'

'I don't know. What does a captain's servant do? I never had one. You will have to ask him, but do not count on a lengthy explanation. I would not call him garrulous. He was at Camperdown. He's a good first. Maybe a bit stiff, bit hidebound, bit of a Bligh . . .'

'*The* Bligh? Bligh of the *Bounty* Bligh? Dear God!'

'I exaggerate. But you probably would not wish to cross him if you were much below him in rank. Not much in the way of a sense of humour. Served before the mast. He has done well.

'The second is Delancey—the Honourable Lionel Delancey.'

Nathan winced.

'Do you know him?'

Nathan shook his head.

'Second son of Viscount Sunbury,' said Tully. 'He was the third on *Leviathan.* Very keen, eager to please, be good with the guns, I think, though 'tis early days. Bit of a—well, I was going to say puppy. Probably not fair, but I long to throw him a stick sometimes, preferably well out to sea.'

Tully could be even less tolerant than Nathan on occasion. It was usually eager young pups that annoyed them the most, though old dogs came in for a fair amount of abuse, too.

'Third is Venables. Signals officer on *Sirius.* I have given him signals again. Seems his strong point . . .'

And so it went on, down through the long list of commissioned officers, marine officers, warrant officers.

'And the crew?'

'A surprising number are rated able. I have had the best part of a month to work them in Gibraltar Bay, and while there is always room for improvement, especially at the guns, they are by no means as rusty as I had thought they would be.' There was a small pause. 'However, I think I need to talk with you about the Americans.'

'Ah, yes.' Nathan sighed. 'I have only just heard about them myself.'

'The admiral said they would be a special concern of yours, but he did not elaborate. There are twenty-six of them, collected from among the various crews at his disposal.'

'So I believe.'

Nathan told Tully what the lieutenant governor had told him, which necessitated revealing their destination, despite an injunction to wait until they were out to sea.

'So, we are going to Washington?'

'We are.' Nathan summarised the commission he had been given by the foreign secretary. 'And I have three diplomats with me in the capacity of advisers who I am afraid will have to be accommodated.'

He did not tell Tully that one of them was newly escaped from the Tower of London, on the grounds that it would be better for him to remain in ignorance.

'One of them you know,' he said. 'Gilbert Imlay.'

He kept his tone flat, but for the first time Tully showed some emotion. Like Nathan, he had served with Imlay before, or against him, and he knew how little they could trust him.

'Have you discussed what he tried to do to us in the Gulf of Gonads?' he said.

'Gonâve,' Nathan corrected him mildly. He probably knew this. 'I have not. Nor will I unless he raises the matter. I am afraid there is a great deal concerning my relations with Gilbert Imlay that is best left in the realms of myth and mystery.'

'Well, I expect we will manage,' said Tully. 'But as to the other Americans—do you have any special instructions regarding them?'

'No, I do not believe so. What do you mean? In the way of accommodation?'

'I was thinking more in the way of discipline. If it should be required.'

'I had not thought about that.' He did now without coming to any helpful conclusion. 'You probably will not be able to flog 'em, not with Imlay and Levy aboard.' He knew the chances of Tully having anyone flogged were slim. Making post might have changed him, but he doubted it. 'Well, let us deal with that problem should the need arise.'

They looked at each other and Tully shook his head, the twitch of a smile again. There were a great many problems he had given Tully over the years; the Americans were probably not the worst of them.

'So—anything else I should know?'

'Yes. I have a son.'

This was clearly a jolt.

'I see. Good grief. Has that been on the cards for a while?'

'Nine months, same as with everyone else, so far as I know.'

'I was thinking more of planning for it.'

'No. No planning for it. Total surprise, in fact. But not . . . unwelcome.'

Tully nodded consideringly. 'Ah. Well, then, I am very pleased for you.' He reached for the bottle. 'He has a mother?'

'He does. Again, it appears to be obligatory at present. In fact, you have met her. Her name is Louise de Kerouac.'

Tully's eyes definitely grew wider. 'By God. The woman you met on Jersey. The beautiful sculptress.'

'Well remembered.'

At least he did not call her the beautiful assassin, Nathan reflected, as Sir Sidney Smith had. Tully had known that Nathan was much smitten at the time, and quite devastated by her sudden departure for France. But it was two years since then.

'We met again when I was a prisoner in Paris,' he said. 'In fact, she helped me to escape. And as a result, became pregnant.'

'Ah.' Tully nodded to himself a few times as he absorbed this intelligence. 'As one does. And how old is the child?'

'Oh, getting on for two weeks now.'

This was clearly more of a surprise.

Nathan explained the circumstances of the birth.

'She gave birth on *ship*? On the way here?'

'She did. It was quite—tense.'

'Yes, I imagine it would be.' Tully's voice was faint. 'More for her than you, I imagine. Not that I mean you were not—tense.' He drained his glass and poured another. Nathan reached out his own.

'Are they both . . . all right?'

'They appear to be. They are still with the convoy.'

'What—*here*—in Gibraltar?'

'Well, they had little alternative. We could not drop them off in Spain.'

'No. I suppose not.'

As if this was not enough for Tully to deal with, Nathan added that his mother was with them.

'Your *mother* . . .'

Tully uttered an expletive which had not been part of the vocabulary lessons on the journey back from India. He knew Nathan's mother of old.

'You got her to leave London?'

This seemed more of a surprise to him than that a woman in the final throes of pregnancy should put herself to the risk of travelling on a ship from England to Gibraltar.

'I did not get her to leave anywhere. This was her doing, not mine.'

'But—*why*?'

Nathan told him. In as much as he could put it into words.

'Louise is convinced that Sir Sidney Smith is the only man who can clear her name,' he explained. 'And as she would not be persuaded otherwise, my mother insisted on coming with her. They have formed . . . an attachment.'

Nathan could see Tully was still struggling to make sense of all of this. He felt for him. He could not make sense of it himself, and he had been working at it for a great deal longer.

'But—Smith is not here,' Tully said. 'He is in Naples. At least, he was when *I* left.'

'You were with him?'

'Not *with* him. Though I suppose I would have been part of his command again if I had not been recalled to Gibraltar. We left the day after he arrived. I heard he had set up his headquarters at the Palazzo Sessa.' He gave Nathan a look. 'You know, where Sir William Hamilton lived when he was envoy there.'

Nathan knew what the Palazzo Sessa was. He had stayed there himself.

'Where Nelson met Emma,' he said softly. 'After the Nile.' He shook his head again. 'That man. He aspires to everything that Nelson had—or was. If Emma were younger, he would have aspired to her, too.' This, however, was beside the point. 'And how long is he likely to remain in Naples, do you know?'

'I was not consulted in the matter. He has something of a diplomatic role, I believe, as you . . .' Tully let the sentence die. 'But I do not think you will see him back in Gibraltar for a while. Perhaps she could write to him. Or you could.'

Nathan made no reply.

'Can you send them back to England?'

'Not as things stand. Louise is adamant that she will be arrested if she returns to England before she clears her name. Or someone does.'

'Well, she may be arrested here,' Tully pointed out. 'It is all army and navy on the Rock, and they are in a great fear of spies.' There was a short silence. 'You are not married then?' he enquired tentatively.

'She will not let me marry her. I have offered.'

'You cannot take her with us—to America?'

'Impossible. A woman and child—a babe barely out of the womb—on a ship of war. And the French fleet at sea.'

He thought there might have been a glimmer of relief in Tully's eyes, but it was probably in his imagining.

'If she would take your name . . . she might be waiting on your return,' Tully ventured after a moment. 'There are a number of wives and families of British officers in Gibraltar.'

'That is what I am thinking of, but it is something I will have to arrange before we set sail, and I am not sure how to go about it.'

'Do not concern yourself.' Tully's voice had recovered some of its former decisiveness. 'We have staff.'

Chapter 21

A House above the Sea

And so it was that late the following afternoon, with the minimum of aggravation, Nathan's extended family, servants, baggage, and all was installed by members of the ship's crew in a large villa on the slopes above Rosia Bay.

'I hope this meets with your approval,' he said to his mother when they were settled in the withdrawing room, Louise being occupied upstairs with the child.

His mother stood at the window, looking over the bay with a disparaging eye.

'How long are we going to be here?' she enquired gloomily.

'Well, that is somewhat in the lap of the gods,' he answered.

'I take it that the man Louise has come to see is no longer on Gibraltar, if he ever was.'

'No.' He did not know how much his mother knew of Louise's affairs. Probably a good deal more than he would have wished.

'So where is he?'

'I believe he is in Naples.'

Her cool grey eyes showed a flicker of interest. 'Naples?'

'That is the intelligence I have received.'

'And is he going to be there long?'

'That is again . . .'

'In the lap of the gods.'

'Quite.'

'These gods appear to have quite a lot in their laps, do they not?'

Nathan made no comment.

'I have always desired to visit Naples,' she mused. 'I would like to lay a wreath on the grave of Eleonora Fonseca Pimentel. Or if she has no grave, the site of her execution.'

'Ah,' said Nathan. 'A friend of yours?'

'I never met her. But I treasure her memory.'

'Ah.'

'Revolutionist, poet, martyr. Her last words before they hanged her were "Can I have a cup of coffee?"'

She would be one of the victims of the massacres, he guessed, when Nelson brought the royal family back from Sicily and they unleashed the fury of the *lazzaroni*, the royalist mob. It was not a subject he cared to discuss now, especially not with his mother.

'In fact, I think she then said, "Perhaps it will please people one day to remember these things." I would like to remember her.'

'Yes, but . . .'

'It was one of the glories of the Grand Tour before the present wars. See Naples and die, I believe people said.'

'Mother . . .'

'Well, in the circumstances . . .'

'What particular circumstances do you have in mind?'

'At least we would not be in daily danger of arrest.'

'Are you in daily danger of arrest? I mean, any more than usual?'

'I might be done for aiding and abetting,' said his mother, who was something of an expert on this aspect of the law, or indeed, most aspects.

'I am sure that you will both be perfectly safe in Gibraltar,' declared Nathan, with rather more confidence than he felt, 'provided she takes my name—and the status of a British naval officer's wife awaiting her husband's return.'

'Ha,' his mother scoffed. 'Well, if you say so.'

'Do you wish to return to London? It can be arranged.'

'Perhaps in a few weeks' time,' she replied warily. 'At present, to be frank, there is nothing I desire less than another sea voyage.'

'How were you planning on traveling to Naples?' he asked provokingly. 'Overland?'

It was always a mistake to provoke his mother.

'Why not? Neither of us is English. There is no reason why we should not travel across Spain, or France, or down the length of Italy. We could visit Florence on the way. And Rome. It might be very pleasant.'

'Mother . . .'

'But I guess Ewen is a little too young for coach travel,' she conceded with a sigh.

'This is really a very nice villa,' he said, looking around the room. 'The best that was available. It was until recently occupied by a colonel of artillery, but he died of a condition of the liver. And Mr Makepeace is at your disposal should there be anything you particularly require.'

'Mr Makepeace?'

'The agent I have commissioned.'

This again, was Tully's doing, or the purser's.

'I have told you this. And I have arranged for funds to be deposited in the Bank of Gibraltar, in your name.'

'How much?' Again, a glimmer of interest.

'Enough for your immediate needs,' he said flatly. 'Louise will not take my name, or my money.'

His mother pursed her lips. 'Well, I expect she has her reasons,' she said. 'Are you going somewhere?'

He was shrugging into his uniform coat.

'Yes. I am returning to my ship, and then I am going to sea.'

He had not told her where he was bound. If she knew he was going to America, she might want to come with him. She had brothers in New York. And New York, for all its inconveniences, was probably a lot more to her liking than Gibraltar, or even London at present.

He could see the squadron waiting for him in the bay below, each ship held by a single anchor in six or seven fathoms of water, like horses straining at the leash. He could sense their restless impatience from here. The wind remained easterly, and the tide would soon be on the turn—not that this was an issue in the Strait of Gibraltar. They would leave as soon as he was aboard.

He looked towards the staircase. 'And now, I must take my leave of Louise,' he said.

She was sitting on the bed in her room, fastening up her dress with the child sleeping in the cradle beside her.

'I never thought he would go to sleep,' she said.

Mr Makepeace was supposed to be finding her a wet nurse, among his other duties. If he could not find one on the Rock, he would bring one over from Spain, he had said. It did not appear to be an insurmountable problem. But then, nor did the breastfeeding for Louise, though it was not something they had discussed.

There was a great deal they had not discussed.

She looked tired but so beautiful he felt as if someone had drawn a hook through his insides, dragging everything out. There was no pain, not even a dull ache, just a great emptiness.

She came to him and put her arms around his neck and they kissed.

'I cannot bear this,' he said.

'I said you would always be going away.'

And that he would leave her with his mother, if he thought he could get away with it.

But this was her fault, he told himself, her fault entirely.

They stood there for a while like that. And then gently he moved her away.

She lifted her chin and he saw that although her eyes were wet, she was smiling.

'A house on the sea,' she said. 'Just what I have always wanted.'

'Just as you always feared.'

'Come back to me,' she murmured. 'Wherever I am.'

He would remember this for a long time—the feel of her body and the baby asleep in the cradle, and the press of her lips on his, and most of all, the last thing she said to him. That, and his mother's remarks about Naples.

He thought about this on the way out to his squadron. He thought about it all the way out to America, off and on, and of how different it might have been.

Chapter 22

The Voyage Out

SCIPIO. *MARCH 25, TUESDAY. COURSE NWBN. WIND NE. LAT 32.18N Long 70.75W. Gentle breeze. Studding sails alow and aloft.* And as close to the wind as it would allow—although Nathan privately considered that it would have been worth trying for another half-point had he been consulted in the matter, which he was not. Instead, having little else to occupy his time or energy, he stretched out his legs in the canvas chair provided for his greater comfort on the weather side of the quarterdeck, tipped up his hat a trifle, and contemplated an empty sea under a cloudless blue sky with a strange sense of complacency soured by the feeling of being as superfluous to requirements as when he was a passenger aboard the *True Briton*.

The Atlantic Ocean might have been as full of French predators as General Fox had supposed, but none had been recorded in the ship's logs of the *Scipio* and her consorts during their long passage to the Americas. In fact, they saw very few ships at all, for Tully had chosen a route that was at the very northern edge of the trade winds. His decision appeared to have paid off, however, the squadron clocking as many as two hundred and fifteen nautical miles from one noonday casting of the log to the next, and never less than a hundred, their peaceful progress shattered only by the regular gunnery practice imposed by their new captain. This was not entirely satisfactory exercise, but by the fourth week into their voyage they had achieved a best time of five minutes, twenty-six seconds, for two complete broadsides, which, as Tully remarked sardonically to his officers, at least gave them an outside chance of fighting their way out of a bag.

Nathan meanwhile did what commodores usually do when their lofty position precludes them from the daily running of the ship, which is to say, very little. He slept, he read, he paced the deck, he climbed the rigging, studied the sky at night and his fellow man by day, ate and drank considerably more than was good for him—and made friends with Lieutenant Levy.

His contact with the American had been minimal while they were aboard the East Indiaman. He had seen him on deck occasionally after dark or in dirty weather, a solitary figure in the vicinity of the foremast shrouds, or less often at the stern rail in private converse with Imlay, which Nathan had not wished to interrupt. He had assumed he was disinclined to be friendly, his imprisonment in the Tower doubtless having prejudiced him against the British in general and the British navy in particular. In any case, Nathan had enough to concern him with his own affairs.

Once they had transferred to the *Scipio*, however, they found themselves in the peculiar position of being the only two naval officers aboard with time on their hands, and after several short exchanges while strolling about the deck, Nathan invited him for a drink in the great cabin, where after some initial reticence, he managed to get Levy to talk about himself and his family.

His father had been born in Hamburg, one of the free ports on the Baltic Sea, collectively known as the Hanseatic League, where the family was heavily involved in shipping and finance, and he had been sent to Boston to represent their commercial interests.

'My father was not the most obvious example of the destitute European exile,' Levy admitted. 'He came to avail himself of the opportunities provided by the expanding British Empire.

However, he soon became aware that most of the opportunities went to those with connections in London and other major British ports.'

His arrival in Boston coincided with the period of discord and dissent that preceded the Revolution, and the young immigrant had associated himself with the 'hotheads,' as they were known by their more conservative fellows, and among themselves as the Sons of Liberty. The British authorities used harsher names.

'I expect you would use them, too,' he observed wryly, 'as a loyal officer of the king.'

'Not all loyal officers of the king would have supported the repression of the people of Boston,' Nathan replied dryly, though, in fact, his father had.

Perhaps it was the use of the word 'repression,' or 'the people of Boston,' but Levy clearly felt encouraged to express himself more freely than he might normally have to a commodore in the king's navy. From Nathan's point of view, it was instructive to hear the story from someone other than his mother, or one of her radical associates.

When protest flared into open conflict in 1775, Levy's father had joined the colonial militia, fighting at Bunker Hill, Valley Forge, and Saratoga, where he was wounded. By the end of the war, he was a captain of artillery in Washington's continental line, and he was present at the British surrender at Yorktown, 'which some called the German Battle,' Levy confided, 'because there were so many Germans involved in all three armies.'

Nathan knew of the mercenaries from Hesse and other German states who had fought with the British in America, but not of the large numbers in the French army, or those who fought for the rebels.

'Many were immigrants like my father,' said Levy, 'but many others were deserters from the British army. There were so many Germans in Washington's army by the end of the war, my father found a new occupation as an interpreter.'

During the war, his wife and children had moved to Rhode Island to live under the protection of his wife's family, who were merchants and shipbuilders like his own people back in Hamburg. When he came out of the army, Levy's father joined them there, but within a couple of years they had moved south to set up a branch of the family business in Charleston, and did well enough to purchase a cotton plantation with almost a hundred slaves.

'He treated them well by the prevailing standards,' said Levy. 'There was no flogging or any other physical punishment, unlike on a ship of war. Even so, I was always opposed to slavery; it was one of the many things on which I and my father could never agree.'

His father wanted him to train for the law, but at the age of fifteen he ran away to sea on a ship bound for Europe and spent the next two years serving before the mast. Following desperate pleas from his mother, however, he agreed to come home and carry out his father's wishes, provided he was permitted to join the American navy when he passed the bar exam.

'My father thought I would have changed my mind by then,' he said. 'But when I made it clear that I was still determined to go to sea, to his credit, he did not stand in my way. I was taken aboard the USS *Constitution* as an ensign, and within the year we were packed off to the Mediterranean to fight the Barbary pirates. By the time it ended I was a lieutenant, but the navy was more interested in my skills as a lawyer than those of a seafarer, and ever since I have been serving in that capacity, in one way or another.'

Nathan assumed this covered a multitude of sins, such as his recent mission to England, but this was clearly a more difficult subject than talking about the War for Independence.

Levy did not appear to resent the way he had been treated in England, but he did express doubts that the squadron would be permitted to sail up the Potomac to Washington.

'It will not surprise you to know that there is still a great deal of antipathy towards the British in Washington and elsewhere,' he said. 'I simply cannot conceive of a British naval squadron being allowed within a hundred miles of the federal capital, not with the number of armed men and heavy ordnance that are aboard.'

Despite the assurances he had been given by Imlay, Nathan was inclined to agree.

There were other issues, too, that had not been satisfactorily explained to him, and on the thirty-fifth day out of Gibraltar and within a few days' sail of the Chesapeake, he convened a meeting with Carteret and Imlay in the great cabin.

First on the agenda was the exact means by which Carteret's appointment as British minister *ad interim* was to be accomplished.

'I assume you have the necessary paperwork to hand,' he remarked lightly, though in fact he did wonder.

'I do indeed.' The diplomat tapped his breast as if it were concealed in his jacket pocket or locked in his heart. 'Signed and sealed by His Majesty, and with an accompanying letter from the foreign secretary apprising Mr Merry of the reasons for his recall. Or at least, those we would wish to make public,' he added with a mirthless smile.

After the best part of two months at sea Carteret had recovered something of the composure he had displayed at the foreign minister's home in Chertsey, and rather alarmingly for Nathan, he appeared to have developed an understanding with Imlay.

Since their transfer to the *Scipio,* the American had been almost invisible, at least to Nathan. He had been given a small cabin adjacent to the gunroom, and Tully had made clear that he was allowed access to the quarterdeck only by invitation of the officer of the watch. But as they approached the shores of his native country, there were troubling signs that he was preparing to reassert himself.

'Let me explain the situation to you,' he said now. 'I take it you have heard of Mr Aaron Burr?'

'Vaguely,' said Nathan, who had heard his mother talking about him, but had not taken much of it in. Something about shooting his political opponent in a duel.

'Yes, well, I will not bore you with the whole story,' said Imlay. 'Suffice to say that he has concluded that he was cheated of the presidency at the last election and is plotting to create a breakaway dominion in the western territories. An independent nation under his own presidency—or dictatorship. I do not know exactly what he has in mind.'

'Is that not treasonable?' Nathan enquired mildly.

'Of course it is—if it can be proved. Which is where your Mr Merry comes in.'

Nathan glanced at Carteret, who was studying a spot on the table with apparent fascination. He wondered just how much plotting had been going on between them both during the long passage from Gibraltar. A considerable amount, he imagined, but then, what else did they have to do? He should have devised some physical exercise for them. Swimming off the side, in Imlay's case, in the shark-infested waters of the Caribbean.

'Merry has his own reasons to be displeased with the president, who has treated him with total contempt, he believes, since his arrival in Washington. So, when Burr came to him with his proposal, he gave it more attention than it deserved. At any rate, he wrote to Pitt, who was then the king's minister, suggesting that the British should give it their secret support, initially with money.'

Neither of his companions had anything to say to this.

'Unfortunately for him, and of course Burr, the letter did not arrive until after Pitt's death. So, it was passed on to the new foreign secretary, who has rather a different attitude to Anglo-American relations. Which is why we are now on our way to Washington, and why Mr Merry will shortly be on his way back to England, under a considerable cloud. If not right away.'

It struck Nathan, not for the first time, that Imlay knew rather more about the internal deliberations of the British foreign office than might have been expected of an American agent. It was quite possible, of course, that Fox had confided with him as part of his own strategy of pursuing an American alliance.

'Why not right away?' Nathan put the question to Carteret, but it was Imlay who answered.

'Because it has been deemed advisable to encourage Mr Merry in further indiscretions—on his part, but more particularly, Burr's. If they were to believe, for instance, that the proposal has met with London's approval and that funds were to be made available—even brought out on the *Scipio*—it may provide the evidence against Burr that is currently lacking.'

'I see.' This was not entirely true, but what Nathan did see was not at all to his liking.

If word got out that the squadron had arrived in Washington to distribute bags of British gold to the president's chief political rival, a man whose actions might be deemed treasonable, Fox's goodwill mission would turn into a gross provocation at the very least.

'So, who is to convey this information?' he demanded.

Imlay flicked another glance in Carteret's direction but took his silence as an invitation to continue.

'Shortly after our arrival in Washington, all three of us will meet privately with Mr Merry, and that is when the trap will be laid, so to speak.'

'You will accompany us?'

'I will. If you have no objection, of course.' Imlay smiled.

'Will that not give the game away? Or does he not know you are an agent of the federal government?'

'Ah, as to that, Mr Merry believes me to be a friend and ally to Mr Burr.'

Nathan leaned back and regarded him with interest. 'Now how would he have come to that conclusion?'

Imlay looked a little pained, though he was, in Nathan's view, as shameless as any man on Earth.

'You will recall that I own a tract of land on the Ohio River?'

Nathan did. In the past Imlay had devoted some considerable time and energy in attempts to increase its value.

'And I will go so far as to say I am considered to be something of an expert on the western territories.'

Nathan knew this, too. Imlay had written two books on the subject: one, a topography aimed at encouraging settlement and further adding to the value of his investment; the other, a lurid novel also set on the American frontier, but aimed at a wider market. In fact, Imlay's interests in the western territories were as mysterious as most of his activities. Nathan had no idea if he still owned land there, but it was worth bearing in mind.

'Accordingly, Burr believes that it is in my personal interests to support his ventures in the West,' Imlay went on. 'Indeed, to encourage him in this belief, I have even advanced him a significant sum of money.'

Nathan wondered where that had come from; it was unlikely to have been from Imlay's own pocket.

'So, he does not know whose side you are really on?'

'That is correct.'

And nor, of course, do we, thought Nathan.

'So, we are going to tell Merry that this proposal has the approval of the British government, and we have the funds to support it.'

'That is about the measure of it, yes.'

Nathan addressed himself to Carteret. 'Was the foreign secretary privy to this, before we left London?'

'Of course. How could he not be?'

'And he did not consider sharing that information with me.'

'It might have slipped his mind. There were many other things to discuss, if you recall. Also, I am not sure how much he knew himself at that stage. He had only just assumed the office of foreign secretary. You remember all the papers that were scattered about. There was a lot of reading to catch up on.'

Nathan supposed he should have been prepared for an element of subterfuge given his past dealings with the political class, but it still rankled somewhat. He had expected better of Fox.

'So, how are we to proceed with this stratagem, if I can call it that?'

Imlay exchanged another glance with Carteret. It was not quite relieved, but Nathan thought he had the air of a man who has cleared a major hurdle.

'When we arrive at the mouth of the Potomac, I will disembark with Lieutenant Levy and the American seamen and make my way to the capital, in order to give notice of your arrival and prepare a suitable welcome.'

Nathan did not at all like the sound of this, either, but he was at a loss to suggest an alternative arrangement. They could not sail four foreign ships of war up the Potomac and into the heart of the federal capital without giving notice and receiving permission. This was one of the reasons they had brought Imlay and Levy along. But if he was planning on any mischief, this would give him ample opportunity. And Nathan had not known a time when Imlay was not planning mischief.

'And you are confident that this will not be a problem?'

Imlay considered. 'Quietly confident.'

Nathan wondered at the distinction.

'The release of the seamen cannot be made public, of course, but it will be conveyed to both the president and the secretary of state as a sign of your good intentions. I am not saying it will be plain sailing from then on, but it will considerably smooth the waters.' Imlay smiled at the analogy.

'Why cannot it be made public?' Nathan demanded.

'Because it is not official British government policy to countenance the return of American seamen illegally detained on the high seas,' Carteret pointed out. 'It should be, one might argue, but it is not—at least, not yet. It is possible that the current negotiations in London will include a clause to that effect. However, in the meantime, it would only give ammunition to our opponents to hear that two dozen American seamen had been returned *un*officially to their homeland.'

This had been intimated by General Fox in Gibraltar, of course, when Nathan had first heard about the plan, but now they were due to be handed over he could see difficulties ahead. The Americans were not registered on the muster roll, according to the lieutenant governor's instruction. However, if the president wanted to make political capital of their release, and it was announced in the American newspapers, it could be extremely embarrassing—not least, to him personally. Certainly, it would be much resented by many of his colleagues in the service.

'And what about Lieutenant Levy?' Nathan looked to Imlay. 'What if he talks to the newspapers about his role in all of this—including his arrest and his escape from the Tower of London?'

'Lieutenant Levy is a senior intelligence officer and a trusted adviser of the president,' the American replied. 'He knows the value of discretion.'

'So, this story about him being a spy was not so far from the truth?'

'There is a significant difference between the role of an intelligence officer and a spy,' Imlay retorted. 'As I believe we have discussed previously.'

'And I would love to discuss it further with you someday,' Nathan needled him, 'as you are an acknowledged expert on the subject. However'—he turned to Carteret—'could I not have been told about all of this, at the time of my appointment?'

Carteret looked unusually embarrassed. 'You have to understand there was a certain amount of confusion at the time, not to say chaos. Mr Fox was new to the job and not in the best of health. He inherited various problems that were not of his making, and was occasionally obliged to make a rapid decision without consulting everyone involved. There was the business of Lieutenant Levy, which was something of a covert operation known only to a very few people. And I have to say, we had no idea that you would be personally involved'—another quick, possibly accusing glance in Imlay's direction—'but up to the day of your departure, we had several distractions to contend with, including reports of an operation by government agents directed at certain individuals who were suspected of being French agents . . .' Another awkward pause, but with both pairs of eyes upon him, he continued: 'One of whom was, I believe, an acquaintance of yours.'

'Louise de Kerouac.'

'Precisely.'

'You knew about this—when we were in London?'

'It was brought to my attention on the day of your departure—and the fact that the lady in question was aboard the *True Briton*.'

This could only have been conveyed to him by Imlay.

But now Nathan had something else to worry about, something much more serious than 'the business of Lieutenant Levy.'

If Carteret knew about Louise before he left London, there was every likelihood that he had passed the information on to the authorities in Gibraltar. In which case, Louise, and possibly his mother, would have been arrested within hours of Nathan setting sail for America.

And when his help was most needed, he was—as Louise might have predicted—an entire ocean away.

CHAPTER 23

Journey's End

AN HOUR INTO THE FORENOON WATCH, FORTY DAYS AND FORTY nights after leaving Gibraltar, they sighted land. Cape Henry, to be precise, on the southern entrance to Chesapeake Bay. They were now only eighty-six nautical miles—a day's sailing in current conditions—from the mouth of the Potomac and the gateway to Washington. Journey's end.

Nathan was under no illusions, however; he knew the most difficult stage of the journey still lay ahead. If he needed any reminder, a few miles off the larboard bow, though presently just beyond their vision, was Yorktown, where only twenty-three years previously a British army had surrendered to the combined forces of the rebel Congress and the French king, leading directly to the loss of the thirteen colonies and the creation of the United States of America. This would be the first time that a British squadron had been here since. It would not change what had happened then, and it would take a great deal more to reverse it, but it might herald a change of course. It might even change history.

But first they had to get there.

'I am afraid they will not permit more than one ship of war to enter the Potomac,' a somewhat subdued Imlay admitted a few days later when he re-joined them after his short visit to the federal capital, 'and that of sixteen guns or less.'

Nathan derived some small satisfaction from knowing that Imlay's confidence had been misplaced—though he did wonder if the American had always known this would be the case—but it left him with a problem; several problems, in fact. The first was whether he was to stay with the squadron in the Chesapeake or accompany Carteret and Imlay to Washington.

'There is no question but that you must accompany us,' Carteret pronounced firmly. 'The foreign minister depends upon it. Indeed, it was the principal reason for your appointment,' he added unflatteringly, 'for we know that you enjoy the favour of the president—or at least,' he corrected himself, 'we know he is not especially antagonistic, which is rare, if not unique, among subjects of His Majesty. Besides which, we need you to assist in the exposure of Merry and Burr.'

'So that is to go ahead, is it?'

'Is there any reason why it should not?' Imlay looked surprised that it should even be in contention.

'And what is the squadron to do in the meantime?'

'The State Department has indicated that there would be no objection to the presence of a British squadron in the Chesapeake,' Imlay assured him, as if this solved the problem to everyone's satisfaction.

And if there was such an objection, what would they propose to do about it?

This was what Nathan was tempted to say, but he retained an uncharacteristic restraint, merely rattling the bars of his cage a little by remarking that this was very nice of them, which probably made his feelings clear, even if it did not entirely relieve them.

'The existence of the squadron has been noted,' Imlay confirmed, 'and I believe it will have a significant impact on our negotiations.' Seeing that this failed to have a significant effect on the present atmosphere, he added with the pomposity that came naturally to him whenever he thought he had been found out: 'Besides which, the goodwill visit of even a single British ship of war to the federal capital at this time and in these circumstances is an event of historic importance, given the unfortunate *contretemps* between our two nations in the recent memories of many of our citizens.'

To which the only response that occurred to Nathan at the time was a noise very like the release of flatulence.

But the following day he moved his flag to the *Falaise*.

It was with considerable misgivings. While the *Falaise* had brought him good luck with the bad over the years, and a not inconsiderable amount of income, her past record did not make her the best ship to choose for a goodwill visit to the American capital. The price of her purchase had almost certainly been paid from whatever secret fund was at Imlay's disposal at the time, and certain individuals in the Treasury Department might be eager to recover it. Even if they were persuaded otherwise, they might well be disposed to resent her appropriation by a captain in His Britannic Majesty's navy. They might even regard her visit to the nation's capital as adding insult to injury.

Nathan would have taken her sister ship, the *Aurore*, but that would have meant leaving Captain Curtis in charge of the squadron in his absence, for he had been made post over a year ago, and was thus senior to Tully. This Nathan was extremely reluctant to do, though he would have been hard pushed to put his objections into words. Fortunately, it did not appear that Carteret knew anything of the *Falaise*'s past history, and Nathan told himself it would be far too embarrassing diplomatically for either Imlay or his associates in government to admit to ever owning the vessel. Even so, he was by no means assured that it was the best decision he had ever made.

However, shortly after sunrise on the day following Imlay's return from Washington, under the watchful escort of a twelve-gun brig of the United States navy, the sloop began her 116-mile journey up the Potomac. It was hardly the grand gesture of reconciliation envisaged by Fox at Chertsey, and certainly not a triumphant expression of British sea power after Trafalgar, but Nathan knew enough of Americans from his mother and his own experience of serving with them to have ever thought this was any more than a remote possibility, long before Lieutenant Levy expressed his doubts on the subject.

In the event, he soon discovered there were plenty of practical reasons for leaving the *Scipio* in Chesapeake Bay, for though the Potomac was a good eleven miles wide at its mouth, it swiftly narrowed to three or less, and they were in frequent danger of running aground. Over the first couple of days they made steady progress with the aid of an experienced pilot and a brisk south-westerly, but the current ran strong, and whenever they were obliged to come up into the wind, they would feel the force of it tugging at their prow as if it was trying to force them back down again towards the sea. Nathan dismissed the thought that the gods were trying to tell him something.

As usual since his promotion, he had little to do with the technical running of the ship and was a mere passenger, though rather less comfortably accommodated than on the *Scipio*. He and Carteret divided the stern quarters between them while Captain Curtis moved into a humble abode off the gunroom. They were spared the attentions of the dreaded Kidd, however. It turned out that he had been supplemented by an entire staff of servants, including a personal valet, a cook, and a barber, Curtis being of that rank in society that could not imagine life without such attendants. As a consequence of which, Kidd had apparently skipped ship at Naples and must now be added to the list of Nathan's followers who had gone astray or been otherwise mislaid.

There were a number of old shipmates who appeared to remember Nathan fondly, however, and recalled their time together in the waters off Saint-Domingue, and more recently, the English Channel during their involvement with Fulton's infernal machines, but he gathered from Curtis's glowering brow that conversing with members of the crew was not encouraged under the present regime, and for the most part he spent the long hours of daylight seated in a canvas chair on the little quarter-deck, exchanging views with Carteret or gazing out at the mostly wooded shores of Virginia and Maryland, observing the constant flow of barges and larger vessels while doing his best to ignore the jeers of their crews and the not infrequent shaking of a fist when they saw the British flag.

Besides this appropriate reminder of the difficulties that lay ahead of them, the course of their journey soon took them between miles of plantations, mostly of tobacco, with a multitude of African slaves working in the fields, supervised by mounted white overseers with whips, and at one point they saw a gallows at the water's edge.

Nathan knew from his previous discussions with Carteret that he was a proponent of the Foxite view that Britain should support liberal causes in every country of the globe, America included, unless they clashed with the interests of British commerce, which of course they invariably did. The one exception to this rule appeared to be his dedication to the abolition of slavery, which Carteret and his mentor considered to be an unmitigated evil and an affront to civilised society. This must put him in a difficult position when it came to dealing with Jefferson, Nathan suggested to his companion, for despite his public condemnation of slavery, he gathered from his mother that the president was a slave owner himself.

'There has always been an element of hypocrisy in his approach to the problem,' Carteret acknowledged. 'It is not rare in a politician.'

'And you do not mind that?'

'Good God, man, I am a diplomat. Who am I to mind anything?'

'Is that the definition of being a diplomat?'

Carteret took this proposition seriously. 'You have to take people as you find them,' said he. 'I am not personally in favour of the Tsar of Russia or the Emperor of Austria, but if they offer to put half a million troops in the field against Bonaparte, well—do not look a gift horse in the mouth, so far as I am concerned, better than having it fart in your face.'

'Is that what Fox thinks?'

Carteret considered. 'It is not something we have discussed, possibly because after the recent French victories, there is no prospect of them putting a single infantryman in the field, let alone half a million.'

Thus encouraged, Nathan put it to him that Jefferson was known to be an admirer of Bonaparte and certainly favoured him over King George, or indeed, any other European monarch.

'So, what is your point, sir?'

'Well, it does not make our mission any easier, does it?'

'Whatever gave you the opinion that it was going to be easy?'

'And what if we get into a discussion about slavery?' Nathan persisted.

'We do not get into a discussion about slavery,' Carteret replied firmly. 'Any more than we would about politics or religion or the sexual preferences of the Duchess of Devonshire.'

Nathan viewed him with amusement, for this appeared uncharacteristically bold of him, not to say undiplomatic. He wondered if Carteret would show a different character in Washington, far from the influence of the foreign office, and emerge from his chrysalis not as a butterfly but a wasp.

'And if we are pressed for our opinion on the subject? Of slavery, that is.'

'We reply that we have *no* opinion, and that it is not for us to comment on the practices of less civilised nations. That was a joke,' he added, when he saw Nathan's expression. 'Come, sir, you as a naval officer must have had years of practice at avoiding subjects that would provoke dissent. You practise it every time we have dinner.'

This was true. In fact, it was truer aboard the *Falaise* under her present command than on any other ship Nathan had served upon. The three lieutenants and all but one of the midshipmen were recent appointments, and they all seemed to be kinsmen of the Curtis family, or beholden to them in some way or other. Not that he knew much about them besides that. They were so coolly restrained at dinner as to make conversation an extremely laboured exercise, and not even generous quantities of wine appeared capable of loosening their tongues or easing their starched collars.

Their main inhibition, Nathan thought, was not so much himself or Carteret, although this was certainly a factor, but their presence on American territory, for it was clear that they nursed a deep resentment of the former colonists for having the temerity to dispute King George's benevolent rule and to side with his mortal enemy, the French, to achieve what they called their freedom. Not that this was a total surprise: His own father felt much the same way and continued to express himself forcefully on the subject whenever Nathan visited him at the family home. Sailing up the Potomac on a goodwill visit to the capital of the new nation made them about as comfortable as sailing up the Seine to Paris to pay their respects to Napoleon Bonaparte.

But there was something else that worried Nathan. It was more in the atmosphere than in their conversation—apart from one overheard remark between two officers during the night watch when they did not think he was within hearing—but he suspected that they had become aware of the squadron's mission to support President Jefferson in his attempt to outlaw the transatlantic slave trade, and that they were as determined in their opposition as they were to the similar measures that had been brought before Parliament by Fox and his political allies in England. Whether they were capable or willing to do anything about this was a different matter, of course, but it did not encourage him in the belief that he could rely upon them for moral support if his stay in Washington proved at all contentious.

As for Captain Curtis himself, he probably vied with Simpson for being the most rigid, unbending, and humourless naval officer Nathan had ever encountered, though it was a tight bet on which of them had a higher opinion of himself. Moving into a small cabin off the gunroom so that Nathan and Carteret could be more comfortably accommodated would not have reconciled him to his role as their subordinate, and he was unlikely to be a supporter of Charles James Fox. Tully had disclosed that his family were wealthy plantation owners in Jamaica, possessing hundreds of slaves, and that his uncle, the present admiral, was a strong opponent of abolition.

But then he was not alone in that. Nathan had not conducted a survey on the subject, but he would have guessed that opinion in the service was more or less evenly divided. There was a considerable feeling, certainly among the officer class, that slavery was essential to the economy of Britain and her colonies, and the slave ships a vital training ground for the royal navy. On the other hand, there was great pride among many men in the service, officers as well as crew, that as slavery was legally banned in Britain itself, a slave had only to step aboard a king's ship to be assured of his freedom, whatever country the ship was visiting at the time.

This would presumably lead to further complications on their arrival in Washington. He noted that Curtis always had at least two of the ship's boats out on picket duty with armed marines aboard when they were moored at night, and although he had thought initially this was a worthwhile precaution, given the continuing hostility towards the British flag, he was now inclined to think it was to prevent any escaping slaves from swimming out to them from the adjoining plantations.

In fact, there were at least half a dozen seamen of African origin among the crew of the *Falaise*, and Nathan had brought George Banjo with him, too, despite some misgivings, for until

Nathan had purchased his freedom, he had been a slave in Louisiana. However, George had expressed a wish to accompany him on the journey up the Potomac, partly out of curiosity, but mostly because he had a friend there, an Armenian he had worked with when they had both been in the employ of one of the most powerful spymasters in the Levant. When George revealed that this gentleman now worked as a lawyer for the Federalist Party, Nathan had suggested that he might care to ask him about Aaron Burr and, while he was about it, Gilbert Imlay. George did not seem to mind, but inevitably Nathan was now feeling bad about making use of him in a way that was not strictly speaking part of his duties as coxswain or even bodyguard.

But then, George did not fit into the hierarchy of shipboard life any more than he did into society generally. Most people in Nathan's experience had a problem knowing who they really were, but when you had been the son of a king, a slave, a seaman, and a spy, it probably tested your sense of identity more than most occupations. George seemed to carry this lightly, but you could never tell. Even so, Nathan did not tell him not to bother.

It took them five days to reach the capital, including one whole day towing the ship behind the boats when the river made a dogleg and they had to fight the wind as well as the current, but they moored on the fifth night within three miles of their destination. And the following morning, with the Stars and Stripes flying above the Union Jack as a mark of respect, the broad commodore's flag at the mizzen, and bunting hanging from every available halyard and stay, they came at last to Washington.

Chapter 24
Washington

Nathan had known many great cities. When you were married to the sea it formed part of the dowry, as it were—if it didn't drown or otherwise dispose of you shortly after the formal betrothal. He had seen Venice rising from its lagoon in a shimmering haze of domes and cupolas, Revolutionary Paris with the guillotine shrouded in black tarpaulin in the rain, Naples sweltering under the smoking dragon of Vesuvius . . . Aleppo, Bombay, New Orleans . . . All magnificent in their way, even if they were also redolent of death and decay.

Washington was not like any of them. Not so much a city as a work in progress—a cluster of disparate villages scattered over a vast plain. Houses half built, swathed in scaffolding, preserving a shabby illusion of majesty amid the stumps of trees and a cross-hatching of pits and trenches. Baked earth and dust littered with what could as well be debris as building materials. As if the bits and pieces of a kit for constructing a model city had been pulled out of their boxes and thrown in a temper on the ground by the baffled builder. If it had not been for the domes of the capitol building on its slight elevation and the president's house opposite, you would not have known it was meant to be a city at all.

They saw it from the deck of the *Falaise* a good hour or so before they berthed, for the wind had failed them at the last minute and the current ran strong. The sails were furled, the flags and pennants hung limply down, and the ship's boats were out again, the sailors sweating cobs as they tugged at the oars under a breathless sky. Insects came in clouds—flies, mosquitoes, bugs of all kinds and colours, even grasshoppers making use of their tiny wings—for the shores pushed in on both sides. The river had narrowed considerably as they approached Washington, which was apparently as far as was navigable for an ocean-going vessel, and it was less than a mile wide at the capital itself.

They moored off the newly built naval yard, which was presently bereft of ships, either under construction or in service. President Jefferson was not much taken with the notion of a navy, Carteret reported, despite its success in the Barbary Wars. Navies only provoked conflict, he maintained, and he was probably right.

They fired the twenty-one-gun salute due to a head of state, and as the compliment was returned, the two representatives of His Majesty, Nathan in full dress uniform and Carteret in a frock coat and top hat, took their places in the cutter for their first formal steps on American soil. A small party of dignitaries had been assembled to greet them, accompanied by a number of servants or slaves bearing parasols, a marine guard, and a brass band, which struck up as they approached the wharf, though the tune was not familiar to either of them.

'I think we may assume it is not "Rule, Britannia,"' Carteret murmured.

Despite this characteristic aside, he showed signs of nervousness, as well he might. This was a huge career move for him, and it could hardly have been more fraught with complication. As for Nathan himself, he was surprisingly relaxed. He could not think quite why this was. It was certainly not in any expectation of success. Possibly, his deep pessimism had inculcated a devil-may-care attitude. He was also extremely curious to be visiting what was, after all, the land of his birth, even if it had been part of the British Empire at the time. He had been in Louisiana before, but it had then been a province of New Spain. This was the first time he had actually set foot on United States territory, and there was enough of his mother's son in him to feel a degree of empathy.

First to greet them was Imlay, accompanied by a tall, lean individual in a splendid uniform with a great deal of gold lace and a cocked hat with a large plume attached. He did not have to be introduced for Nathan to know that it must be Mr Anthony Merry, the British minister. Apart from the uniform, his stiff smile and somewhat strained expression was exactly what Nathan had been led to expect. He was otherwise somewhat florid in complexion with a long straight nose, thin lips, and a chin that looked as if it had been forcibly compressed into the confines of a stiff white collar and a tightly tied stock.

More introductions followed. Most of the names passed Nathan by apart from the navy secretary, Mr Robert Smith, which was an easy enough name to remember. The formalities concluded, they were escorted through an imposing Greek arch that looked as if it should lead somewhere more dramatic than an empty shipyard. Although it was still under construction, like most of the city, it did contain an administration building where Nathan was relieved to find refreshments had been provided, including a species of grog which the navy secretary informed him was made of good American whiskey, not rum. It was not noticeably poorer for that, however, though in the circumstances and the heat, Nathan would have drunk most anything that was offered to him.

The navy secretary made a short speech welcoming them to the United States and expressing the hope that it was a sign of improving relations between their two countries. According to Carteret, he was one of the few members of Jefferson's cabinet who favoured the British over the French interest. Nathan gave an even shorter reply, mentioning that he had been born in New York and that his mother was American, which seemed to go down well. He considered adding that he hoped their two great nations would enjoy rather better relations than she and his father since their estrangement but decided to reserve it for a more convivial occasion.

'Excellent,' Imlay congratulated him when it was over. 'Could not have gone better.'

'So, now what?' Nathan asked.

'We go to Merry's for dinner, where we can talk more openly.'

'Then are we not to meet the president?'

This was pure mischief on his part, but if it stung, Imlay did not let it show.

'Not today,' he answered shortly. 'He is at Monticello.'

'Monticello?'

For a moment he thought this was a different country, and that he would not meet the president at all.

'His home in Virginia. He is not always in residence at the presidential house. He will return shortly, I believe.'

'And Madison?'

'The secretary of state is presently indisposed.' He leaned in a little closer, dropping his voice. 'It would be better if you met them later, when our primary business is settled.'

'Our primary business' was clearly the conspiracy involving Mr. Burr, the goodwill nature of their visit being much lower on the agenda, Nathan gathered. He braced himself for further subterfuge, as Imlay would doubtless call it.

A waiting landau conveyed them on a short drive to the Merry house. This was on another construction site, which the envoy described, without any apparent irony, as the diplomatic area. There were in fact more than a few foreign flags in evidence, including that of the French.

'I take it you received my most recent missive concerning a certain person and his requests for assistance,' Merry began, once they had reached the comparative privacy of his drawing room.

'That is why we are here in Washington,' replied Carteret, as he flicked an imaginary speck from his frock coat. But perhaps it was not imaginary. There were almost as many insects indoors as out.

'And the funds he has requested?' demanded Merry.

'Will be made available when we know more of his plans.' Carteret raised a brow a fraction short of a put-down. 'Has he divulged any more details to you of late?'

'Not since my last dispatch, but I believe Mr Imlay has had more recent dealings with him and may have a better notion of his intentions.'

The flicker of surprise on Carteret's face indicated that this was the first he had heard of this, though he might well have been faking it for Merry's benefit.

Imlay nodded with the air of a Greek oracle who has all the answers and has merely been waiting for someone to ask the right questions.

'He is keeping his cards close to his chest,' he said, 'but he did tell me that he has been in contact with a number of gentlemen in Natchez and New Orleans, and that they are ready to take up arms in the cause of independence.'

'Can that be true?' Carteret looked somewhat alarmed at the pace at which events were moving.

'It would not surprise me.' Imlay replied. 'They have reason enough. They are proud Spanish hidalgos and have been passed from one country to another like a parcel of Russian serfs on a country estate. First Spain, then France, now the United States.'

'I would have thought that was an improvement,' Nathan suggested. 'From their point of view.'

Carteret shot him a warning glance, but if this discussion was part of the pretence to put Merry off his guard, he should have been properly briefed.

'The King of Spain and the Emperor Napoleon were distant entities who let them do much as they liked,' Imlay said. 'Washington is neither so remote, nor so disinterested. The proposed ban on the import of slaves, for instance, is a direct threat to their investments, both as slave dealers and as plantation owners.'

'And how many of these gentlemen are there?' asked Carteret.

Imlay considered. 'Not many. No more than a dozen or so, I would imagine, with perhaps three or four hundred followers between them. But according to Burr, they are in contact with people in Mexico—people of their own kind, and of their own families, in some cases—who would like to be free of Spanish control. The new territories purchased by the United States could form part of an independent nation which would extend from Mexico to the Canada border and westward to the Pacific.'

'That could be a threat to Britain as well as the United States,' Nathan pointed out.

'Not in the foreseeable future. The territory has hardly been explored, much less settled.'

'And did Burr say what his role would be in this enterprise?' Carteret wanted to know.

Imlay turned out to be remarkably well informed.

'He has assembled a small army on the Ohio,' he revealed. 'Or, to be precise, on a large island owned by a supporter of his, a wealthy German immigrant by the name of Blennerhassett. Once the insurrection is declared, they are ready to travel downriver to the Mississippi, and thence to Natchez and New Orleans, on the pretext of offering support to the federal government. If the revolt is overthrown, or even fails to materialise, this can only advance his claim to succeed Jefferson as president—the man of action, as it were, as opposed to the man of indecision. If not, he will be on hand to seize power himself and declare an independent republic in the West.'

'He told you that, in so many words?' demanded Carteret.

'He did not have to,' replied Imlay smoothly. 'He will wait to see how the president reacts. He is aware that the success of the new nation would very much depend on British support.'

'And did he indicate how much support this would involve?'

Carteret's tone was critical. Nathan wondered if it had finally have dawned on him that Imlay might have his own agenda—or if it was not as precise as an agenda, that he could be as much of a loose cannon as Burr himself.

'He did. Half a million American dollars and the presence of a British fleet in the Gulf of Mexico.'

Carteret formed his lips into a silent whistle. 'That is a great deal of money.'

'Not to speak of the ships,' put in Nathan.

'A fraction of the fifteen million paid to the French for the Louisiana Purchase, which as you will know, stretches from New Orleans to the Canada border, and as far west as the Rocky Mountains. A prime chunk of real estate.'

Which Imlay would not at all mind having a piece of, Nathan reflected. Not for the first time, it occurred to him that he had a lot more in common with an adventurer like Burr than with President Jefferson. But perhaps they were *too* alike.

'So, where do we go from here?' Carteret asked.

It was clear that Imlay had taken control of the operation, and that Carteret was as much a puppet as Nathan himself—perhaps more so. At least Nathan knew what Imlay was capable of and was on his guard for it. It did cross his mind that Imlay might be a lot closer to Fox than he had imagined, and that their association might go back a few years. And it was possible that Carteret knew this.

'I think Mr Merry should arrange a meeting with Burr,' Imlay proposed, 'at which time he can explain his strategy for himself—and take delivery of whatever funds you are prepared to advance.'

'And how much would that be?' Merry said, making his first contribution to the discussion since Imlay had taken it over.

'For his immediate needs, the figure he mentioned to me was fifty thousand.'

'Pounds?'

Imlay smiled thinly. 'Dollars.'

Merry looked to Carteret. 'Are we authorised to advance such a sum?'

'If such a sum were available, but I do not have it about me at the moment. Do you?'

Merry apparently did not take this as a joke. 'I have already advanced Burr fifteen hundred dollars of my own money,' he said. 'I would be reluctant to give more without an assurance of recompense.'

Nathan saw the flicker of concern in Carteret's eyes before he assumed his usual mask. Merry had admitted lending money to a man who was, according to Imlay, plotting treason against the United States, and Merry was the official representative of King George. If Imlay was playing a double game here, and it was not beyond the realm of possibility, he had just been handed the ace of trumps. There was a tangible silence while the four of them sat there like figures in a tableau at the House of Wax.

Then Imlay spoke. 'I can arrange a draft for that amount on the Bank of Manhattan,' he said, 'if that is your wish.'

He was looking at Carteret, who nodded almost imperceptibly. Nathan wondered if he was aware of the danger he was in if Imlay played them false, but given what Merry had just said, he probably knew it was too late to make any difference.

'But the meeting with Burr must be arranged by Mr Merry,' Imlay said, 'as the official British envoy.'

'I will write to him this evening,' said Merry.

Nathan had the impression that the discussion had gone better than he had expected.

'And now perhaps you would care to join myself and Mrs Merry for some light refreshment,' he proposed.

Nathan tried to catch Carteret's eye as they followed Merry into the dining room, but he was staring straight ahead of him with the benign look of a man who did not have a care in the world. Nathan had his doubts about Carteret, but he had to admire his composure. Then again, he had seen men go to the scaffold with the same nonchalant expression.

'Some light refreshment' turned out to be the famous Potomac River caviar on crisp unbuttered toast followed by the sturgeon itself, or a near relative, lightly broiled in oil and vinegar and cut into thick steaks, and then a procession of waterfowl, the poor birds basted in their own juices and reassembled with their feathers and heads back on, eyes gleaming hopefully as if about to dine themselves instead of forming part of the menu. The analogy was not lost on Nathan, but he tried not to let it spoil his appetite.

There were no swans in the procession; instead, they had Mrs Merry, dressed all in white at the head of the table, with her long white neck rising from a profusion of bosom, a noble nose, and somewhat beady eyes which fixed upon whomsoever had engaged her attention with a rapt if almost carnivorous interest. It was she, of course, whose initial meetings with Burr had set this whole conspiracy in motion, and Nathan could see several reasons why he might have taken her into his confidence. He was aware that Jefferson had described her as something of a virago, haughty and condescending, but Nathan had heard this said before of women with an interest in politics, or other subjects regarded as the exclusive preserve of the male. They had said much the same of Mary Wollstonecraft, and even crueller things of Emma Hamilton, when she was the wife of the British envoy in Naples.

Even so, he had to admit Mrs Merry was a difficult woman to like. She was a remorseless name dropper, and within minutes of being introduced she had given them to understand that when her husband was the British minister in Paris, she had been the intimate acquaintance of some of the great statesmen of Europe, Napoleon included. She clearly considered Merry's present appointment a considerable step down from this lofty perch.

They did not discuss the current political situation in Washington or make any reference to what Nathan now thought of as the Burr conspiracy—presumably, the new capital was no different from those of more ancient lineage in having spies planted in the houses of everybody who was anybody. Merry, himself, had very little to say about anything, other than the food and the drink, and that, sparingly. Nathan found himself feeling a little sorry for him. He clearly had no idea that Carteret had been sent to replace him. All things considered, he was glad when the meal ended.

They had been offered accommodation at the Merry house but declined on the grounds that they needed to stay with the ship. In fact, Nathan did not care to leave the stern quarters unoccupied whilst Captain Curtis was confined to a cupboard off the gunroom, and Carteret was reluctant to trespass on the hospitality of a man he was about to stab in the back.

It was after sunset when they left, and the city looked all the better for it. Dusk drew a veil over its less attractive features, and the lights of the houses made them appear more complete than they were. The air was filled with myriad dancing lights from the fireflies and other luminous bugs that were native to the area, and there was a welcome breeze from the north, which not only kept the temperature down, but would speed their return downriver.

This could not come soon enough as far as Nathan was concerned, for he found the business he was involved in more distasteful than he could have imagined, and even with the best part of two bottles of wine and a large glass of excellent cognac numbing his senses, he was still uncomfortably aware that he might well end up as one of its principal victims.

Chapter 25

The President's Dilemma

'Something must have gone wrong,' Carteret fretted to Nathan over an otherwise excellent breakfast of coffee, eggs, and bacon in the stern cabin of the *Falaise*.

It was two days after their dinner at the Merry house and there had been no word either from him or from Imlay. Nothing about the proposed meeting with Burr; nothing, as Carteret complained, about anything.

'It is probably the heat,' Nathan declared complacently as he buttered another piece of toast, preparatory to ladling it with an excellent preserve. 'Washington is closer to the equator than Naples, you know. And latitude is closely linked to lassitude.'

He did not think it was bad for the time of morning, but Carteret's expression was pained.

'What on earth are you talking about?'

'Only that the closer one is to the tropics, the more enervated one becomes. No-one ever makes a decision. I am surprised they chose it as the federal capital. New York would have made much more sense, or Boston. Nothing will ever be done in Washington, not unless they find some means of cooling the air.'

He signalled the captain's steward that he was ready for more coffee.

'Does it not bother you that we are left kicking our heels like this,' Carteret enquired with an unconvincing air of ennui, 'with the fate of our entire mission hanging in the balance?'

Nathan would have laughed had it not been so discourteous.

'In my experience, it is more often the case than not,' he said.

In his experience you often did not know the true purpose of a mission until it until was over—if you were lucky—and by then the people who had sent you off on it, who as often as not did not know themselves, were either dead or disgraced, or both. And if they weren't, then *you* probably were.

In fact, he very much hoped that there would be no meeting and they could depart Washington without a major diplomatic incident.

He tried to explain his reservations to Carteret, but without success.

The diplomat gave it as his opinion that Merry's conversations with Burr had already compromised them beyond hope of recovery, so they had no alternative but to proceed as agreed with Imlay, who was, when all was said and done, an agent of the federal government.

'And if it compromises us even further?' Nathan enquired reasonably.

'That would require Mr Imlay to act in a manner so devious as to be unimaginable.'

To which Nathan could make no response other than a sardonic grunt.

And so they waited.

Finally, towards the end of the afternoon watch, whilst sleeping off the effects of dinner, Nathan was aroused by the steward with news that a Mr Imlay was come aboard and desired an audience at his earliest convenience.

He dressed hurriedly and sent for a jug of lemon juice.

They met in the stern cabin. Carteret was there, looking pretty much as Nathan felt, but Imlay himself was wearing a smile of satisfaction.

'The bird has flown,' said he.

Either dinner or the heat or a combination of the two had made them stupid, for they both stared at him dully.

'Burr. Flown.' Imlay flapped his arms in the interests of clarity. 'The Burrd has flown, ha ha. Left town at crack of dawn in a covered wagon. Heading west.'

'A covered wagon?' Carteret blinked.

'A drollery on my part,' confessed Imlay. 'I do not know what conveyance he used, nor do I particularly care.'

'You seem remarkably cheerful about it,' Nathan remarked.

'And why should I not be? 'Tis the best outcome we could have hoped for.'

'And why is that?' Nathan waved him to a chair.

'Why, sir, it has forced his hand. I imagine he had information that we were on to his little game, and he is headed for the hills. Or possibly the Ohio. Either way, it has done for him.'

'I thought you said he had a small army on the Ohio.'

'A very small army. I doubt they can number more than seventy men. And he has no money to pay them. He is finished, sir, dead and buried, or soon will be. Is there any whiskey in that?'

He meant the jug of lemon juice. There was not, but Nathan called for his steward to bring some, or if he could not find any, rum.

'So—you think he got wind of the plot against him?'

'I would not call it a plot,' said Imlay.

'What would you call it, then?'

'I have not thought to call it anything.'

'An entrapment?'

'Well, whatever you care to name it, it has served its purpose. It has drawn him out before he is at all ready. No money, no army—no Burr. Ha.'

'Could he not have gone to see a sick aunt? Or at least, say that he has?'

'I do not particularly care what he gives as his reason for leaving Washington. The point is, he has left. Fled. Cut and run. His plans in disarray.' It was obviously a day for idiom as well as drollery. 'With federal agents at his heels. And the governor of Ohio has been alerted to move on Blennerhassett Island.'

'Blenner-what?'

'The island where his troops are being trained. Named after the German immigrant I mentioned to you. The Battle of Blennerhassett Island, they will no doubt be calling it in the journals.'

'How did he know?' Carteret enquired. It was impossible to tell from his reaction what he made of the news.

'Know what?'

'That he was under suspicion? If that is indeed the case.'

'I am afraid Washington is that kind of place. Secrets are hard to keep.'

'And Mr Merry? Does he know about this?'

'I doubt it. Unless Burr let him know. I suppose that is a possibility, but Merry is not a problem.'

'He might be for us,' said Nathan. He looked to Carteret. 'What do you think?'

'I will deliver the letter of dismissal from His Majesty,' Carteret declared, 'and advise him to make arrangements for his return to London.'

'Rather you than me,' Nathan observed helpfully. 'And then what are we to do?'

'I will tell you what you are to do,' said Imlay, happily pouring himself another glass of grog, the required addition having been supplied. 'You are to accompany me to meet the president, who is anxious to express his appreciation for your assistance. Unofficially, of course.'

On the way to the presidential house, Nathan found himself wondering if they would share the same experience as Merry was said to have had on his first visit there. He was rather hoping they would, but in fact, they were escorted directly to the cabinet room, where Jefferson awaited them at the head of a long table, dressed like any respectable Virginia gentleman in a plain but well-fitting brown jacket and breeches with slightly wrinkled but otherwise decent hose and silver buckles on his shoes. He looked younger and fitter than his sixty-three years might have proposed, with a healthy outdoor look, despite the unfashionable grey wig that sat upon his head.

'I am delighted to make your acquaintance,' he said to Nathan when Imlay had made the formal introductions. 'I have heard warm report from our mutual friend, Mr Paine, who sends his best wishes and is sorry he cannot be here to meet you and exchange fond memories of your last experience together.'

'I hope he is happy to be back in his adopted country,' Nathan murmured politely, though he was far from comfortable at having Tom Paine as his advocate, or even being described as his friend. It was true that he had helped Paine escape the guillotine when they were in France, but although he quite liked the man, he had never warmed to his politics. He recalled that among his more recent works was an essay advising the French on the best ways of invading England. His mother called him the Great Revolutionist, and Nathan had always pictured him in his mind as something of a human Catherine wheel, going round and round, shooting off sparks and never really going anywhere, but this was probably unfair. He had taken part in both the American and the French Revolutions, and his *Rights of Man* was said by many to be one of the great books of the age.

He had heard it said that Paine had grown disillusioned with Napoleonic France some years before his return to America, and that he had not been widely welcomed by his adopted countrymen. He had written an open letter to George Washington a few years back, denouncing him as a hypocrite and an incompetent general. But apparently, he still had a friend in Thomas Jefferson.

It was a timely reminder, in fact, of Jefferson's own background as a revolutionist. As well as being the principal author of the Declaration of Independence, he had expressed his enthusiasm for the principles if not the methods of the French Revolution, and more recently he was known to be an admirer of Bonaparte. Nathan had heard that he kept a bust of the French leader in the presidential house, but it was not to be seen in the cabinet room; perhaps it had been discreetly shoved in a cupboard for the visit of the British emissaries, though this would not fit with what he knew of Jefferson's character. It was difficult for Nathan to understand how you could be an admirer of the ideals of the French Revolution *and* of Napoleon Bonaparte, but then, as his mother had oft informed him, Jefferson was more than the sum of his contradictions, whatever that meant.

Shortly after their arrival they were joined by two of Jefferson's allies in government, the secretary of state, Mr Madison, who had apparently recovered from the convenient indisposition to which Imlay had alluded, and the navy secretary, Mr Smith, whom they had already met. The meeting began awkwardly with a discussion on whether Mr Merry should be deported or allowed to leave the country at his own expense and convenience. The latter course being finally agreed, 'provided it is in the very near future,' Carteret moved to the main reason why they were there, as Nathan had originally understood it, and expressed the hope that they might agree to co-ordinate their efforts not only on banning the transatlantic slave trade, but of policing the ban with ships of both navies.

Jefferson exchanged a glance with his two colleagues.

'That would raise quite a storm in Congress,' he said, 'particularly whilst the king's navy persists in seizing American seamen for their crews.'

So there it was.

Talk your way out of that one, thought Nathan, glad that it was not his job.

Carteret did his best. 'There are those in the British government who are resolved to end this practice as soon as possible,' he countered, 'but I will not pretend it is going to be easy, given the strength of opposition, particularly in the navy. However, I think we have made our views clear to you by returning a number of American seamen as a gesture of goodwill . . .'

'Gestures are all very well, sir, but they represent a fraction of the total number, and they should never have been detained in the first place,' Jefferson retorted sharply.

'We are obviously not going to resolve either of these issues right now,' Madison intervened. 'And we do have other things to discuss. May we bring in Lieutenant Levy?'

The president nodded, but there was a tightness about his lips and jaw that did not bode well, Nathan thought. He was looking at Carteret, whose brow was shining with sweat. Nathan knew what he was thinking because he was thinking the same thing himself. What did Levy have to do with these proceedings? Was he now going to regale them with his treatment in the Tower of London? Or would he describe how agents of the British government had facilitated his escape?

Imlay was back within the minute, Levy in his wake.

'Lieutenant Levy has information about the French fleet currently cruising off our shores,' revealed Smith. Nathan saw a visible easing of the tension on Carteret's face. He knew how he felt. 'Information we thought advisable to share with you. Lieutenant?'

Levy was wearing his naval uniform and looking every inch the young presidential aide. He gave no indication of having met Nathan before, let alone of being on friendly terms with him.

'You will be aware that a number of French ships evaded the British blockade of Brest and escaped into the Atlantic,' he began.

Nathan acknowledged this with a cautious nod, but said he was not aware they were anywhere near the United States.

'Our information is that shortly after leaving Brest they divided into two squadrons,' Levy went on. 'One under Admiral Leissègues, headed for the Caribbean, where it was hunted down and destroyed . . . You had not heard this?' He had noted Nathan's sharp glance in Carteret's direction.

'No, but it is obviously very welcome,' Carteret declared. 'And the others?'

'The other squadron was originally headed for the South Atlantic, but for some reason it has diverted north, and several large ships of war flying the French flag have been sighted off the Carolinas.'

This was seriously alarming. All Nathan could think of was his squadron, cruising about the Chesapeake as if the war was a million miles away.

'Do you know where in the Carolinas?' he asked Levy.

'One report has them off Charleston, another off Hatteras Island.'

There was a considerable distance between the two, but Hatteras Island was barely a day's sailing from Cape Henry with the wind in the right quarter.

'And do you know how many ships?'

'One report said three, another four. What we do know is that one of them is the *Vétéran*, of seventy-four guns.'

All four Americans were watching Nathan closely, as if this might mean something to him, but he had never heard of the *Vétéran*. Or had he? Like all British captains he made it his business to know everything he could about every French ship capable of putting to sea, on the basis that he might have to fight her one day.

The *Vétéran*? Yes, it came to him now. She had been launched in '98 as *Magnanime*, but renamed twice. The French had a habit of doing this; it was hard to keep up with them. A matter of current political philosophy, apparently, and who was in and who was out. She was a development of the *Téméraire* class of seventy-fours, armed with twenty-four-pounders on an enlarged upper deck instead of the standard eighteen-pounders. A formidable foe, even alone.

He had a sudden memory of the bearded warrior coming straight at him out of the mist off Ushant. Had that been the *Vétéran*?

'The sighting off Hatteras—this was how long ago?' He addressed Levy, who was the most junior among them, but the most likely to know.

'It would have been a week or more.'

'And the direction they were headed?'

'Of that we have no information,' Smith answered for him. He glanced at the president, who gave a slight nod. 'What we do know is that their commander has been in communication with certain people in Charleston and Savanah.'

'In communication?' Nathan repeated with a frown. By what means, he was wondering, and perhaps more importantly, for what purpose.

'We know that letters have been exchanged. Unfortunately, in cipher.'

Nathan exchanged another quick glance with Carteret. For a French ship of war to exchange coded messages with people ashore was a hostile act, at the very least. 'This is surely of some concern to you,' he said.

'You might well say that,' agreed the president. 'Particularly as these people have never been wholehearted in their approval of the federal government. Or even the concept of one.'

'Friends of Mr Burr?'

'We have no evidence that Burr is involved, though it would not surprise me. However, the proposed ban on the Atlantic slave trade has encouraged certain of these gentlemen to seek greater independence from Washington. There is even talk of secession from the Union. So, yes, the suggestion that they are in contact with a French squadron off the Carolinas is indeed a cause for concern. Especially as we have information that the *Vétéran* is commanded by Napoleon's brother, Jérôme.'

This was another shock, but Nathan tried to keep it from showing. He was in dangerous waters here. To be precise, in the Golfe de la Gonâve off the French colony of Saint-Domingue during the year of peace, where they had been surprised by a French two-decker in the act of landing arms to the rebel slaves under Toussaint L'Ouverture. The encounter had ended with a lucky shot from one of their *obussiers* that caused an explosion in the French magazine and almost literally blew the ship out of the water. They had picked up a dozen survivors, and one of them had been Jérôme Bonaparte.

He wondered if Jefferson knew this. And how much else besides. Nathan was fairly sure the encounter had been contrived by Imlay in the hope of ending the fragile peace between Britain and France and setting them at each other's throats once more. He doubted he would have done that without orders from his superiors in Washington. Possibly Jefferson himself.

'Young Bonaparte is not unknown to you, I believe,' Madison prompted him.

'We pulled him out of the sea when his ship was wrecked off Saint-Domingue,' Nathan said, avoiding Imlay's eye. 'He was in a state of shock, and I do not think we exchanged more than a few words. He was a mere officer cadet at that time. I must say I am surprised he is now the captain of a seventy-four-gun ship of the line.'

'I believe it helps when your brother is emperor of the French,' Jefferson remarked dryly. 'However, after the incident you described the young man fled to the United States under an assumed name, which for the moment escapes my memory. Mr Imlay, do you recall?'

'Albert,' said Imlay, with the hint of a smile. 'Mr Albert.'

'Ah yes, Mr Albert.' Jefferson's expression gave little away, but there was something in his tone that suggested this was of more than casual interest to him—either the cause for irony or ire, possibly both. 'Apparently he feared he had incurred his brother's wrath in some way, though I cannot imagine why, can you?'

Nathan shook his head again, but now he was being disingenuous. He had used young Bonaparte as a hostage for the release of certain friends of his who had been arrested by the French army in Saint-Domingue and were in danger of being torn apart by wild dogs—a form of execution employed by their commander at the time. During the exchange, on a remote stretch of beach, they had been ambushed by French dragoons, but Jérôme had intervened to ensure Nathan's escape. Possibly this explained his brother's wrath, though there may have been other reasons.

'I believe he intended to remain here until his brother's temper cooled,' said the president, 'but alas . . . Mr Imlay, perhaps you would be good enough to tell Commodore Peake the rest of this wretched story.'

Imlay sighed. 'It is somewhat confused,' he said, 'but it appears he became involved with a number of young—and not so young—women, incurred a great many debts, and was obliged to take to his heels again to avoid fighting a duel, or being horsewhipped, for ruining one young lady's honour. He next appeared in Baltimore, seemingly because a naval associate had told him that it boasted the most beautiful women in the country.'

Nathan stared at him in wonder. This was a side to Jérôme that he had not imagined during their brief acquaintance, but then there had been few opportunities for him to reveal it.

'Whether this is true or not, Jérôme was sufficiently impressed to marry one of them, a Miss Elizabeth Patterson—though it might have been for her money rather than her looks. Her father is reputed to be the second-richest man in the United States.'

Imlay, as usual, appeared to be well informed. It occurred to Nathan that he may have met Jérôme in Saint-Domingue and continued their association in the States. Certainly, he would consider the Bonaparte connection useful to him personally. It was the way he operated.

'The couple were of much the same age,' he continued. 'The girl, eighteen, Jérôme, a year older, but her father, being informed of his womanising and his considerable debts, was much opposed to the marriage. As was Napoleon, by all accounts. Apparently, he has hopes of marrying him into royalty, like all the Bonapartes, apart from himself, of course, and establishing a dynasty.'

'A young American lady not being good enough for him, apparently,' growled Jefferson.

Napoleon had obviously suffered a fall in favour at the presidential residence. Perhaps this was why his bust was not on display.

'However, unlike the woman's father, Napoleon was in a position to do something about it,' Madison interrupted. 'First, he tried to get the pope to annul the marriage, but failing in this—yes, that is a surprise'—Jefferson had snorted in derision—'he did it himself by imperial decree. So, Jérôme came back to Europe with his wife, who was then heavily pregnant, in hopes of persuading him to relent. He landed in Portugal and set off for Italy, where Napoleon was on campaign, while his wife tried to land in France. However, the emperor, hearing of this, barred the ship from entering harbour and she was obliged to go to England, where she had the baby. Upon which, Jérôme submitted to his brother's demands and agreed to end the marriage, not that he had any choice in the matter, and was rewarded by being made an admiral in the French navy.'

The president caught Nathan's eye.

'Are you wishing you had left him in the sea?' he enquired, with a sardonic smile.

'I thought he was only a captain,' said Nathan, though this was by no means the only reason he had been shaking his head. It was difficult to believe that the frightened young cadet he had picked up out of the sea had led such a life since, even if he was the younger brother of Napoleon Bonaparte.

'No, an admiral, I believe.' Madison seemed to be enjoying this. 'Also, a general and an imperial prince. And now he is cruising off the southern states where he apparently has connections that were made during his stay with us. Not women in this case, but gentlemen of some standing in society. Again, I imagine it must be the name. So many Americans are in thrall to the achievements of his brother.'

Including his own president, Nathan reflected, at least until recently.

'He has a number of senior naval officers with him,' Madison went on, 'and, more significantly from our point of view, one of Talleyrand's most trusted diplomatic aides to advise on more political affairs—a man called Martinez. The Marquis of Martinez, in fact. Is he known to you?'

He was looking at Carteret now, who shook his head. He looked almost as bewildered by all of this as Nathan.

'But what would the French hope to gain from this?' he said.

'I am surprised you have to ask,' Madison replied. 'Your intelligence of French intentions is usually so much better than ours.'

'Not in this case,' Carteret admitted.

'Well, be that as it may, our own intelligence is that he has been instructed to exploit tensions between the federal government and certain individuals in the southern states, to the ultimate advantage of his own nation, of course.'

'But the French have just sold their holdings in America,' Carteret objected. 'Bonaparte made it clear that he saw them as a diversion from his ambitions in Europe. Are you saying he now wants them back?'

'I would not go so far as that, but he is keen to maintain French influence on this side of the Atlantic—and certainly to weaken the hold of the federal government on the individual states. It would be useful for him to have facilities for his ships in the southern ports, for instance.'

'To attack British commerce, no doubt.'

'I expect that is one of his motives, yes.'

'But that would be an act of war,' Nathan put in.

'I understood you were already at war,' Jefferson said. 'Surely, I have not been misinformed.'

Nathan acknowledged the jest with a polite smile. 'I meant, sir, between Britain and the United States,' he clarified.

Out of the corner of his eye, he saw Carteret wince.

'If we remain united,' Jefferson remarked. 'If one or more of the southern states were to secede from the Union, it would become more—complicated. This is why we are anxious to keep the French out of it.'

'But lacking a single ship of the line . . .' The secretary for the navy uttered what was possibly a habitual reproach.

' . . . you would like us to do it for you,' Nathan concluded.

Carteret applied a soothing hand to his forehead.

'It would surely be as much in your interest as in ours,' Smith observed.

'I have only one ship of the line myself,' Nathan reminded him, assuming Imlay had mentioned this to him.

'But there are others in the region. Our information is that half the British navy is cruising off our shores.'

This was a considerable exaggeration, but Nathan let it pass. He considered. There was a squadron at Halifax, another in the Caribbean, which would be harder to locate but closer to the southern states—and whatever ships had been sent in pursuit of the French. But in the meantime, he would have to do what he could with the ships he had at his present disposal. If the French had not already dealt with them.

'I should leave at once,' he said.

'As you wish.' The president exchanged a quick glance with Madison that persuaded Nathan he had achieved the object of the exercise. It had not escaped Nathan's attention that they had ducked any further discussion of the joint slave patrols.

'And perhaps you would care to take Lieutenant Levy with you,' said the president.

Nathan showed his surprise.

'As a liaison officer,' Jefferson added. 'Should you need assistance in dealing with any of our own citizens you encounter in your travels.'

Or be tempted to press them into the service, his look implied.

But Nathan did not need the warning look from Carteret to keep this thought to himself.

Chapter 26

Sturm, *Drang*, and *Zerrissenheit*

'Forgive me for mentioning it,' said Nathan to Levy when he welcomed him aboard the *Falaise*, 'but the place seems to be falling apart.'

'Washington?' Levy gave him a quizzical grin. 'It may give that impression, but it is, in fact, in the process of being built.'

'I meant the country.'

'Ah yes. The country. Well, it probably does give that impression at times. *Zerrissenheit*.'

Nathan frowned.

'It is a German word,' Levy explained, 'meaning a tendency to fragment, to pull apart, to go in different directions.'

Perhaps it was America that had sneezed. One could only hope it was not a sign of the plague. Unless, of course, like many of his countrymen, His Majesty included, you wished it *would* fall apart, and stop being a problem for them.

'And does that not trouble you?' Nathan ventured. 'That you might pull apart and become a number of separate nations, mutually antagonistic?'

'Oh, it does, but . . . I suppose it is in our nature, as Americans. If there is such a species. It is a little too early in our evolution to say. We are not one big, happy family, that is for sure. We unite only against a common enemy, and without that'—he shrugged and smiled—'*Zerrissenheit*.'

Nathan feared the common enemy might be Britain, in the past, present, and future. But that was the pessimist in him. If he was to be as good a diplomat as Fox thought he was, he had to adopt a more hopeful approach.

'Is there anything you can do to stop it?'

'Oh, that depends on a number of things. Burr and the West, I think we could handle, if 'twere the only issue, but with this trouble in the South . . .'

'Could they be linked? The two?'

'It is possible,' Levy conceded. 'I suspect the president thinks so.'

'And yet Burr is opposed to slavery, is he not?'

Levy gave him a look. 'So, you are not as ignorant of American politics as you sometimes pretend.'

'That is because I have been spending a lot of time with my mother of late,' Nathan told him.

'Well, it is true that Burr is opposed to slavery, but he is a strong advocate of states' rights. And he knows the proposal to ban the import of slaves will be fiercely contested in the South. The federal government will have enough on its hands without having to fight a war in the West.' Another humourless smile. 'We think Europe is a cesspit of intrigue and conflict. We appear to be headed the same way.'

It was a lot faster going in the opposite direction, and they reached the Chesapeake on the evening of the second day out of Washington, just a few hours before the next rendezvous Nathan had agreed with Tully before they parted.

Nathan was up well before sunrise, for he was unusually anxious. He knew that Tully would have been inclined to stay close to the mouth of the Chesapeake, close to the major trade route between North and South, which would increase his chances of catching a French blockade runner. But if the reports Levy had heard were true, he might have hooked a bigger fish than he could handle.

It was with some relief, then, that halfway through the morning watch there was a hail from the maintop that had him swarming up the ratlines as swiftly as any midshipman, at least in his own mind, if not theirs. He took out his glass and a few moments' scrutiny assured him that it was *Scipio*, heading back for their rendezvous, and behind her, the *Panther* and the *Aurore*, looking pretty much as he had left them ten days before.

Within the hour, he was back in his flagship, having coffee with Tully in the great cabin.

'So, you did not encounter any French gentlemen in your travels?' he began. 'Or even ladies.'

'Not so much as a single hooker.' This was not as vulgar as it sounded, a hooker in nautical terms meaning one of the smaller coastal traders, with a single mast and a couple of foresails. They had done very well out of them in the Mediterranean during their time there, but they were unlikely to be found cruising off the east coast of America, at least not the French variety. 'Were you hoping I would?'

Nathan told him Levy's story of the three or four ships of the line that had been sighted off Cape Hatteras.

'We were off Cape Hatteras just a few days ago,' said Tully. 'They were not there then.'

'Perhaps that is just as well.' Nathan had told him not to stray far from the Chesapeake. Cape Hatteras was a hundred and fifty miles to the south. But like him, Tully considered most orders to be no more than useful advice—or not, as the case may be.

He told him what he had heard about Jérôme Bonaparte and the *Vétéran*.

Tully's astonishment was if anything greater than Nathan's.

'My God, he is hardly out of linen clouts. And last time we saw him, if I remember rightly, he was in urgent need of someone to change them for him.'

'He was probably not at his best,' Nathan remarked dryly, 'and he must be at least twenty-one by now. And, of course, he *is* a Bonaparte.'

'Is this what the Revolution was about?'

'Well, it puts a new gloss on *fraternité*.'

'So, why has his big brother sent him to America, do you think?'

'For much the same reason that Fox sent us.'

'Oh yes, and what reason is that?' Tully regarded him archly. 'Do you have a better idea now you have been to Washington?'

'It comes under the general heading of interfering in American politics,' Nathan said. 'Big brother has a particular interest, it appears, in the southern states.'

'So, are we to go looking for them, these ships of theirs?'

'We will have a sniff around Charleston, I think, perhaps Savannah. Unless you can think of something better to do.'

'No, no, that seems perfectly . . . agreeable. And if we find them?'

Nathan gave him a look.

'I mean, given that there may be three or four of them. Do you have a particular plan of attack?'

'Not really. Do you?'

'No, but I have not had as long to think about it as you.'

'Well, obviously going straight at 'em, Nelson fashion, would probably not be the best approach in this instance. So, I was thinking more of harassing them—from a distance.'

'Harassing from a distance. Yes, I must say that has more of an appeal. Not the same ring perhaps, but . . .'

'If we can provoke them into a chase, towards the Caribbean, for instance, we have a good chance of running into some of our own ships. There are enough of them about, from what I have heard.'

'Well, I had better set a course for Charleston.' Tully began to rise.

'There is no hurry. It is nearly a fortnight now since they were sighted off the coast. One must assume they have moved on by now. How is the rest of the squadron, by the by?'

Tully frowned. 'Much as you left us,' he said.

'Crew all right?'

'Shaping up. Haven't had to flog anyone yet.' Nathan assumed this was a joke. 'Gunnery has improved. We cracked five minutes yesterday, for two complete broadsides. *Panther* can do better, of course, but they have been longer at it.'

'And how have you been getting on with the other captains?'

Tully shrugged. 'No complaints. I had them over for dinner once. Simpson is as fond of me as I of him, but we deal with each other cordially enough.'

'I could say the same for me and Curtis,' Nathan reflected. 'What a happy crew we are.'

'We few, we happy few, we band of brothers,' declaimed Tully.

Nathan blinked a little, this being somewhat out of character.

'Shakespeare,' said Tully. '*Henry the Fifth*.'

'I know that.'

Did he? It was instructive to know this was the source of the expression 'band of brothers.'

'I was not aware you were an admirer of the Bard. When did you see *Henry the Fifth*?'

'Not yet had the pleasure,' said Tully, being at sea for the last two years. 'Borrowed it from your library.'

Nathan glanced in the direction of his 'library.' Two shelves on the farther bulkhead, with thirty or so books in them, secured by fiddles against rough weather. Most were on astronomy and navigation, but there were one or two dedicated to more frivolous subjects, including a volume of the plays of Shakespeare which his mother had given him upon hearing of his promotion to commodore, on the grounds that it would improve his understanding of human nature.

'Have not had a chance to look at it yet,' he remarked. 'Any good?'

'Mixed,' Tully advised. 'I like the histories best. There are some good characters. You would like Falstaff. And Richard the Third. Top villain, but a good sense of humour.'

'Well, I suppose I should have them over to dinner myself, now I am back,' Nathan mused. He saw that Tully was looking puzzled. 'The other captains,' he said. 'The band of brothers. What can we give them? I suppose you have eaten most of my supplies.'

'Not touched a morsel, not even a bottle. Would not dare.'

'How we doing for fresh meat?'

'Not bad. Took a couple of hogs off an American the other day. Bound for Philly.'

'Did you pay for them?'

'Of course I paid for them, what do you take me for?'

'A pirate like the rest of us. Well, that is good to know. Anything else?'

'Caught a shark on the way here. Sandbar, but a fair size. Six foot at least. Oh, and there is a turtle we caught off Cape Charles a few days back. Leatherhead. I have been saving him for you. I know you like turtle.'

'How many days back?'

'Never fear, it is still alive. We have been keeping it in a cage slung off the stern and feeding it on crabs and ship's biscuit.'

'Dear God,' Nathan muttered. Standards had clearly dropped since his departure for Washington. 'What if we have to fight an action?'

He wondered if a turtle dangling from the stern would affect the ship's performance. Probably not.

'Then we will cut it free or haul it in and chop its head off,' Tully announced blithely. 'I was thinking of a soup, with a bottle of your precious Jerez, if you can spare it.'

Nathan began to cheer up. 'We will have them over for dinner,' he said. 'And I can bring them up to date. But let us set a course for Cape Henry in the meantime.'

Then he saw the barometer. He stood up and took a step closer, rubbing his eye.

'Dear God,' he said. 'Can that be true?'

They reached the Atlantic a few hours before the storm. By then the barometer was down to twenty-nine inches and still falling, so they had some idea of what they were in for. They had taken what precautions they could, striking the royal and topgallant yards and battening down the hatches, the guns lashed fore and aft across the ports, lifelines rigged, reliever-tackles on the tiller . . . the turtle hauled aboard. But Tully kept as much canvas aloft as he dared in hopes of gaining sea room before they hit the worst of it. He had George Banjo assisting at the helm, being by general consent the strongest man on the ship, and four more below at the tiller, to assist the promptings of the wheel. The rest of the squadron were making their own preparations, and while Nathan still could, he sent the cutter to instruct them to rendezvous off Cape Hatteras, or if they were driven back to the north, Cape Henry at the southern mouth of the Chesapeake.

In fact, the wind was currently from the north, but it was as warm as in the tropics, which was almost certainly where this storm had sprung from, and if it was the kind of storm Nathan feared, the wind would come at them from more than one direction. He and Tully had discussed their options. There were only two: to scud or to lie to, staying close to the wind but making very little headway. There were dangers in both, but their greatest fear was being caught broadside to the waves and rolled over. So, they agreed the safest option was to run before the wind with just the fore lower topsail and the jib to keep the bow steady. It had the advantage of taking them in the direction they wanted to go, and very likely out of the path of the storm. But the jib was carried away in an instant, and they were obliged to strike the topsail and run on bare poles with just the wind resistance in the rigging itself driving them forward. Even then, Tully worried they were in danger of yawing, and he had a length of hawser hung out from the stern in hopes of giving them more control of the helm.

They were barely into the afternoon watch, yet the sky was black as night, shot through with distant lightning that briefly showed the sea as a boiling wrath of waves, violent, venomous, frothing with manic rage. Nathan thought of a pit of serpents, but this was deeper and denser, a more concentrated fury, more muscular, a thing possessed.

The lightning came again, closer, as if directed at them personally, and the air was rent with a terrible thunder. Then the rain came, and in the glare of the lightning it shone like claws and felt almost as sharp on the exposed skin if you were foolish enough to lift your face to the wind.

They had a tarpaulin in the weather rigging, and he and Tully hunkered beneath it in their oilies, exchanging pleasantries from time to time at the top of their voices with their mouths pressed to the other's ear.

Then someone came climbing up the lifeline to join them, and when he was close enough, they saw it was Lieutenant Levy.

He appeared to be laughing.

'What are you doing on deck?' yelled Tully fiercely.

He had sent most of the crew below to save them from being swept overboard, keeping on deck only those he needed to man the helm or deal with a minor crisis. Anything major, the boatswains would call all hands.

'I came to see if you needed any help,' yelled Levy.

'No. Get below,' said Tully shortly.

'Do you have a word for this in German?' Nathan enquired out of kindness before he left.

'*Sturm!*' Levy screamed, disappointingly, in his ear. He must have considered that this was something of a let-down, for after a moment, he added '*Sturm und Drang.*'

This seemed to Nathan as good a name as any for the demonic orchestra in the rigging, with its drumroll of thunder, and a moaning and a groaning, a creaking and a shrieking that seemed to be coming from the ship itself, like a living creature in mortal pain, or a worthy attempt at the Greek orchestra in one of the tragedies his mother insisted on dragging him to.

Nathan should have gone below with the lieutenant, for he was of no use on deck, but he could not bear to, and Tully had the tact not to suggest it. He had secured himself to the lifeline with a loop of rope, but there was so much water in the air it was difficult to breathe or to see much beyond the quarterdeck and the lower mizzenmast. They could see nothing of the rest of the squadron, of course, and he could only hope they were still with them and coping as best they could.

The waves were lifting the stern rather than breaking over it, which was something to be thankful for, and then passing under the hull, lifting the bows in turn and then dropping them into the trough with a jolt that felt like it would break her apart. But like all fast sailors, *Scipio* had a tendency to roll even as she pitched—she would roll into the troughs and roll out of them, so that it felt like they were riding a wild thing, mad with fear, thinking only to be rid of these reckless creatures who had brought her to this, to pitch or roll them off her back and be rid of them that were so foolish as to challenge nature.

And then just as it seemed to be worsening, if that were possible, the wind fell off and the rain ceased; the waves appeared chastened, confused, running this way and that, their fury spent as if it were they that had been broken. And the sky cleared. It was not blue, more a dirty grey, streaked with orange and mauve and pink, but it was not black.

They had both been here before and knew what this was, and it was not over.

'How long do we have, do you think?' said Tully.

Nathan was looking up at the hole in the sky. It told him nothing, but it was good to see. 'Could be thirty minutes,' he said. 'Could be three.'

If this was a proper hurricane, and it felt like it, it would be moving north, like a spinning top, at a speed that was impossible to measure but faster than any ship. Something else he knew—here, in the northern hemisphere, it would be spinning counter to the clock, and the winds spinning with it. To the west of the eye, the wind would be from the north, but once the eye had passed . . .

'We will have to turn the ship,' he said, 'unless you want to head into it.'

'It might be easier on the helm,' said Tully, thinking about it, 'and we would be out of it sooner if . . .' He let the sentence trail; neither of them wanted to know about the *if*. 'But we would have to make sail—at least one staysail to keep the head to the wind—and you saw what happened the last time.'

'Your decision,' said Nathan, for possibly the first time in his life.

'You do not mind running back to the Chesapeake?'

'*Towards* the Chesapeake,' Nathan corrected him. 'If we stay well out to sea . . .'

But he knew that might be out of their hands. For all their knowledge and experience, for all the precautions they had taken, it felt like they were merely going through the motions, and they were entirely at the mercy of the storm.

Tully called up the fo'c'sle hands, and they rigged the flying jib and the fore staysail and turned her head to the north minutes before they hit the wall again, or rather, it hit them, heeling them over almost on their beam ends before she hauled herself laboriously back to what only a madman or a drunkard would call an even keel. By then both sails had been carried away, and before she would answer the helm, a great sea broke over the stern and ran the length of the ship, taking more than one man with it. But for all the cries of the hands in the fo'c'sle, Nathan knew they could do nothing to help their missing shipmates, for it was impossible to launch a boat, and no-one could swim in that terrible sea.

And now here was Kenwright, the first lieutenant, hatless and streaming blood from a cut in the head, to announce the stern windows were stove in, and there was so much water below they would need all hands at the pumps.

And so the wild junket began all over again, but in the opposite direction, through what was left of the evening watch and well into the night. Somehow the men below managed to stretch a sail over the smashed windows in the stern, and it kept some of the water out, enough to give them at least the breath of a chance at the pumps. But either the storm was less violent to the east of the eye, or all the water they had shipped helped steady them, for it was by no means as rough a ride as before.

And then it was over, truly over, for the storm had but one eye, and there was a memorable moment when looking up into the rainless sky, Nathan saw the first star and blessed it with all his heart, whatever it was.

He slumped down on the deck with his back against the starboard bulwark, for it was as comfortable here as it would be below in his wreck of a cabin, and briefly closed his eyes. When he opened them, it was to find dawn was breaking over the restless sea and George Banjo was sitting next to him, either too jiggered or too elated to maintain the pretence of rank. He had been at the helm since the start of the storm, for though Tully had replaced the other helmsmen twice, he was their rock, their lucky star.

'Well done,' Nathan told him. 'Or was it the cat.'

'That cat take too many chances for my liking,' said George. 'Even for a cat.'

A private joke. Code for surviving another catastrophe, natural or manmade, that should by rights have killed them all. George had developed a fondness for English nursery rhymes once he had detected the meaning in them, but he insisted it was the cat that had jumped over the moon, not the cow. For how could a cow jump over a moon?

Then Nathan's steward was there—his new steward, Kelleher, plucked from the waisters because in another life he had been a pageboy in the household of the Earl of Radnor, or at least said he had, before he ran away to sea. Certainly he had the style of a servant in a great household. He could not cook even as well as Kidd, but he was more trustworthy and respectful, and exuded an impressive calm under pressure. Now, unruffled as ever, he informed Nathan that breakfast was being served below.

'When you say below . . .' Nathan pressed him.

'In the wardroom, sir, as I fear your cabin . . .'

He, too, left the rest of the sentence hanging, but Nathan could imagine it.

'Come and join us,' he invited Banjo. Then, seeing the look of doubt: 'Come, sir, we invite the midshipmen to dine with us at times, and you have done a lot more than they in the last few hours. At least.'

He could not think of a midshipman who had done more in the entire course of his career as a midshipman, including himself, apart from catching the odd rat.

'Even so, I think it would be better for both of us if I had breakfast with the others that were at the helm,' George said, 'with respect.'

There was a distant roll of what might have been thunder, a parting shot from the storm that had just passed, but then it came again, and they both knew it was not thunder.

Breakfast, it appeared, wherever it was to be had, would have to wait.

Chapter 27

Cape Henry

Nathan viewed the distant battle with Tully from the foretop of *Scipio*. From what they could see for the smoke of the guns, the *Panther* and the *Falaise* were engaged with a French two-decker a few miles to the south of Cape Henry. This was reckless to say the least, and somewhat out of character, according to what Nathan knew of their two captains, but as they drew closer, a few more details became clearer and put rather a better gloss on it.

The French ship was acting most odd. Although some of her quarterdeck guns were firing, she looked to be having a problem bringing her broadside to bear, and the smaller British ships were standing off her weather quarter, firing shot after shot into her exposed flank. Indeed, as Nathan watched, they were in the process of passing across her stern, raking her with their larboard guns, almost without reply.

'Why does she not fall off the wind?' he wondered aloud.

Tully speculated that her rudder had gone. The tricolour and the smoke of the guns obscured what view they might have had of her helm.

The wind was east-south-east and still fresh, the sea restive, not yet settled after the show it had made of itself, and low, scudding cloud with rain squalls coming in from the Atlantic. Tully figured she must have lost her rudder in the hurricane and was limping into the Chesapeake in hope of repair when she had run into *Panther* and *Falaise*, who looked to be in far better shape. Even so, she should have done better. She was a ship of the line, of seventy-four guns at least, and the combined weight of their two broadsides was less than half hers. They were like a pair of bull terriers snapping at the heels of a wounded bull; but one false move and she'd have 'em.

'I think she is running for the cape,' said Tully.

'What good will that do her?'

He had taken a long look at Cape Henry on their way to Washington, and all it had was a lighthouse and a load of rocks—and a wooden cross to mark the landing of the first English settlers two hundred years before. The way she was going on, it was as like to mark her grave.

'Do they not have a border—a limit?' said Tully.

Nathan looked at him, then swore an oath as his meaning became clear.

'Do you know what it is?' Tully asked.

'Three miles, I think, same as ours.' He swore again.

'And do you mean to respect that?' His experience of Nathan would suggest not.

'I am thinking about it,' said Nathan. He could see the Virginia coast, like a layer of dark cloud to westward. Cape Henry was further north, obscured by the warring ships. They were probably in American territorial waters already.

'And we have Levy with us,' Tully said.

They both looked back and down towards the quarterdeck. They could see the lieutenant halfway up the mizzenmast shrouds with his own glass. Nathan knew he would not let Levy's presence stop him if he made up his mind to it, but it would be embarrassing all the same. He had a commission from the president himself, to keep an eye on them.

On the other hand, there was the prize money. A French two-decker shared between the three ships, even badly damaged. Between twenty and thirty thousand pounds at least, and then the head money.

He looked down again. They were already cleared for action, the guns run out, the gun crews at their stations, the ship's boats over the side . . . The hands were tired, exhausted even, after weathering the storm and a sleepless night at the pumps, but the thought of all that prize money would keep them going. And with any luck she'd throw in the towel when she saw *Scipio* coming up.

He brought the glass up to his eye again and saw that this was wishful thinking. She was standing on for Cape Henry, and unless she lost a mast or a yard or something else untoward occurred, it would be at least an hour before *Scipio* was within firing distance. He wondered if they thought she was a French ship coming up to their rescue. Parker and Simpson were keeping a respectful distance and firing long, and for all his frustration, he could not blame them. One broadside and they'd be dead in the water.

'Damn their three-mile limit,' he said. 'I'll not give up on her now.'

'You could send him below,' said Tully, 'out of harm's way.'

It took Nathan a moment, but then he clapped him on the arm, almost knocking him off his perch. 'By God, of course I can! He is an American. We cannot expose him to danger.'

They descended to the deck and made their way aft.

Nathan put on a grave face, avoiding Tully's eye.

'I fear I must ask you to go below, Mr Levy,' said he. 'There is a fight in the offing, and I cannot in all honour put you at risk of injury.'

Levy looked at him in astonishment. 'She can barely set sail, let alone fight,' he objected. 'Where is the risk in that?'

'Even so, she still has guns to fire, and I could not look the president in the eye if you came to harm.'

He did not know how he had the face for it. He supposed one-eighth of thirty-odd thousand pounds played some part in it.

Levy appealed to him. 'Sir, I beg you, I cannot go skulking below deck. What of *my* honour?'

'I tell you what, you can help the doctor in the cockpit,' declared Nathan, inspired. 'There is honour aplenty in that.' He looked about the usual crowd of officers and men on the quarter-deck and caught the eye of a young midshipman who was paying more attention to their converse than he should have been.

'You, sir, what is your name?'

'Me, sir?'

'Yes, you, sir.'

The midshipman flushed a deeper pink than the usual shade for small boys of his age and breed.

'Reed, sir,' he managed after one false start.

He could not have been more than ten or eleven, if that. What was he doing on the quarterdeck, he wondered. Taking messages, probably, but you would think they would have picked someone whose voice had broken. He could not recall seeing him before, but he must have been with them since Gibraltar. One small boy looked pretty much the same as any other to Nathan. He wondered if that would change now that he had one himself.

'Well, Mr Reed, kindly escort Lieutenant Levy down to the cockpit. You know where it is, do you not?'

'Yes, sir.'

Of course, he knew where the cockpit was. Probably had nightmares about it, and a drunk surgeon sawing his leg off while his shipmates held him down.

'Well, away with you then. Give the doctor my compliments and ask him if he would find a use for Mr Levy, as he is anxious to do his bit. Or would you rather not, Mr Levy?'

Levy shook his head, but in resignation rather than refusal. He knew when he was beat.

Nathan was looking at the boy. Last time he had asked, the minimum age for a midshipman was nine, but they were rarely that young.

There was something else about him, too . . .

'Wait a moment,' said Nathan. 'What is that you have under your coat, Mr Reed?'

'N-n-nothing, sir,' said Reed, looking down.

' 'Tis never one of them new life vests?'

He was half amused, half indignant. He had seen them advertised in *The Sporting Magazine* and was not, generally, in favour. Life vests made of cork, designed especially for seamen. They might work in the water, though he doubted it, but he considered it divisive unless everyone had one, and that was not to be thought of.

'N-n-no, sir.'

'What is it, then?'

'Please, sir, I am not wearing anything, sir, save my undervest.'

He began to pull open his uniform coat.

There was an explosion from two of his messmates over by the larboard rail, but they turned away when Nathan turned a wrathful gaze on them.

'Do you hear that?' he said to Tully when the boy had gone, taking the resigned Levy with him.

'I was trying not to,' said Tully.

'Well . . . I did not know it was all him. I have never seen a midshipman so stout. What are they giving him to eat?'

'I really have no idea.' Tully did not quite roll his eyes, but it came close. 'His mother probably gave him a few extras.'

'Do you know his mother?'

'I have met her once, yes. She is the wife of a naval officer in Gibraltar.'

'What is she doing sending him to sea at that age?'

But before Tully could hazard a guess, there was a shout from the lieutenant on the upper gundeck and he turned away.

Nathan looked out towards the fighting ships, though all he could see from deck level was the smoke of battle. They would soon be within range, a quarter of an hour, maybe less. But the conversation with the midshipman had troubled him. He was thinking of the danger he would be in if there was a fight. He hoped he had always had a concern for the youngest of his crews, barely out of the nursery, some of them, but never as strong as he felt it now. He knew it was the thought of Louise and his own son, though he was not four months old. It had made him soft; he had known it would. Perhaps he would stay in the cockpit with Levy where he would at least be safe, even if he saw things that would haunt the rest of his childhood.

Then a gust of wind took the smoke away and he saw the three ships plainly, even without the glass, no more than a half-mile now, surely. The *Panther* and the *Falaise* still off her quarter, still firing their rippling broadsides, and the French ship, now unmistakeably heading for the cape. He could even see the name across her stern. *Impétueux*. For once his research failed him. He could not recall another thing about her. It would be a huge feather in his cap if they could take her, though, even if it had little enough to do with him. It would go somewhere towards compensating for the fiasco in Washington.

The shore was close, too, closer than he had thought, with the lighthouse and a small jetty and even a crowd of figures at the end of it, and the flag of the United States on a small mast above. As if he needed reminding.

Venables came to him with a signal from *Panther*.

'Permission to pursue.'

What was that supposed to mean? He must mean pursue into territorial waters, though he was very likely in them already. Typical of Simpson, he thought, trying to pass the blame.

'Send "Heave to and stand by,"' he said. Then he called him back. 'And add "Cease firing."'

What had made him think again? Seeing the flag perhaps, and the small cluster of spectators. If either *Panther* or *Falaise* were to fire from their present position, it might well carry to the shore. And if they killed an American citizen, there would be hell to pay.

There was a shout from the foretop.

'She is aground!'

Nathan brought the glass to his eye to see for himself. She lay dead in the water but on an even keel, as if she were at anchor, or just settled on the bottom, about two cables' lengths from the shore. They were taking in sail, and making a pig's ear of that, too. There did not seem to be many men aloft; he wondered if she was short-handed. The maintop and the foretop both looked a bit odd, too. It could be that she had been in a fight before, not so long ago. She was a winged bird, waiting for the dogs to pick her up.

But already there was a boat putting out to her—and a large Stars and Stripes at her stern, which suggested an official presence, even if it was only a revenue man.

What was he to do? He could send his own boats in and cut her out. And argue about it later, whether they were three miles out or less. He was thinking about this when there was another cry from up top—the mizzentop now, directly above his head.

A sail, two points off their starboard quarter.

By the time he was up there, he could see there were two ships, not one. Ships of the line, by the look of them. They were about three miles to the sou'sou'east and coming on steadily, with the wind at their quarter. But whose were they? He could not afford to wait and see.

'Shout out as soon as you see their colours,' he told the look-out before he slid back down to quarterdeck.

'Mr Tully, we will go about, if you please. And Mr Venables, signal the *Panther* to follow.'

'Only the *Panther*, sir?'

'Only the *Panther*. And when you have done that, signal the *Falaise* to stay in position.'

The *Falaise* would never stop the *Impétueux* if she came out fighting, crippled though she was, but could at least keep a watch on her until Nathan could bring his other ships back.

He looked to see what the tide was doing.

Still on the ebb, but not for long. They would surely try to float her off when it turned, but he would have to take a chance on that. He reckoned he would have two hours at least.

Now here was Tully with another problem.

'We will be between them and the shore, and they with the weather gauge,' he said. 'If they are French . . .' He did not need to spell it out. They would have the wind with them, and *Scipio* on a lee shore with precious little room to spare.

'Then we will wear ship and come up on the starboard tack,' Nathan told him, as if that was all there was to it.

There was another cry from the lookout that he did not catch, but one of the midshipmen relayed it in his piping voice.

'Tricolour at the main, sir.'

He saw that Reed was back on the quarterdeck. Why did he not have the sense to stay below with Levy?

'False colours or French?' Nathan said.

Tully had no opinion on the matter.

'Well, I know what I would put my money on,' Nathan said.

Chapter 28

The Seat of Ease

He knew they would be French, and they were. The look-out confirmed it when they were still a mile or so off, but Nathan and Tully went up to the foretop again to take the measure of them. Two-deckers like the one they had left at Cape Henry, but with no problems steering from what Nathan could see. And now he had a proper fight on his hands.

'The first one has a warrior at the prow,' said Tully. 'With a helmet and a shield.'

Nathan looked for himself and swore softly. 'The *Vétéran*,' he said. 'Jérôme Bonaparte.'

It was no better than a guess. There must be other ships with warriors at the prow. *Scipio* had one, too. But he felt it in his bones. It was the ship that had come out of the mist at Ushant.

'Everywhere I go there is a damned Bonaparte,' said Nathan. 'It is like a curse.'

'There are a lot of people in Europe who feel like that,' said Tully.

Nathan was already calculating what moves he could make, and how his opponent might react to them.

It was reasonable to make several suppositions.

One was that the French would think they had the advantage. They were two ships of the line against a single ship of the line and a frigate. That meant a broadside of seventy-four heavy guns against fifty-five. If all four ships continued as at present, the French would exchange fire with *Scipio* in passing and then concentrate their combined broadsides on *Panther* at close range. This would very likely leave the frigate dead in the water, and the two of them would be able to focus on *Scipio*.

This could not be allowed to happen.

However, there were other factors to consider. One was the presence of Jérôme Bonaparte aboard *Vétéran*. The other was whether they were close enough to see their crippled shipmate stranded on Cape Henry. Because if they could, the likelihood was that they would want to save her.

He looked back. He could just about see *Impétueux* from his present vantage, but could they be from the *Vétéran*? It seemed unlikely, even from their topmasts. They would have to come closer.

'Wear ship,' he said to Tully.

'What—now?'

'Now,' he said. 'I will explain in a moment.'

For a moment he considered the lubber's hole, but then he tucked the glass in his pocket and went down the futtock shrouds like he always did. Then, while Tully gave the order to wear ship, he figured out what to signal to *Panther*.

'Keep it simple,' he told Venables. He did not wish to leave any room for doubt, but he could see Venables struggling.

'Is there a flag for Do As I Do?' Nathan asked.

He left him to work it out and crossed to the weather rail to keep the enemy in sight. Still coming on in line ahead. The second ship seemed to have moved up closer so there was less than a cable's length between them.

Scipio was starting to fall off the wind and come round. She was a lovely ship. She did not quite spin like a top, but there was nothing laboured about it either. He watched *Panther* anxiously, but whatever Venables had signalled, Simpson seemed to have grasped it because he could see them starting to brace the yards.

'He will think we are running,' said Tully at his shoulder.

'Let him,' said Nathan. 'So will they.'

He waited until they were on their new course to the north-east and then explained his reasoning to Tully.

'I want them to be close enough to Cape Henry to see *Impétueux*,' he said. 'When they do, I figure that *Vétéran* will press on to the cape, leaving the other ship to engage us.'

'Why would they not both engage us?'

Nathan suppressed a sigh.

At least in a game of chess, he thought, *you only had to figure out what your opponent was going to do; you did not have to explain it to the pieces.*

'If you were the French captain,' he said, 'and I mean the real captain, the one who knows what he is doing, not Jérôme Bonaparte, would you want to go back to France and tell the emperor "Sorry, mate, but your precious little brother got his head blown off in a bit of a barney we had with the British off the Chesapeake"?'

He saw Tully was thinking about it.

'No, you would not,' Nathan told him firmly. 'You would not want to risk Jérôme's life in a scrap with another seventy-four if you could possibly help it. If you are going to pick a fight, you will pick a fight with a much smaller ship—like a frigate, or even better, a sixteen-gun sloop. Then you get all the honour without the risk, or not much of a one, any road.'

Tully looked a little doubtful at this assessment of his character.

'So, when we are a mile or so closer,' Nathan went on, 'we will turn again and go back and fight them. But my guess—my informed opinion—is that the *Vétéran* will press on and leave us to engage the second ship.'

Tully nodded. It was difficult to know if he agreed or not. He often thought Nathan tried to be too clever by half.

The *Panther* had followed them round and was off their quarter, a little to starboard. The two French ships were a mile to the south, maybe a little more, but all four ships were now moving back to Cape Henry at a speed of three or four knots.

Nathan could see the *Impétueux* and the *Falaise* clearly now from the quarterdeck. There were a lot of small boats in the sea. This bothered him slightly, but there were other things on his mind.

'If anything happens to me,' he said, 'will you look after Louise?' They were standing at the weather rail a little apart from the other officers, but he kept his voice low.

Tully looked startled. In truth, Nathan was a little surprised himself. He had not meant to say that.

'Really?'

He was sounding doubtful again. Perhaps because he knew Sir Sidney Smith had declared an interest? Or perhaps you always sounded doubtful if your closest friend asked you to look after your lover when you were about to go into battle.

'Ewen, then,' he said.

'Who?'

'My son.'

'Oh.' Tully thought about this for a moment. 'I do not think I can do that,' he said. 'Legally.'

Nathan called his clerk over and scribbled it down on his pad.

In the event of my death, I hereby appoint Martin Tully, Captain, RN, executor of my will and trustee of my property and possessions until my son Ewen Nathaniel Peake comes of age.

He signed it and instructed his clerk to sign as witness.

'What is this?' Tully said to him privately. 'You have never been like this before.'

'Probably having a son,' said Nathan.

He thought that the conversation with Reed may have had something to do with it, too.

'Now, let us go back,' he said.

They fell off the wind and turned to the south.

The lead French ship fired with both bowchasers, but he ignored them.

Must be nervous. *Good.*

He climbed the weather shrouds a little way and focused his glass on the second ship. She was a little to leeward of the *Vétéran*, and about a cable's length behind—but now he saw something he had not seen before. She was listing. She was listing heavily to larboard.

He thought of pointing this out to Tully, but Tully had enough to think about.

They were quite close now.

'We will wait until they are close enough to see the heads,' he said, 'then wear ship and rake her as we cross her bow.'

'The heads?'

'The seat of ease,' Nathan said, to avoid misunderstanding.

The seats the hands used were just under the cathead on each side of the prow, and you could see them without a glass at a distance of about three hundred yards if you knew what you were looking for. A broad plank with a hole in it; three holes, to be precise, so the men could sit in a row and make a party of it if they so wished. Nathan had noted this on a previous occasion and considered it might come in useful someday.

'Like they say in the army,' he said. ' "Wait 'til you see the whites of their eyes." I wait 'til I see the seat of ease.'

Tully shook his head a little as if to clear it of some lingering doubts concerning his friend's sanity. Now was not the time.

'And if she comes up into the wind?'

'We take her out to sea with t'other in her wake.'

The two ships were closing fast. He could see the ancient warrior with his naked eye, and the catheads to either side. His whole body was tensed as if for a spring. He made himself relax. And then he saw them, just below the lee cathead, presently vacant . . .

'Now!'

'Prepare to wear ship!' Tully was back at the con, raising his voice to issue a stream of orders. A rush of hands to the braces. 'Port your helm!

And hard over they went, falling off the wind and turning the bow for the not-so-distant shores of Virginia. Their stern was now turned towards the French ships, and Nathan thought he could hear cheering, even a snatch of 'The Marseillaise.' The inevitable *Vive l'Empereur!*

He looked about the quarterdeck, at his own officers and men. Tully at the con, George Banjo making some adjustment to one of the quarterdeck carronades which he considered his own personal property, a gaggle of midshipmen, Reed among them, trying to look as bored as if they were at their Latin. Looking up into the rigging he could see the marine sharpshooters distributed about the tops—they even had a small swivel gun up there for sweeping the enemy quarterdeck; the French probably had one, too. He looked down the length of the gundeck at the gun crews standing ready at the eighteen-pounders, silent and ready; sometimes they sang, but not today.

He felt the familiar twist in his guts. They probably all felt it. He had been in over a dozen battles, ship-to-ship engagements, fleet actions. It did not get any better.

He caught the eye of the second lieutenant, Delancey, who was in charge of the upper deck guns. His lips formed the word 'Steady' and he raised his arm, turning his gaze to the *Vétéran* as she came rushing on. The *Scipio*'s bow was coming up into the wind; he felt her heeling over to leeward.

'Now,' he said, and heard the command repeated along the upper deck and on the deck below.

'Fire as you bear!'

Then the guns did the talking.

They might not have been the fastest gun crews he had ever known, but they had been drilled to perfection. There was no need of further orders. They would not have heard them anyway, the rippling roar working its way aft until the quarterdeck guns came to bear and he was immersed in it, his ears deafened, his nostrils filled with the acrid smell of the powder and the smoke stinging his eyes 'til the wind took it and he could see the *Vétéran* still coming on at a distance of less than a cable's length, the ancient warrior still as fierce and proud as he had been off Ushant.

But on his starboard side, just beneath that fearsome gaze, the seat of ease had been entirely shot away.

And now *Vétéran* was beginning to turn, turning into the wind, exactly as he wanted her to do.

He braced himself for what was coming next. They were sister ships, built in the same yard within a year of each other, and matched gun for gun. A wall of smoke and flame exploded outwards and rippled down her hull. A hail of langrel and chain swept through the rigging, and he felt the solid blows of the heavy round shot on her hull like the beating of some deathly drum. But he had felt worse, and likely would again.

'Now back,' he said to Tully.

And they fell off the wind and came back to the south.

'Look!' They were closing fast on the second ship, and he could see the hole now, just above the waterline. They had wrapped a sail round it, taking it under her keel like a huge bandage round the ship's hull, and it had been sucked into the wound, which was about the length of two gunports and almost as wide. They must have been in a battle, probably the same one as the *Impétueux*, or else one of the guns had come loose during the storm and been hurled about like a battering ram; whatever it was, it need not concern him now.

'She cannot open the lower gunports,' he said, though it must be obvious now to Tully and anyone else who had eyes to see. 'And she must have half the hands at the pumps.'

But Tully was off again, shouting his orders. That was one thing about being a commodore; you did not have to shout as much. The problem was, he had *Panther* to worry about. Having fired that one broadside she had been exposed to *Vétéran*'s full attention, and when he looked back, he saw that she had fared very badly from it. Even as he looked, her foremast came down across her bow with a great deal of canvas, dragging her head into the wind and laying her aback, and the French ship was preparing to cross her bow and rake her at the range of a pistol shot.

He turned away, storing the guilt up for another day, and gave his attention to his own battle. The French captain had seen the danger they were in, and he was falling off the wind to bring their starboard broadside to bear, but they had left it far too late, and her list was a massive hindrance. She lumbered about like a herring buss with a heavy net over the side and *Scipio* was bearing down on her from the north, as close to the wind as Tully could take her.

Both ships were firing now with their foremost guns, the distance between them closing by the second, and at the last minute Tully fell off the wind in a bid to keep some space between them. But they were too close. The French bowsprit pierced their foremast shrouds, and they came together with a jarring crash that threw men to the deck and even one or two down from the mastheads, then a terrible crunching and a grinding as the two ships grated along each other's sides, firing their larboard broadsides muzzle to muzzle as they came to bear. They might have passed in opposite directions, but the French list carried her spars into their upper rigging, and they stayed together like a pair of rutting stags with their horns locked.

This was less of a problem for Nathan than for his opponent, for *Scipio* had both gundecks in action, and the thirty-six-pounders on the lower deck were firing at maximum elevation, ripping through the enemy gunports and up through the deck above. From his vantage on the quarterdeck, he could see long, jagged splinters of wood, gun and body parts flung high into the rigging, and the continuing groan and grind of the ship's timbers was matched by the screams of the wounded.

It was not all one-way, however, for the French were firing down from the tops and hurling grenadoes like Lucas's men at Trafalgar. He felt the wind of the shot past his ear like so many buzzing hornets, and the grenadoes were exploding in the netting above his head. Men were falling all around him—falling from above, too, for most of his marines were aloft and they had their own battle going on in the rigging. His clerk was hit, still clutching his hat with one hand and his pad with another.

Then he saw Reed go down. He was at his side in an instant, cradling his head off the deck and calling for assistance. His eyes were open, but there was a great wound in his neck. Nathan tried to staunch the blood with his cravat, but a sailcloth would not have done it. The poor boy was trying to speak, choking on his own blood, and all Nathan could say was 'Hush now, hush,' like he was trying to get him to sleep.

'Help over here,' he cried again. But even as men ran towards him, the poor boy died in his arms.

He stood up, feeling more at a loss than at any battle he had ever fought, even Trafalgar when he was on the wrong side. The French ship had taken the wind out of their sails, and they seemed doomed to pound each other to death while they slowly drifted down on the coast of Virginia.

But then he saw that Tully had ordered a hawser roused up from below, and some of the hands had wrapped the ropes around the French bowsprit and taken them back to the *Scipio*'s main capstan. They had no sooner made it secure than there was a great snapping of yards like branches in a storm, and then the wind filled their sails again and they pulled their opponent round by the head until she lay almost dead astern of them on a short cable, exposed to the raking fire of their quarterdeck guns.

George Banjo had taken the four carronades there under his personal supervision, and the two that could be brought to bear were firing a lethal hail of grapeshot down the length of the enemy upper deck.

Then, through the smoke and flame, Nathan saw her foremast come toppling down towards him. He fell to the deck, and looked up on all fours to see it poised a foot or so above his head. When he crawled out from beneath it, he saw it was lying across their stern board forming a perfect bridge between the two ships, and he called at once for boarders.

They poured up from the lower deck in a great roaring mob, armed with whatever came to hand: cutlasses, tomahawks, pikes, and pistols, and behind them a more disciplined wedge of marines in their red coats with muskets and bayonets. They swarmed across the makeshift footbridge and fought their way up the enemy deck from stem to stern, stabbing and slashing and roaring blue murder, Nathan among them, mad as any. He fired both pistols, hurled them at the nearest enemy, and drew his sword, but he was borne up in a press of bodies, having neither the room nor time for finesse.

Banjo, he saw, was at his side. He had made it his principal role when boarding, but Nathan felt a mindless irritation.

'Why are you not at the guns?' he yelled at him.

'What use are they now,' Banjo yelled back, 'with this mob in the way?'

He had a point, for the enemy deck was a struggling, surging mass of humanity, if that was not too fine a name for it. There was something in the British character that lent itself to this form of fighting, Nathan had often thought, though in truth there were almost as many foreigners in the king's navy as natives, and the French were no slouches when it came to savagery. They might have taken a battering, but they put up a hell of a fight, and their marines were still firing down from the tops.

But the boarders were gaining ground. The front ranks were up on the quarterdeck now, and Nathan was crossing swords with a French officer, the two of them going about it like virtuosos at a fencing school, up and down the deck, lunge and parry, circle-beat and counter, until Nathan slipped in a patch of blood. For a moment he lay helpless on the deck, looking up at his opponent as he drew back his sword for the final, killing thrust. Then George Banjo was there with his cutlass, and that was the end of the fencing lesson.

The end of the whole brutal business, in fact. Perhaps there was something in the wild rush of boarding that favoured attack over defence, or else the broadsides had taken their toll, reducing the French in number and in spirit, for they began to throw down their weapons and cry for quarter.

Nathan found a French cadet, not much older than Reed had been, and asked him in French where his captain was.

The boy pointed to the weather side of the quarterdeck, and Nathan saw an officer lying in a pool of blood, stuffing a paper in his mouth.

'*C'est quoi, ce bordel?*' he said, astonished.

'*C'est le code secret,*' said the cadet.

He died before they could reach him.

A marine brought what was left of the paper to Nathan, but it was not the *code secret*; it was the poor man's commission. His lower body was shattered by grapeshot, and in his agony he had got hold of the wrong paper. They found the secret code in an inside pocket of his uniform coat, and Nathan kept it for future reference.

His immediate concern now was the *Vétéran.*

It had been his great fear that contrary to his reasoning, she would come up on their leeward side while they were engaged with her consort, but this had not happened. Now he saw at least one good reason why. She had run athwart the *Panther* and both ships were as hopelessly entangled as they had been themselves. With the disparity in size, this could have only one ending, and it was already apparent that the frigate was close to it. She had lost all three masts and most of her guns were silenced, yet she continued to put up a fight with what was left. Not for long, though, unless *Scipio* could come to her assistance.

Nathan left the prize in charge of Lieutenant Venables, with half the marines and all the hands he could spare, and headed back over the bridge with the rest of his boarders.

'Cast off the hawser,' he told Tully. 'And get us under way.'

They had men poling them free of the other ship and hacking at the mass of rigging draped over the quarterdeck, but now there were others shouting down from the foretop and pointing to the south.

Nathan's ears were deafened by gunfire—he could not hear a word—but he ran partway up the mizzen shrouds to see what they were on about.

It did not take long. There was another sail hull down to the south.

Chapter 29

Fire on the Chesapeake

Levy had said there were three or *four* French ships of the line cruising off the east coast.

Was this the fourth?

They had to be prepared for it, but Nathan did not have to be a pessimist to rate their chances at close to zero—not with two French ships of the line to contend with in anything like fighting shape, and his own crew so much depleted.

His only hope was to board the *Vétéran* while she was still engaged with *Panther* and take her before the other ship came up. He began to explain this to Tully, but then he saw the *Vétéran* drawing ahead of the shattered frigate and crossing her bow. He looked to see how the boatswain and his men were getting on with freeing them from the shambles on their quarterdeck, but they still had some way to go, and *Vétéran* was barely half a mile to windward. She would either wear ship and come down on their starboard quarter or carry on towards the cape to deal with *Falaise* while he confronted the new enemy from the south.

But she did neither of these things. She was coming further into the wind and heading out into the open sea.

He looked to Tully, who shook his head, as mystified as he, but failing divine intervention, it could only mean one thing. There was no fourth French ship. They must think the newcomer was British, and they no more favoured odds of two to one than Nathan had. Less so, in fact, for they were clapping on sail and bearing away to the northeast.

'I told you,' said Nathan, as if there had never been a grain of doubt in his mind. 'They fear the emperor's wrath.'

'Do you want to go after her?' asked Tully.

'Let us see what this other one is first,' said Nathan, shifting his gaze to the south. If she turned out to be French, he did not want her taking both his prizes along with the *Falaise* and the shattered wreck of the *Panther* while he was off chasing young Bonaparte back to France.

But she was not French. She was the *Aurore*.

Tully was the first to smoke her, even at two miles distant, for he had commanded her for the best part of two years after they took her in the bay of Vauville. The news quickly spread through the ship, and a great cheer went up that quickly spread to the prize.

Nathan caught Tully's eye.

'Let us have a list of the dead and wounded,' he said. 'And signal to *Panther* to ask what the damage is.'

But that would not do. She had lost all three masts and would be hard put to hoist a single flag. He sent Venables over in the cutter, and he came back to say they had lost more than thirty dead, including Simpson, with fifty-six wounded. Almost half her crew. The ship herself would not fight again, he thought, without major repairs.

Nathan doubted that would happen. The right decision would be to transfer her crew to the prize and fire her, but she had a proud record of service going back more than thirty years, and he did not want to be the one to pronounce the death sentence.

The nearest naval dockyard was in Bermuda, six hundred miles or so out into the Atlantic. A six-day voyage with a jury rig, if they were lucky, and there was the prize herself to think on. He knew her name now. She was the *Jupiter*, one of the older

Téméraire class, launched in 1789. She was in better shape than the *Panther*, but he would not care to sail her back across the Atlantic without plugging that hole in her side, and she needed a fair bit of work aloft.

And then there were the French prisoners, around five hundred of them, presently herded below under guard.

The best thing, he decided, was to shift most of *Panther*'s crew to *Jupiter* and have her tow the frigate to Bermuda. Then he could take most of *Scipio*'s crew back with the marines, leave *Impétueux* to the Americans, and take off after *Vétéran.*

By then he had the butcher's bill on *Scipio*. Twelve dead, sixteen wounded, including Delancey, who was like to lose his leg. The remains of the enemy rigging had been cleared from the quarterdeck and Tully reported, with a straight face, that they were ready for action. And *Aurore* was in plain sight to the south.

Nathan was beginning to feel on top of things, perhaps for the first time since leaving Gibraltar, when there was another cry from the lookouts, and he turned his face northward to see the smoke rising from Cape Henry.

It was *Impétueux*.

'I saw the other ship coming up from the south,' said Parker when Nathan came aboard from the cutter. 'I thought if she was another Frenchie, it was best not to take any chances.'

'So, you set fire to her,' Nathan said flatly. He could scarce believe it, though it was plain enough. Her upper deck was enveloped in smoke and flame, and her gunports were like the open vents of a furnace.

'I did,' said Parker, who seemed quite pleased with himself. 'Sent the boats in and put her to the torch.'

'Even though she is in American waters.'

'I did my duty,' said Parker stiffly. 'As I understand it.'

Nathan watched her as she burned down to the waterline, burning Fox's peace treaty with it, and probably a lot more besides.

'It was not by my order,' he told Levy when he was back on the *Scipio*.

The lieutenant was still bloodied from his time in the cockpit, and his face when he looked on the burning hulk of the French ship was grim.

'Even so,' he said. 'It was done by British seamen—and there will be a price to pay.'

'I will have to go back to Washington,' Nathan told Tully. 'I owe it to Carteret to tell him what has happened, and how.'

'Can you not write to him?' Tully was all for cracking on after the *Vétéran*. He seemed to have a particular animus for Jérôme Bonaparte, for reasons Nathan did not entirely comprehend. Possibly it was his rapid promotion.

'I think I need to do it face-to-face,' said Nathan. 'There is the president to think of, too. And Imlay.'

'Imlay?' Tully had known Imlay almost as long as Nathan had. 'What has he to do with anything?'

'He was involved in this mission from the start,' said Nathan. 'It might even have been his idea, and for once he has behaved well. It is the only thing I have known him to believe in besides himself.'

Tully looked slightly stunned. 'What?'

'Abolition,' said Nathan. 'Or at least banning the Atlantic slave trade. He has invested a great deal in it.'

'Oh, I will give you that,' said Tully. 'Have you spoken to George Banjo about this?'

'What has George Banjo to do with it?'

'I thought you had him ask a friend of his in Washington. About Imlay.'

'This is true,' said Nathan. It had slipped his mind entirely. He supposed there had been other things to think about. 'How do you know?'

'Because he told me. On our way out of the Chesapeake—before the storm hit. He thought I should mention it to you.'

'What?'

'That Imlay has been investing in African slaves.'

'*Investing* in them. In what way?'

'He has joined a consortium to buy up as many as they can while the price is low.'

'But—that makes no sense,' Nathan protested. 'Not with the bill about to go through Congress.'

'Makes plenty of sense to Imlay. If Britain and the United States combine in banning the Atlantic slave trade, what do you think will happen to the price of slaves that are already in America?'

Nathan stared at him.

'They are buying up all the young men and women they can find, boys and girls, aged twelve and over. Breeding stock, they call them.'

'And Imlay is involved in this?'

'From what Banjo heard, he is the brains behind it.'

'I will kill him,' said Nathan quietly. 'I will call him out and this time I will kill him.'

'That will help Anglo-American relations.'

'He has played us all false—Fox, Carteret, me, even the president. What else can I do?'

'Well, we could go after the *Vétéran*,' said Tully.

Nathan looked out to the northeast, across the empty sea.

'Really?'

'I suppose it depends on what you consider to be the most important.'

Being a diplomat or a naval officer. Tully would never say that, not to his face, but Nathan knew it was what he meant.

'We might have to chase her all the way back to Europe,' he said.

'There is that,' said Tully gazing at him evenly, as if he knew what he was thinking, and perhaps he did.

'Europe it is, then,' said Nathan.

Europe—and Louise. Come what may.

'Have Lieutenant Levy put ashore,' he said, 'and when the boat is back, set a course to the northeast.' He turned to Venables. 'Signal *Falaise* and *Aurore* to follow in line ahead.'

'And that?' Tully was looking back at the burning hulk on the Virginia shore.

'We will leave that for the diplomats,' said Nathan.

THE END

Author's Note

Fact and Fiction

The action at the mouth of the Chesapeake was the last of a series of engagements between units of the British and French navies known collectively as the 1806 Battle of the Atlantic. It occurred when several French ships that had been damaged in the great storm of 1806 were obliged to run for ports in the Chesapeake and came under attack by a British squadron. It is true that the seventy-four-gun *Impétueux* deliberately ran aground on the Virginia shore to avoid capture and that the pursuing British ships sent in boats to burn her.

Although this led to protests from the French consulate and was regarded as a breach of sovereignty in Washington, as a cause of tension it was secondary to the continuing practice of stopping American ships on the high seas and seizing members of their crews for service in the royal navy. This practice so angered US president Thomas Jefferson that he refused to ratify a trade agreement with Great Britain and imposed an embargo on shipborne commerce between the United States and Europe. In 1812 continuing tensions over incidents at sea led to the 1812–1814 war between Britain and the United States.

Jérôme Bonaparte

It is true that Jérôme Bonaparte commanded one of the French ships that broke out of Brest and became involved in the Battle of the Atlantic. He left the squadron to which he was attached to go off on a cruise along the eastern seaboard of the United States as described in the novel, but neither he nor his ship, the *Vétéran*, were involved in the action in the Chesapeake, and there is no evidence that he tried to stir up trouble in the southern states over opposition to the ban on the Atlantic slave trade.

However, it is true that Jérôme had already stirred up a fair bit of trouble in America by eloping with the eighteen-year-old heiress Elizabeth Patterson, their marriage clearly in defiance of her family's wishes. Unable to secure a reconciliation with her wealthy father, Jérôme sailed with his pregnant bride for France, but his big brother, Napoleon—who had just had himself declared emperor of the French—had already arranged his marriage to a German princess and refused to let Elizabeth land.

While she sought refuge in London, Jérôme pursued Napoleon to Italy in hopes of changing his mind. His pleas fell on deaf ears. Napoleon had the marriage annulled by imperial decree—his own—and married Jérôme off to the woman of his—Napoleon's—choice, after making him king of Westphalia to give him a title. This appears to have mended Jérôme's broken heart, though of course we cannot know for sure. However, he made no mention of his ex-wife or son in his will and left them nothing.

Elizabeth had her child in London where he was named Jérôme Napoleon Bonaparte. His mother returned with him to America, where his grandson Charles Joseph Bonaparte later served in the cabinet of President Theodore Roosevelt—as secretary of state for the navy.

The Burr Conspiracy

The 'facts' of the so-called Burr Conspiracy are still contested by historians, but nothing I have written about him is seriously disputed. Burr believed he was cheated of victory in the 1800 presidential election, and for this he blamed Thomas Jefferson and Alexander Hamilton (among others). After shooting Hamilton dead in the famous duel, he challenged President Jefferson by attempting to form a breakaway state in the western territories. He fled Washington when the conspiracy was revealed and was arrested by US army officers in Mississippi Territory on February 19, 1807, and charged with treason. Although he stood trial in Richmond, Virginia, Chief Justice John Marshall, presiding, ruled that he could not be found guilty unless he had committed an act of war. His secret correspondence with the British minister, Anthony Merry, and the Spanish envoy in Washington were deemed evidence of conspiracy, but not insurrection.

Despite his acquittal, Burr fled the United States for Europe to escape his creditors, residing mainly in London until 1812, when he returned to New York and resumed the practice of law. At the age of seventy-seven he married a wealthy widow nineteen years his junior who divorced him four months later when she became aware of her rapidly dwindling resources due to his land speculations. Alexander Hamilton Jr. was her divorce lawyer. Burr died in 1836, aged eighty.

It is true that Mr Merry considered himself slighted by President Jefferson, for the reasons I have described (though what Jefferson was wearing at the time is still disputed by historians), and that his wife Elizabeth encouraged him to meet with Aaron Burr, who outlined his plans for insurrection. It is also true that his dispatches on the subject were read by the new pro-American foreign secretary, Charles James Fox, who had him recalled to London for his involvement in activities that could be deemed treasonous. Merry served in several other diplomatic postings and died in 1835.

The Atlantic Slave Trade

The bill to outlaw the Atlantic slave trade was passed by Congress in March 1807, and became law in Great Britain three weeks later. The trade continued illegally, but between 1807 and 1860, the West Africa squadron of the royal navy seized 1,600 slave ships and freed 150,000 Africans.

However, it is true that the value of slaves rose appreciably in the southern states when it became more difficult to bring in Africans from abroad, and large profits were made by dealers.

The permanent involvement of the US navy in suppressing this illegal trade (the purpose of Nathan's mission) was not achieved until 1842, and it continued until the American Civil War and the subsequent abolition of slavery throughout the United States.

Childbirth and Death

The chapter on childbirth at sea and the character of Dr Munro are based on the real-life character of Dr Alexander Gordon (1752–1799), a former royal navy surgeon who developed the theory that the infections which caused so many deaths of both mother and child were very likely passed on by the birth attendants, whether doctors or midwives. In the 1790s Gordon returned to his hometown of Aberdeen, where he practised as an obstetrician and specialist in infections at the Dispensary, making detailed observations of dozens of pregnant women in his care during an epidemic of puerperal fever. He concluded: 'It is a disagreeable fact that I, myself, was the means of carrying the infection to a great number of women.'

Gordon suggested that the woman's bedclothes should be burned, and that the doctors and nurses involved in the birth should carefully fumigate themselves, or at the very least, wash their hands. This was taken badly by his medical colleagues, and he was hounded from Aberdeen and obliged to go back to sea.

This was fifty years before the better-known work of Dr Ignaz Semmelweis, the Hungarian physician at Vienna General Hospital who became known as the 'saviour of mothers,' and was the subject of a 2023 play at the Harold Pinter Theatre in London, with Mark Rylance in the title role. Despite his success in almost eliminating deaths from puerperal fever during childbirth (from 30 percent to less than 1 percent), Dr Semmelweis, too, was pilloried by his colleagues for proposing that they wash their hands before treating their patients. Rather more ruthlessly than the Scottish doctors, they had him committed to a mental asylum, where he died of septic shock, possibly after being beaten by the guards.

Lieutenant Daniel Levy

Lieutenant Levy, though fictitious, is based on several real-life characters taken from notes made by my friend Jim Guggenheim of Virginia on his own family background. These comprise a fascinating insight into the Jewish community in North America at the time of the War of Independence and the early years of the United States, and I have not been able to do them anything like enough justice. Hopefully he might be able to do so himself sometime in the future.

The background of Lieutenant Levy is formed from the various records Jim assembled on that of his own family, including Jacob Phillips, who emigrated from England to the Caribbean as a youth, and then, in 1780, still young, to South Carolina, where he joined the militia to fight with the Patriots in the American Revolution; and Isaiah Moses, who originated from Hanover, moving first to England and then to Charleston, where he became a merchant and then a planter.

But the main influence on the backstory of Daniel Levy is yet another of Jim's ancestors—Uriah Phillips Levy—who fought in the 1812–1814 war with Britain and rose to the rank of commodore, then the highest rank in the US navy.

Uriah Phillips Levy was born in Philadelphia in 1792 and ran away to sea at the age of ten, to serve as a cabin boy on a trading ship. By the time of the 1812 war, he was an experienced merchant seaman, and he began his naval career aboard the USS *Argus*, an eighteen-gun sloop of war. When the ship was taken by the British, Levy was incarcerated with the rest of the crew in the notorious Dartmoor prison in Devon, England, where he remained for sixteen months. After his release and the end of the war, he rose through the ranks of the navy to become flag officer of the Mediterranean squadron, and in the 1850s he played a prominent role in the abolition of flogging in the navy. In 1836 he purchased Thomas Jefferson's house and estate at Monticello, which he restored and opened to visitors. In 1923 the Levy family sold the estate to the Thomas Jefferson Memorial Foundation.

And as a final note on the subject of fact and fiction . . . the bizarre events described at Nelson's funeral are much as they were reported at the time, including the ripping up of the Union Jack that draped the coffin, to provide mementos for the bearers. It was, as Hallowell remarked, the only bit of the ceremony that was really Nelson.

—Paul Bryers

March 18, 2024

Acknowledgments

A SINCERE THANKS TO GEORGE JEPSON AND HIS TEAM AT McBooks Press, especially Brittany Stoner and Melissa Hayes, and my literary agent Bill Hamilton at A M Heath for all their encouragement and the efforts they have put into getting this series published. Thanks to Sharon Goulds for her expert research into early nineteenth century childbirth, especially when it came to the specialist subject of having a child at sea, to Jim Guggenheim for sharing his family history, which I've referenced in more detail in the Notes at the end of the story, and Bruce Reed for sharing his knowledge of the Georgie accent, though in Admiral Lord Collingwood's case I was more restrained than I was tempted to be. And finally, thanks to Martin Fletcher and to Alex Skutt for launching the series in the UK and United States, and to all those readers who have made the journey with me.

Acknowledgments

Milton Keynes UK
Ingram Content Group UK Ltd.
UKHW032125111024
449602UK00016B/306